THEODOSIA
and the
LAST PHARAOH

THEODOSIA
—and the—
LAST PHARAOH

R. L. LaFevers

illustrated by Yoko Tanaka

sandpiper

HOUGHTON MIFFLIN HARCOURT

BOSTON   NEW YORK

www.hmhco.com

The text of this book is set in Minister Book.
The illustrations are acrylic on board.
Map of 1905 London used courtesy of the Harvard Map Collection.

The Library of Congress has cataloged the hardcover edition as follows:
La Fevers, R. L. (Robin L.)
Theodosia and the last pharaoh / by R. L. LaFevers.
p. cm.
Summary: When eleven-year-old Theodosia and her cat, Isis,
travel to Egypt to return the Orb of Ra and the Emerald Tablet,
she hopes to learn more about her origins but finds, instead,
the Serpents of Chaos and a precious treasure that suddenly
appears and disappears.
[1. Adventure and adventures—Fiction. 2. Magic—Fiction. 3. Blessing and
cursing—Fiction. 4. Museums—Fiction. 5. Family life—Egypt—Fiction.
6. Egypt—History—20th century—Fiction.] I. Title.
PZ7.L1414Tgl 2011
[Fic]—dc22
2010032224

ISBN: 978-0-547-39018-5 hardcover
ISBN: 978-0-547-85086-3 paperback

Manufactured in the United States of America
DOC 10 9 8 7 6 5 4
4500556605

This book is dedicated to librarians everywhere,
the few, the proud, and the learned,
and most especially to Amy Clarke,
my grandmother and a most exemplary librarian,
who instilled in me her love of the written word.

CHAPTER ONE
THE WRETCHED RETICULE

NOVEMBER 1907

EVEN WITH THE WINDOWS CLOSED, the sand still managed to creep into the railway car and find its way into the most *inconvenient* places. I shifted uncomfortably on the seat, blew the dust off the pages of my journal, and focused on the list I was composing. Seeing things laid out in black and white often helps me think better.

Things to Do in Egypt

1. Avoid the nefarious Serpents of Chaos, a secret organization determined to obtain any and all cursed artifacts and use them for their own ill gain.

2. Locate Major Harriman Grindle, my contact at the Luxor branch of the Brotherhood of the Chosen Keepers, the honorable group of men dedicated to stopping the Serpents of Chaos.

3. Help Mother find the temple of Thutmose III. While my research had indicated there might be such a temple, I had overstated the case in order to convince Mother to return to Egypt so I could—

4. Return two powerful artifacts, the Orb of Ra and the Emerald Tablet, to the wedjadeen, a shadowy organization that not even the Brotherhood of Chosen Keepers had heard of. According to the Egyptian magician Awi Bubu, they are charged by the Egyptian gods to guard and protect the same magic and are just as committed to protecting ancient, powerful artifacts as the Brotherhood of the Chosen Keepers are.

5. Convince the wedjadeen that I should not be punished for having their powerful artifacts in my possession.

6. Also convince them that since my friend Awi Bubu had sent me to return these powerful

artifacts to them, he should be forgiven for his past mistakes that had caused him to be expelled from their ranks.

7. Learn the circumstances of my birth. Awi Bubu seemed to think my peculiar talents of being able to detect ancient magic and curses had been given to me for a reason.

I studied the list. It didn't look quite long enough, frankly. A mere seven things shouldn't feel as if the weight of the known world were resting on my shoulders, should it?

A low, unhappy warble emerged from the basket on the seat next to me. I glanced anxiously at Mother, who raised a warning eyebrow. *Oh, yes.*

8. Keep Isis out from under Mother's feet at all times.

I slipped my pencil into my pocket, then put my fingers through one of the slats in the basket to reassure Isis that I was still there. When I felt the feather-light touch of her soft, warm nose, I inched my fingers around to scratch behind her ears. That seemed to appease her somewhat. She didn't quite purr, but she *almost* purred, and that was victory enough for me.

Mother had been furious when she'd learned I'd snuck Isis

along on the trip. Luckily, we'd been far out to sea and it was too late to turn back. I know it was wrong of me to smuggle her along and not only because it annoyed Mother (although I do try to avoid needlessly annoying my parents whenever possible—there are enough times when I simply have no choice). The reason it was wrong had more to do with Isis herself. She wasn't fond of cooped-up spaces, nor was she fond of long journeys on the ocean. I knew she would be miserable until we arrived in Egypt. But I also knew *I* would be even more miserable without her company for months and months. Besides, she had some . . . power, a special quality that had a strange effect on people that might come in handy on the trip.

If I was going to be thousands of miles from everyone I knew and needed to tackle dangerous duties on my own, then it seemed to me I ought to have at least one ally I could count on. Honestly! Mother was lucky I hadn't tried to smuggle Sticky Will along on the trip. Although it was difficult enough smuggling a cat—smuggling a twelve-year-old street urchin with a talent for picking pockets would have been impossible.

With an earsplitting screech of metal and a final sickly chug, the train pulled into the Cairo station. I had to brace my feet to keep from pitching to the floor, and flung my arm out to prevent Isis and her basket from tumbling off the seat. Across from me, Mother rocked backwards as the train braked, then pitched forward, her head nearly landing in my lap.

She quickly sat back up and adjusted her hat. "We're here!" she said cheerfully.

"We're here," I agreed, carefully setting the basket to rights.

"Collect your things, dear. We'll be de-boarding in a few minutes."

"Yes, Mother." I took my hand from Isis's basket, annoyed to find that the silken cords to my reticule had gotten wrapped around my wrist again. I must say, fashion is a mystery to me. How on earth can ladies stroll around with a beastly reticule wrapped around their wrists? The cords get twisted and tangled, then grow so tight it feels as if they have cut off all the circulation to one's hand. Not only that, but the horrid thing bumps and thumps against one's leg with every step. Sighing with annoyance, I jerked at the silken cords, trying to get the blood flowing back into my hand.

"What are you doing?" Mother asked.

"Straightening this wretched thing out," I muttered, watching the reticule spin round and round as I untwisted the cords.

"I thought you loved that little purse! If I remember correctly, you begged and begged for me to buy it for you."

I bit back a sigh of frustration. Why do grownups always remember the things you wish they wouldn't? "Well, that was before I knew what a lot of bother it'd be." What I'd really wanted was a muff, but even in November, Egypt was too hot for one. It would have made a wonderful hiding place, though. One where I could have kept my hands safely wrapped around the—

"Here, give me that." Mother reached for the purse.

"No!" I jerked it out of her reach. "I need to practice, don't you think? I'll be a grownup before you know it, and I'll need to know how to carry a reticule properly. If I don't learn now, when will I?"

Mother stared at me for a long moment, then shook her head. "Your grandmother is right. You are a peculiar child."

Her words stung me to the quick. Peculiar? *Peculiar!*

Seeing the stricken look on my face, she gave me a smile she meant to be comforting. "Don't worry, dear. We all go through peculiar stages, but we grow out of them."

It did not make me feel one whit better that she was hoping—counting on the fact—that I would grow into someone different from who I was.

All the joy and promise of this trip evaporated. One part of me longed to explain the true reasons I acted so peculiar, but I didn't think the true reasons would make her feel any better. In fact, she would most likely ship me off to a sana-torium if she knew that I spent most of my time removing black magic and ancient curses from rare and powerful arti-facts in the Museum of Legends and Antiquities that my parents oversaw back in London. Or that I spent quite a lot of energy avoiding secret societies that would love to get their hands on those artifacts and use them for their own evil ends. No, I was fairly certain Mother wouldn't consider those reasons any less peculiar.

Completely unaware of the turmoil inside me, Mother stood and brushed off her skirts. "Get your things, dear."

Another low-throated warble emerged from the basket on the bench next to me. "Isis doesn't like being called a thing," I pointed out.

Mother stopped her grooming and speared me with one of her stern looks. "Since Isis was not invited on this trip, I do not particularly care what she likes and does not like. Do not try my patience, Theo. The travel and the delays have done that well enough. Now, come along."

Feeling that perhaps coming to Egypt with Mother was a very bad idea, I grabbed my traveling satchel in one hand, Isis's basket in the other, and pushed to my feet.

"Your hat," she reminded me, motioning to the pith hel-met on the seat cushion. *Bother.* I set down my satchel, plunked the hat onto my head, picked up the satchel again, then followed Mother out of our compartment and *thump-bumped* my way down the narrow, cramped aisle.

In the station, faint traces of *heka* and ancient magic hung in the air, mingling with the soot and steam from the train. I sneezed, then gingerly picked my way down the steps to the platform, the small weight in my reticule heavy against my leg. The Orb of Ra within was a constant reminder of why I was here and the promise I had made to Awi Bubu when he'd been on his deathbed. (Or so I had believed at the time; if I'd known he hadn't really been at death's door, I would never have made it.) However, while Awi Bubu hadn't died from the injuries, he hadn't recovered enough that he could travel to Egypt himself.

Thinking of the Serpents of Chaos made me uneasy. My shoulders twitched, itching for the safety of our hotel room. "Is Nabir meeting us?" I looked around the crowded station, hoping to spot the familiar face of Mother's drago-man.

"Not this time," she said. "He's in Luxor putting together a team for the dig. We'll find a porter and obtain transportation to the hotel ourselves."

Easier said than done, I thought, trying to push through a knot of people milling about the station. In truth, it was more of a mob. And while I remembered Cairo station being busy,

I didn't remember it being *this* busy. "What are all these people doing here?" I asked over the rising hum of the voices. "Is it a holiday of some sort?"

"I'm not sure, dear," Mother called over her shoulder, "but stay close so we don't get separated."

I squeezed around a group of men, all wearing long white robes and arguing forcefully with one another. With a stab of surprise, I found myself longing for Father. He was quite efficient at coaxing people to give way. Of course, that was due to the cane he wielded with such devastating effectiveness. Even so, I had not expected to miss his solid presence quite so much. Unfortunately, the museum's current exhibit had become so popular that the board of directors wouldn't let him leave.

Unfamiliar foreign voices filled the station, sounding angry and frustrated. Mother gripped her satchel more firmly and glanced back to be certain I was still right behind her. I was glad to see that, peculiar or not, she didn't want to lose me in this crush. I gave her a smile of reassurance, then turned my attention back to looking for a break in the crowd through which we could slip.

That was when I noticed an odd, spindly man fighting his way through the throng. His eyes darted over the heads of the jostling crowd, searching for someone. Thoughts of the

Serpents of Chaos immediately filled my mind. I glanced over at Mother to see if she had noticed—or recognized—the fellow, but she seemed reluctant to take her eyes from the baggage car, afraid our trunks would disappear from sight if she so much as looked away.

The man was quite tall and long limbed. His hair was so fair as to be nearly white, as if all the color had been washed out of it. There was something a bit twitchy about him that made me wonder if his bones didn't quite fit in his skin.

His searching gaze landed on Mother and me, and a determined gleam appeared in his eyes, like someone zeroing in on a target.

Just as I was trying to decide if Mother and I could give him the slip, he gave a vigorous shove past one last barrier of bodies and popped through the crowd like a cork out of a bottle to land neatly in front of us.

His pale blue eyes blinked rapidly as he tugged his jacket back into place and straightened his tie. I saw that there was a bit of hair on his upper lip that wanted to be a mustache when it grew up. He sent a quick, unreadable glance my way, then bowed to Mother. "Mrs. Throckmorton?" he asked.

I gripped the satchel and reticule more tightly.

"Yes?" Mother asked with chilly politeness.

"I am Jonathan Bing of the Antiquities Service. I've been

sent to escort you to your appointment. When I stopped by the hotel to collect you, they said you had not yet arrived. I thought I'd best come check on your train since this business"—he nodded his head toward the crowd of Egyptians—"was going on today."

Mother visibly relaxed. "And we are so very glad that you did."

"What exactly *is* this business?" I asked, looking back at the edges of the throng, where a lone man stood on a crate, addressing the others.

His gaze followed my own and his nose wrinkled faintly in distaste. "The Nationalist Party. They're having a demonstration to protest the British presence here in Egypt."

"Yes, well, they are taking up rather a lot of room," Mother said as someone jostled her and sent her stumbling into me. "Would you be so kind as to take this?" Mother thrust her small carry-aboard suitcase at him, then grabbed my elbow in a firm grip.

Some of the tension left me, and suddenly, the teeming masses of humanity seemed less threatening.

Taking Mother's suitcase, Mr. Bing began using it rather like a battering ram and forced a path through the mob. We followed gratefully in his wake.

At first, Bing had little success in getting through the solid wall of bodies. I was quickly surrounded by black robes and turbaned heads. If it hadn't been for Mother's solid hold on me, I'm afraid I might have panicked.

The man on the crate let loose with a new torrent of words, and the crowd erupted into cheers and surged forward, as if to embrace him on their wave of joy. The three of us were carried along with them. "What is he saying?" I asked Bing, nearly shouting to be heard.

"Nothing good," he shouted back. I scowled. He was my least favorite sort of grownup—the kind that never told children anything.

A tall, bearded man bumped into me and knocked my elbow out of Mother's grip. Within seconds, the sea of strangers closed in around me and I couldn't see any sign of Mother's dusty rose traveling suit or the tailored lines of Bing's morning coat. A firm hand grabbed my arm. *Chaos*, I thought, with a hot bubble of panic. I bit back a scream and tried to jerk away.

The grip tightened painfully. "This way!" Bing shouted. *Bing*, I told myself. It was only Mr. Bing. I allowed him to tug me through the wall of bodies until finally we were on the other side. I spotted Mother waiting for us and started to head for her, but a squeeze on my shoulder held me back.

"What?" I asked Mr. Bing.

"Wigmere," he said out of the side of his mouth. "Wigmere sent me."

I stumbled to a stop when he uttered the name of the head of the Chosen Keepers. "Really?" I asked.

He nodded and turned his attention back to Mother, waving to her to let her know he'd found me. For the first time since stepping off the train, I relaxed. I should have known Wigmere would have arranged for some sort of help here in Cairo. Especially with the burden I was carrying.

Mr. Bing deposited me next to Mother, then braved the crowd once more to oversee our luggage.

Outside the train station, the smell of old magic was stronger and mixed with the heat and the dust and something a little bit . . . gamey. I turned to find a small herd of donkeys and donkey boys waiting nearby. That was it: the smell of donkey.

Finally all of our belongings were collected and we loaded ourselves and our luggage into the conveyance. The driver slapped the reins and the carriage moved forward.

The streets of Cairo still looked the same as on my first trip. Mostly. They were lined on either side by high narrow houses with second and third stories that jutted out over the street. Windows were covered with elaborate latticework that looked like exotic lace. And the colors! Violet, mulberry, olive, peach, and crimson, with the occasional flash of silver or brass. It was as though someone had spilled a paint box in the sand. Even so, it seemed to me that the shadows were darker, deeper, and more threatening than on my last visit.

I kept a careful eye on the men in the street—barefoot Egyptians in tattered cotton, Bedouin in long, billowing robes, effendis in their red fezzes—looking for any sign of the Serpents of Chaos, but everyone seemed as he should.

When at last the hotel came into view, my sigh of relief was cut short as a swarm of vendors and street sellers descended upon our carriage like one of the Ten Plagues of Egypt. They pressed around on all sides, trying to sell whips, fly swatters, cork-lined hats, or locally crafted fans. One man carried an enormous stick covered with dangling shoes and nearly beaned us with it as he tried to show us his wares.

The hotel doorman—a giant, burly fellow—waded through the bodies, shooing them aside as if he were brushing crumbs from a table. He reached our carriage and cleared enough space for us to get out. Then he planted himself on one side of us and Mr. Bing took up the other as we made our way to the safety of the hotel lobby. The cool quiet was like a balm to our battered souls after the pandemonium of the morning.

Porters were sent to fetch our trunks and we were quickly

shown to our rooms. Mr. Bing offered to wait downstairs while we freshened up, then escort us to the Antiquities Service.

"Don't dawdle, Theodosia," Mother said, when we reached our suite. "We've got to meet Mr. Bing in a quarter of an hour. I don't want to keep Monsieur Maspero waiting any longer than necessary."

"Yes, Mother," I said, then *thump-bumped* my way into the room where the porter had set my trunks. I nudged the door closed with the toe of my boot, then set my satchel and basket on the floor. I knelt down to open the wicker basket. "We're here," I told Isis. "You can come out now."

As soon as I lifted the lid, she shot out of the basket like a black lightning bolt. She stalked around the room, stopping to sniff here and there, trying to determine if the room met with her approval.

While she was deciding, I rifled through my trunk, looking for the least-wrinkled frock I could find. The butterscotch-colored taffeta seemed to have traveled the best, so I took it out and shook the wrinkles from it. By that time, Isis had returned to me and bumped her head against my ankle. "Is everything all right, then?" I asked her.

She meowed, and I bent to scratch her behind the ears. She ducked away from my hand and meowed again, this time prancing over to the window.

"Of course!" I said, horrified that I hadn't thought of it first. "You must be desperate to go out." I hurried over to the window, happy to see that it opened onto a garden of some sort. "But do hurry back," I told her. "I'll need you to stand guard while I'm out with Mother."

Isis gave a short warble of consent, then leaped outside and disappeared among the bushes.

I stepped out of my travel-stained gown and went to wash the dust from my face, neck, and arms. Scrubbed clean, I stared at myself in the mirror, looking for any sign that my eyes might be beginning to turn brown like Mother's. But no luck. They hadn't gotten more blue like Father's, either. They were still the color of swamp mud and unlike anyone else's in my family.

Answers, I promised myself. I would find answers on this trip. That was the other reason I had agreed to keep my promise to Awi Bubu.

I went back to the bed and slipped into my clean frock. I wished desperately that there was some way to carry a five-pound stone tablet on me, but there simply wasn't. I would have to leave the Emerald Tablet where it was. I was very careful to not let myself think of the tablet's hiding place in case someone skilled in Egyptian magic might be able to snatch it from my mind.

Just as I'd finished brushing my hair, Isis appeared on

the windowsill. "Perfect timing—oh, what have you got?" Something small and wriggly dangled from her jaws. I hurried over to shut the window and lock it tightly behind her.

"Theo? Are you ready?" Mother called out.

"Coming!" I called back. I turned to Isis. "Don't let anyone near our treasure. I'm counting on you."

She gave a low-throated growl, then stalked back to her basket, climbed in, and began to make crunching sounds.

"Er, enjoy your dinner." I glanced at the reticule on the bed. I thought briefly of putting it in one of the drawers, but a reticule was the first thing even a common thief would look for. No, it seemed best to bring it with me. Sighing, I slipped the wretched thing onto my wrist and went to find my mother and Mr. Bing.

CHAPTER TWO
THE MOTHER OF ALL MUSEUMS

IF YOU'VE EVER HAD THE EXPERIENCE of being given a lovely apple, all rosy and full of promise, only to bite into it and find a wormy, rotten core, then you will understand the feeling I had when I first stepped into the Egyptian Museum.

It was a large, impressive building full of hundreds—if not thousands—of ancient artifacts I would never see anywhere else. However, when I stepped inside, the force of the black magic, *heka,* and lingering *mut* nearly brought me to my knees. In fact, I actually stumbled as the magic rising off centuries' worth of discoveries pressed down on me. It felt as if every artifact in the place had left a trace of itself behind in the vestibule of the museum, like Mother's perfume when she leaves a room. Only this wasn't the charming smell of lilacs or lily of the valley. This was a thick miasma of magic and curses. Far removed from the source of their power, they buzzed faintly through the air, an invisible swarm of tiny, malevolent insects. With so much of it contained in such a confined space, there was the distinct sense of pressure building—like the air just before a thunderstorm.

"Theo, are you all right?" Mother asked, the worry in her voice overlaid with a tinge of annoyance. The word *peculiar* lay unspoken in the air between us.

"Yes, Mother. Just missed a step, that's all." I held myself as still as possible and let the noxious brew wash over me, trying to get acclimated to it.

Mr. Bing peered down at me. "Are you certain? You look rather pale . . ."

I waved my hand dismissively. "I'm sure it's the heat. I'm not quite used to the weather here, and then the sudden cool of the museum. It will just take me a moment to adjust."

"Well, if you're sure, Monsieur Maspero's office is this way." Bing led us through the vestibule and past a large, tantalizing room lined with rows and rows of sarcophagi. At the far end of the room sat two large statues, as if holding court over all the tourists who dared to interrupt the rest of the ancient pharaohs. My feet itched to turn down those steps, but Bing was moving along at a brisk clip and I had already been scolded once for dawdling.

We proceeded down a hallway lined with offices until Mr. Bing finally stopped in front of a large door. "Mrs. Throckmorton," he said, "you may go in, as Monsieur Maspero is expecting you. While the two of you meet, perhaps you would allow me to give your daughter a tour of our museum? Find her some cool refreshment?"

"You are too kind, Mr. Bing," Mother said. "That would be lovely."

I was torn. If I went with Bing, I would not hear what Mother and M. Maspero discussed. However, Bing might have an important message from Wigmere. Not only that, this could be my only chance to see all the wonders in the museum. Besides, I already knew the bulk of Mother's plan—it had been my plan first, after all, to come to Luxor and look for clues to what we suspected was a grand temple built by Thutmose III. In the end, I decided I could afford to take Bing up on his offer. "Thank you, Mr. Bing. I would like that very much."

He opened the door for Mother, then closed it after her and turned to me. "This way."

As we made our way back down the hallway, I was dying to ask if he carried a message from Wigmere, but a public hallway didn't seem the right place for such a question.

Especially since I had no idea how many at the Antiquities Service were part of the Brotherhood of the Chosen Keepers. It was a brilliant cover, I thought, hiding a secret organization dedicated to minimizing the corrosive effects of ancient magic and keeping it out of the wrong hands inside the Antiquities Service.

However, the longer I *thump-bumped* along behind Bing, the clearer it became that he was leading me far away from the exhibits. Perhaps we were heading for the refreshment first. I certainly wouldn't refuse something cool to drink and a place to sit down and grow accustomed to the thick pool of *heka* I was wading through.

Except, as we went farther and deeper into the museum, we seemed to have passed all the offices altogether. A faint niggle of concern settled along my shoulders and I remembered the rather maniacal look he'd had in the train station when he'd first spotted us. "Mr. Bing, where are you taking me, exactly?"

He looked over his shoulder at me and I was struck again by his intense eagerness. To make matters worse, his hair had escaped the confines of whatever tonic he'd combed it with that morning and was starting to stick up in odd places, which made him look slightly demented. "We're almost there," he said.

I knew he meant it to be reassuring, but instead it was as

if someone had just flipped a caution switch inside me. I wasn't sure I should be following him.

I mean, what did I know about him, *really?* He said Wigmere had sent him, but surely any of the Serpents of Chaos could pretend he had been sent by the head of the Chosen Keepers. I abruptly stopped walking.

It took Bing a half dozen steps before he realized I was no longer following him. He stopped, then looked around. "What are you doing back there?" he asked.

I folded my arms and tried to look implacable. "I'm not taking another step until you tell me exactly where we're going."

He quickly retraced his steps until he was standing right in front of me. "I told you. Wigmere sent me," he said in quiet tones.

"Yes, but anyone could say that, couldn't he? And I would have no way of knowing whether or not he was telling the truth."

He opened his mouth as if to argue, then closed it again. He looked crushed. "You mean you don't trust me?"

I hated to hurt his feelings, but one thing I've learned in the past few months is that everyone is suspect until proven innocent. I thought briefly of asking to see his wedjat eye tattoo—the one that all Chosen Keepers had—but decided against it. For one, if he was an impostor, I didn't want to spill the beans about their secret tattoo. Second, it was beyond scandalous—even for me—to wander around demanding to see strange men's chests. "Let's just say I have a cautious nature."

His smile put me a bit off balance. "And so you should, but really, there is nothing to worry about. We're almost there and then you'll see. Here, come." As he spoke, he reached out to grab my arm.

I tried to leap back out of his reach, but he had rather longish arms and was able to snag me anyway. "Let go," I said, pulling on my arm with all my strength.

"I told you," he grunted, trying to tug me down the hall. "We're almost there." Suddenly, he seemed to remember something and stopped tugging. Without him pulling on me, I tumbled backwards, nearly landing end over teakettle.

"I forgot! I'm supposed to tell you, *I'm a traveler, come from the West.*"

Hearing the code phrase that Wigmere had given me cleared my suspicions instantly. "Well, honestly! Why didn't you say so in the first place?" I asked, straightening my frock.

"Sorry," he said with a sheepish grin. "I'm rather new at this."

Clearly, I thought.

Bing resumed walking and I fell into step behind him. He

led me down the hall to a door, which led to another hall-way, which in turn led to a back staircase of some sort. "Where are we going?" I asked.

"Lord Wigmere wanted you to meet with one of our senior research and development team members before you left for Luxor." Mr. Bing stopped in front of a small door. At first it appeared to be a closet—a closet full of an amazing collection of ancient Egyptian bric-a-brac. There were medium-size obelisks leaning up against the wall, plinths, busts of ancient Egyptians carved from stone, unused stone tablets and stele stacked atop one another like dinner plates. A fine layer of dust lay over everything. Mr. Bing went over to a towering wooden mummy case propped against the wall. As he went to lift the lid off, I saw that it was hinged, and it swung open to reveal a door.

"Very clever," I said admiringly.

"Isn't it, though?" Mr. Bing beamed and motioned for me to go first.

The passageway led to a large, winding stairway that seemed to disappear deep into the bowels of the museum. As we clattered down the stairs, the orb in my reticule bruised my leg with each step. The stairs were steep, almost a ladder, really, and they were circular. We went round and round, so that by the time we reached the bottom, my brain was spinning inside my head. "Where are we?" I asked. The walls down here seemed to be of rock rather than wood or plaster.

"It's an underground chamber, built under the museum, dug right into the ground itself," Mr. Bing explained. "Most people don't even know it's here." He crossed over to two large steel doors and pressed a buzzer on the wall. There was a loud clunk as something unlocked, and then Mr. Bing pushed open the door. "Here she is, Professor. I'll come back for her in a bit." Then he stepped back out and closed the door behind me with a resounding clang.

I found myself in a large, cavernous room. Dark shadows obscured the high ceiling, and it was easy to imagine hundreds of tons of rock and Cairo streets far above.

A scraping noise came from a distant corner of the room and my pulse quickened.

"Hello?" I called out.

Rows of tables and benches swept out in front of me, stacked high with all manner of strange things: blocks of paraffin wax, rolls of beeswax, crocodile eggs, a mortar and pestle, long skinny reeds, papyrus leaves. There was even a large fish tank in the middle of the room, filled with what I thought might be *oxyrinchus* fish.

Half a dozen mummies in various states of undress lined one wall. Next to them were wine kegs, huge jars of golden honey, slabs of clay and unworked stone—basalt, granite, and alabaster. Thin sheets of gold and lead were scattered on one of the tables like playing cards, while a thick pot of what smelled like bitumen boiled sluggishly nearby.

"I'll be with you in just a moment," a voice called out.

I turned toward the voice, relieved to see a thin man hovering over one of the tables. He was taller even than Father and had stooped shoulders, as if he'd spent his entire life in a room that was too short for him. He wore a white canvas coat that came down to the knees of his plaid trousers. His hair was white and put me in mind of a dandelion just before all the fuzz flies away in a stiff breeze.

"There we go," the man said. "Done." He set whatever he'd been working on down and looked up at me. I gasped and took a step back, ready to run for the door. His face was half metal and leather, and his eyes were enormous, the size of billiard balls, as they swiveled crazily in my direction.

CHAPTER THREE
PROFESSOR QUILLINGS,
I PRESUME?

"OH, SORRY ABOUT THAT." He reached up and pushed the leather and brass up onto the top of his head. As his eyes went back to normal size, my heart started to beat again. He'd been wearing magnifying goggles.

The man came out from behind his table, smoothed down his hair (to no avail, I might add), and straightened his orange bow tie, which was singed at one end. "Miss Throckmorton?" He held out a hand and peered down at me.

I bobbed a quick curtsy. "Yes, sir, and whom do I have the pleasure of meeting?"

"Dr. Seymour Quillings. Head of the Brotherhood of Chosen Keepers Research and Development branch."

"How do you do?" I turned my gaze from the strange man back to the room behind us. "This is a lovely laboratory you have. You must do nothing but remove curses from dawn to dusk!"

He chuckled. "Not exactly. Wigmere's been telling me the most extraordinary things about you."

"Really?" That may or may not have been a good thing, I realized.

"Yes, about your remarkable abilities. Not to mention some of the very clever ideas you've been using in your work with ancient magic."

"Oh. Well. Thank you."

"I was especially fascinated by your use of wax and the moonlight. Fascinating. I've been doing some further experiments on those principles myself."

"Well, that's lovely, and I'm sure you'll find some, er, wonderful results." For all her emphasis on etiquette, Grandmother Throckmorton and her governesses neglected to teach me the proper response when discussing a person's experiments.

He stared at me a moment longer, as if I were a strange mechanism he were trying to understand, then clapped his hands together suddenly, startling me. "Well, I guess you'll be wondering why you're here?"

"I was, rather."

"Knowing the dangers and challenges you'll face, Wigmere did not want you going out unprepared. He wanted to outfit you properly for your mission."

I warmed at his words. Even from thousands of miles away, Wigmere was still looking out for me. "Excellent! What sorts of tools would those be?"

"Well, the first priority is to be sure you don't disappear. Wigmere did say you have an uncanny knack for finding trouble."

"I would have said trouble has an uncanny knack for finding me," I corrected, as the distinction seemed important.

"Either way, we don't want to lose track of you. Here, let me show you." He led me to a cluttered worktable that was full of springs and cogs and small chisels and screwdrivers the size of sewing needles. He brushed aside some brass shavings and tiny silver screws. "Here we go," he said triumphantly.

"A watch?" I inquired politely, although in truth, it was the largest, strangest, *ugliest* watch I'd ever seen. It was more than two inches thick and about three inches in diameter. A half dozen knobs protruded from its case. Honestly, it was about the size of a small wind-up clock.

"No, no. Not a watch. It is a Quillings's Homing Beacon and Curse-Repelling Device." He lifted his eyes from the contraption and gave me a worried look. "I took the liberty of naming it after myself. I don't think anyone will mind, do you?"

"I shouldn't think so. How exactly does it work?" I asked, eyeing the contraption with newfound admiration.

"Using alpha particles," Quillings proudly announced. "We have discovered that dark magic and curses give off something called alpha particles, a mild form of radiation, which is why being around them for too long can be so corrosive. I've only just this year invented something that allows us to use that phenomenon to our advantage. If you must work around a particularly vile curse, turn this knob here and it sends out a small electromagnetic pulse that repels the corrosive *heka* and allows you to escape unscathed. However, if you turn the knob this way, it acts as a homing beacon. The pattern of the alpha particles allows us to locate you with this." He held up a huge piece of photographic equipment.

"Is that a camera?"

"Not quite, but it works on the same principle. The alpha particles create a pattern on the thin film of gold inside, allowing us to track your movements that way. Wigmere wants us to keep a close eye on you."

"I daresay it can't hurt," I agreed. I took the clunky watch and strapped it to my wrist. Hoping Quillings wouldn't be offended, I tugged my sleeve down to cover it up. I looked up to find him watching me. "So my mother won't ask inconvenient questions," I explained.

His face cleared. "Ah, of course. And I see you wear gloves."

"Always," I said. "I try to minimize my contact with curses." One can never be too careful—black magic and curses have the most annoying habit of trying to work their way into one's skin.

"You might be interested in these, then." He led me over to a table against the back wall that held a small mountain of gloves. "As I said, I was very interested in the work you'd been doing with wax, and I've been conducting a few experiments. These gloves are made especially with wax-coated thread—"

I gasped. "Brilliant!"

His old cheeks pinkened. "Why, thank you. I thought it was worth a try. It works wondrously well—absorbs the curse right off an object so you can touch it if need be. The only drawback is that the gloves are a little sticky. Here. Let's find you a pair." We spent a few moments sorting through them till we found a white pair that were almost small enough for me. As I tucked them into my pocket, he motioned for me to follow him to yet another workstation in the middle of the room.

"Wigmere wanted you to have some offensive weapons at your disposal as well."

"Offensive weapons?" I repeated, not sure I'd heard correctly.

"Yes. Like this one." He picked up a gold fountain pen. "This contains a curse, a rather nasty one. It causes the recipient to suffer the agonies of a hundred scorpion stings over and over again. If you are backed into a corner, you twist it here, like so, and the inside capsule snaps apart and releases the curse. You'll need to point it at whatever you wish to use it on, then get away quickly, before it has a chance to zero in on you instead."

I stared at the pen, both fascinated and repelled. "How cunning."

"Here, take it."

With great reluctance, I reached out and gingerly took the pen.

"And lastly, this," he said, producing a fetching little silver compact, just like the one Mother uses when she powders her nose.

"Oh, it's lovely!" I said. "But I'm afraid I'm too young to wear powder."

Quillings chuckled. "Oh, trust me. You wouldn't want to wear *this* powder. This is made from ground-up sandstone collected from inside a pharaoh's tomb—"

"Which has magical properties!"

"Yes! You know of it?" He looked duly impressed.

"I do. In fact, I used it once when I was cornered by a very nasty man."

"Well then, I shall hardly have to tell you how it works. Here you go."

I stared at the compact, remembering Bollingsworth's ruined face. Slowly, I shook my head. "I don't think I should, sir."

"Why ever not?"

"It seems wrong, somehow."

"But you just said you'd used it before."

"Yes, but I'd been backed into a corner and outnumbered and there was nothing else at hand. It was a choice of last resort."

The professor looked at me oddly, almost as if he was a little disappointed in me. "I was given to understand you had used Egyptian magic quite comfortably."

"I don't know that *comfortable* is ever the right word to use regarding Egyptian magic." I eyed the pen in my hand. "I have, on occasion, been forced to use magic to ensure my own safety. But it was only making do with what was at hand. Carrying it around with me and planning to use it seems very different. Especially with such vile curses as these. Besides," I said, putting the pen back onto the table, "I don't expect I'll need it. I've only to hand off two artifacts when I first arrive in Luxor, and then the rest of my time will be spent working on my mother's dig."

Quillings looked at the pen and compact on the table, then took a step closer to me so that I was forced to tilt my head up to meet his gaze. "Do you really think it will be that easy?" he asked. "With Chaos causing riots in the streets—"

"Chaos is behind that?"

"We believe so. Someone is certainly behind it and Chaos is the most likely. You must understand, Miss Throckmorton. Things are different here on the frontlines of the fight against Chaos. The London operation that Wigmere runs is more of a last line of defense. It is designed to catch whatever slips through our grasp. But here in the field, we take a much more active approach when we come face-to-face with evil."

His words sent a chill down my back.

"Now, take these." He took the pen and compact from the table and put them firmly in my hand. "And do not be afraid to use them. Remember, it is not only your life you are protecting, Miss Throckmorton, but the lives of count-less innocents who do not even suspect that such hideous magic exists or what it would do if unleashed in their midst."

Reluctantly, my fingers closed around the items, and then I quickly dropped them into my pocket, as if they were hot. I was suddenly desperate to be away from Quillings and his sinister laboratory. "Is that all, sir? I should probably get back to my mother. She didn't have *that* much to discuss with Monsieur Maspero."

Quillings looked at me steadily, as if he knew perfectly well why I wanted to leave. "Of course. But do remember one thing. It's different here, where we live side by side with the ancient mysteries." Then he bade me goodbye and wished me Godspeed.

Slowly, with my head whirling, I made my way back to the public part of the museum. I couldn't make up my mind about Quillings and his thoughts on how to combat Chaos. It seemed too much like the methods Chaos themselves used.

I *did* envy him his laboratory, however. Just think of how many curses I could remove with all of that equipment!

I'd reached the door that led back to the storage closet and cautiously poked my head through. Bing wasn't waiting for me in the closet, so I stepped out into the hall.

An unfamiliar gentleman loitered in the corridor. As soon

as he saw me, he hurried over. "Bing sent me," he explained. "He has been detained by Maspero and asked that I escort you back to your mother."

"And who did you say you were?" I asked, giving him a nudge to use the code phrase.

There was a flash of annoyance in the other man's face, just a second-too-long pause before he answered. "I am Carruthers."

That was it. Simply "Carruthers." No mention that he had come from the West. Slowly, I began to back away from him.

The stranger lowered his brow in a scowl and took a step toward me just as Bing himself came round the corner. "Oh, are you done, then? I was just coming to fetch you."

The stranger, realizing the gig was up, leaped forward, grabbed for my arm with one hand, and fumbled at his jacket with the other.

CHAPTER FOUR
Come into My Parlor, Said the Spider to the Fly

I DIDN'T STICK AROUND LONG ENOUGH to see what he was reaching for. I grasped the cords of my reticule, then swung it down—hard—against his knuckles. He gave a shout of surprise and relaxed his grip. I jerked away and darted down the nearest hall. "Be careful!" I called to Bing. "I think he's got a weapon!" Then I clamped my mouth shut and took the next corner at full tilt.

The exhibits, I thought. I needed to get to the exhibits where there'd be loads of people. He'd have a hard time snatching me if others were watching. I ran as silently as I could, which was hard in the echoing marble halls of the museum. I stayed up on my toes as much as possible, which helped keep my footsteps quieter but made my calves scream in agony. I turned a corner, then another, and the shouts of the men faded behind me.

I took another turn and found myself in a gallery, which meant I must have crossed the full length of the museum. Pursuing footsteps sounded behind me. Not waiting to see who it was, I tore down the stairs to the ground floor, afraid a huge, hairy hand would reach out from behind and snatch me at any moment.

At the bottom of the stairs, I darted into a room full of magnificent jewelry (New Kingdom, seventeenth century BC). Unfortunately, the room was empty, so there were no witnesses among whom I could lose myself. However, the display cases were enormous, so I threw myself behind the nearest one and tried to breathe as softly as I could, even though my lungs were begging for air.

There was the squeak of shoe leather on the polished floor and I felt the pursuer's *ka*, or life force, hovering in the doorway. I quickly cast my eyes downward so he wouldn't feel me looking back at him and held my breath.

After a long moment, the footsteps moved on down the hallway. Allowing myself to breathe a little more deeply, I waited another five minutes to be certain he wouldn't double back. Finally, with great reluctance, I crept out of my hiding place and inched toward the doorway, careful to keep close to the wall and out of sight. When I slowly stuck my neck out to check the hallway, I nearly screamed as I came eyeball to eyeball with a pair of rapidly blinking eyes.

"Mr. Bing!" I gasped in relief, putting my hand up to keep my heart from thudding right out of my chest.

"This way, miss," he said, keeping his voice low. "Let's get you back to Maspero's office."

"What happened to Carruthers?" I asked, falling into step alongside him.

"He made his way to the front exit and got out that way. I sent one of the guards after him, but he had a decent head start, so I'm not hopeful."

"How did he get in, do you think?"

Bing shrugged. "He'd just have to pay admission like everyone else."

When at last we reached Maspero's office, Bing rapped quickly on the door. "Come in," a muffled voice called out.

Bing opened the door and stepped aside so I could go in. "I'll go see if the guard had any luck," he whispered, then closed the door behind him.

"There you are, darling," Mother said. "Do come in and meet Mr. Borscht."

My head snapped up. Borscht? I thought she was to meet with Monsieur Maspero. "How do you do, sir," I said as I bobbed a small curtsy.

"Very pleased to meet you, young lady."

Mr. Borscht did not have a lick of hair on his head, and his shaved scalp gleamed faintly in the light coming from the window. It was an odd look, especially when coupled with the dark black mustache that covered the lower half of his face. Behind his gold-rimmed glasses, his eyes were an arctic blue.

"Come sit down, dear. We're almost done."

I wanted to ask Mother what had happened to Monsieur Maspero, but that seemed rude to do in front of Mr. Borscht. Hoping I didn't look too disheveled after my gallop through the museum, I took the seat next to her, my heart still beating rapidly. There was a small tray with empty plates. They'd had tea, I realized, then remembered I'd not gotten the refreshment Mr. Bing had promised me. Looking at the empty plates only made my stomach feel emptier, so I turned my attention to Mr. Borscht.

He was staring at me hungrily. Something about that gaze sent a chill of warning down my spine. Unsettled, I quickly cast my eyes downward.

His hands were encased in black gloves, and his right hand toyed with a letter opener while his other hand . . .

His other hand lay perfectly still. In fact, he held it at a rather odd angle, as if it was useless to him.

A leaden ball of dread began to form in my stomach. I

could think of only one man I knew who was missing a hand—an injury I had caused, more or less. Fear mounting, I lifted my gaze back up to his face.

As our eyes met, he smiled. It was not a nice smile. In fact, it made my heart stutter in my chest.

This was not Mr. Borscht, whoever that might be. This was Count von Braggenschnott, one of the most powerful Serpents of Chaos I had ever met, sitting in front of me as pretty as you please.

And he had been chatting with my mother for nearly an hour.

I was afraid I might be sick.

Trying to be casual, I glanced over my shoulder toward the door, wondering where Bing had gotten to.

"Theodosia? Mr. Borscht is speaking to you." Mother's chiding voice poked through my rising panic.

"Forgive me." I slowly turned back around, my mind scrambling frantically. How could we make our escape? Dare I risk exposing him? Would Mother even believe me?

I doubted it. I gripped my reticule cords more firmly.

"I asked if you were enjoying your trip to Egypt?" von Braggenschnott repeated.

"Er, for the most part." I was embarrassed at the faint tremble in my voice. Refusing to be cowed, I straightened my shoulders and met his chilling blue stare. "I have found there are more vermin in the city than I care for, but other than that, I am finding it most educational." There, that would show him I wasn't afraid.

"Vermin?" Mother sounded puzzled. "Whatever are you talking about, dear? We've only been here a matter of hours, and I have seen nothing that remotely qualifies as vermin."

That is because grownups never see the really important stuff. They are too distracted by the ordinary and mundane.

Von Braggenschnott laughed, cutting off any answer I might have given. "Children. They have such flights of fancy, do they not?"

Mother rolled her eyes delicately. "Don't they, though?"

The humiliation of having Mother and the head of the Serpents of Chaos dismiss me as a mere child was as sharp and painful as a knife.

"And I shall not subject you to Theo's any longer," she continued. "You have been most kind, Mr. Borscht. My husband and I, and the museum, cannot thank you enough for your help."

"It has been my pleasure, madame." He rose and bowed from the waist, his eyes taking on an appreciative gleam as he looked at Mother. That's when I had my second shock of the day. He was sweet on Mother!

While they continued with a few last-minute niceties, I tried to come up with a plan for escape. Finally Mother bade him goodbye and turned toward the door. I held my breath and followed.

It was only a short distance, but it felt as if time held still while we crossed it. I kept waiting for von Braggenschnott to call us back or stop us, but he didn't and we reached the door without incident. Was he really going to let us walk out?

Just as Mother put her hand on the knob, he spoke. "And Madame Throckmorton?"

"Yes," she said, turning to look back at him.

"Congratulations on such an intriguing daughter. I hope her visit continues to be educational. I believe the more education children receive, the better."

Mother smiled, inclined her head, then opened the door and swept out. I followed in her wake, nearly tripping in my eagerness to escape that small office.

CHAPTER FIVE
WHERE TO NOW, DONKEY BOY?

ONCE THE DOOR CLOSED FIRMLY BEHIND US, my heart slowed down from a flat-out race to a mere gallop.

Von Braggenschnott had let us go. He had let *me* go. Why?

There could be only one reason, really. He wanted something I had. Or he was hoping I'd lead him and his men to something they wanted.

All right, that was two reasons. My math skills aren't at their sharpest when I'm under duress.

Bing was waiting for us, calmly as you please, as if he hadn't been chasing assailants throughout the museum just moments before. I studied him, wondering if he had any idea who was in the office. "Mr. Bing?"

"Yes, Miss Theodosia?"

"Have you talked with Monsieur Maspero today?"

Mr. Bing frowned. "Not since this morning, when he sent me to fetch you two from the hotel." I could tell by the puzzled look on his face that he did not understand the reason for my question.

Either that or he was a very good actor. Mother, however, was giving me one of her looks, so I didn't dare risk any more questions. Even so, as we made our way to the exit, I studied Bing surreptitiously. No matter how I tilted my head and squinted at him, his thin, gangly form and scrubbed face did not look sinister in any way.

"Theodosia?" Mother's voice was sharp. "Are you quite all right?"

I swiveled my eyes over to Mother, who stared at me with her hands on her hips. "Just working out a kink in my neck. From looking at the exhibits. Some of those statues are quite tall, you know."

Mother sighed, shook her head, and sent an apologetic smile in Bing's direction.

He smiled back. "If you're ready to return to the hotel, I'll take you now."

"Thank you. That would be lovely," Mother said.

As we stepped outside the museum, I tried to think of a way to alert Mr. Bing to von Braggenschnott's presence without alarming Mother. I was so distracted by the challenge that I didn't even notice the crowd until I bumped up against a woman swathed in black from head to toe. That's when I noticed that the demonstration seemed to have spread from the train station to the streets near the museum. Quillings's words echoed through my head. *Chaos causing riots in the streets.*

Bing looked grimly at the mob. "Let's get you ladies home before it gets ugly," he said, leading us to where he had parked the carriage. It was nowhere to be seen.

"What happened to it?" I asked.

"No doubt all available carriages have been snatched up as people try to get away from the demonstration." He gave Mother an apologetic look. "I'm sorry, Mrs. Throckmorton. It looks as if we must stay here until the crowd disperses or hire donkeys." He grimaced at the second option, his glance flickering to the small crowd of donkey boys gathered at one end of the square.

"How long till the crowd disperses?" Mother asked, eyeing the safety of the museum. Little did she realize, the place held more danger than a mere mob.

Bing shrugged. "Hard to say. Last week there was a demonstration that lasted for two days with the participants camping in the streets."

"Well, we can't wait that long!" Mother exclaimed. "We've

a train to catch in the morning. Plus, we are quite tired from our trip." She glanced uneasily at the crowd. "I suppose we shall have to use the donkeys."

"Why can't we simply walk?" I asked.

"No one walks in Cairo, darling. It just isn't done," Mother said. "Besides, the donkeys will help force a path."

"Very well." Bing gave a resigned nod and strode toward the asses. Not wanting to get separated, we followed close on his heels.

At our approach, the donkey boys converged around us like a cheerful swarm of buzzing hornets. In a loud jumble of Arabic and English, they vied for our business. In spite of the unholy racket they made, they were all smiling and seemed to be having a marvelous time of it.

Bing pointed at a small cluster. "You. There. We'll take you." The boys snapped to attention and four of them jostled forward. "We only need three," Bing said testily.

One of the boys, the smallest one, was pushed aside by the others. As he sent them a hot glare, I saw that he was misshapen, his back hunched up. How wretched! And how cruel of the others to exclude him like that. "Excuse me, Mr. Bing," I said, "but I'd like to ride that donkey." I pointed at the one next to the crippled boy.

Bing sighed in exasperation. "One donkey is not any different from the others, but very well. You heard the girl," he

48

snapped at the boys. One of them sent a scathing glare in the smallest one's direction and shuffled back to wait with the others.

The crippled boy flashed me a grin of thanks and stepped forward to assist me up into the saddle. He had a bright, intelligent face and moved quickly in spite of his infirmity. By the time he had me settled on my donkey, Mother was delicately perched on hers and Bing . . . well, the reason for Mr. Bing's distaste for riding was quite clear. His legs were so very long, and the animal's so very short, that his feet nearly dragged on the ground. He looked utterly ridiculous, and it was hard to keep from laughing. I did not, however, crack so much as a smile.

"Let's get going," he said, shifting uncomfortably in his seat.

My donkey boy lightly flicked his beast about the head with a small, thin whip. The donkey lurched forward, then settled into an ambling walk. The donkey boy turned back and smiled at me. "Miss is wanting to go faster? Gadji's donkey very most fast. Get effendi miss there double quick."

"No, thank you." I held on more tightly just in case he ignored me. "I don't want to risk losing the others."

Looking somewhat disappointed, he shrugged and turned his attention to navigating the busy streets. I risked a glance over my shoulder, not surprised to see Carruthers slinking along behind, trying to hide among the masses of people. I tried to catch Bing's eye, but he was too busy keeping his feet from dragging in the muck.

As we headed away from the museum, the crowd continued to grow, its ranks swelling as more and more people poured in from side alleys and streets. Their mood—not quite menacing, but certainly not friendly—was almost as palpable as the *heka* in the air around us. I steered my donkey closer to Mr. Bing. Besides, I needed to tell him of von Braggenschnott.

Pedestrians managed to fill in the space between us, and I wasn't able to get close enough to avoid being overheard by Mother.

As we turned down the next street, we came to a full stop. The entire thoroughfare was clogged with demonstrators. Mr. Bing gave an exclamation of frustration.

My donkey boy flicked his whip and called out instructions in Arabic, trying to get my donkey to back up, but there was no room. The sea of people had closed in behind us. We couldn't go forward; we couldn't go back.

"Now what?" I called out to Mr. Bing.

His response was lost over the noise of the crowd. Shouts went up as a procession made its way down the middle of the street, the sea of people parting just enough to make room. As the crowd surged back, it drove a wedge of people between me and Bing. I shouted at him for assistance, but he and Mother had been shoved back up against a shop and were stuck in place. The jostling and pushing continued until my donkey, the boy, and I were pushed into a side alley.

Uneasy now, I searched the faces for the man from the museum but saw no sign of him. It would be just like Chaos to engineer a near riot in order to work their own mischief.

Actually, all they needed to do was be in place to take advantage of such a thing, I realized.

There were fewer people in the alley. I could still see the street as the crowd streamed by, but there was no sign of Mother or Bing. The city, which only hours ago seemed charming and picturesque in its exoticness, now felt ominous and threatening. Not knowing what else to do, I looked down at the donkey boy. "Now what?" I asked.

He shrugged. "Now we wait."

"Where does this alley lead? Can we double back?"

The donkey boy studied the stream of people trying to make their way past us to the main demonstration. He gave me a thumbs-up sign and then, holding firmly to the bridle and whispering something to the donkey, he got the poor beast turned around without tramping on anyone's toes. We began picking our way carefully to the other end of the alley. It was very much like trying to force water back up a spigot.

When we reached the street at the far end of the alley, we found it, too, was wall to wall with people. "We is going this way instead." The donkey boy pointed in the opposite direction. "Take longer but we get there still."

We surged along with the crowd for a bit, and then the boy turned down another alley, where we nearly stumbled into a group of wild-eyed men destroying an office of some kind. This wasn't good. "Maybe we should go back," I whispered to the donkey boy.

Too late. One of them spotted us, then nudged his neighbor. Within seconds all the rioters were staring at us with hard, angry expressions. *"Inglaize!"* one of them said.

"Inglaize!" another deep voice shouted.

I did not like the look in their eyes.

Neither did the donkey boy. He turned the donkey around and began running back the way we'd come, pulling the donkey along behind him while I held on for dear life.

CHAPTER SIX
CORNERED!

WE TURNED ONE CORNER, then another. The crowd followed, their voices getting louder as they drew near.

We slipped into the next alley and passed a tiny, narrow lane with barely enough room for the donkey. I stopped, but the donkey boy shook his head and kept going.

"But the alley is a dead end!" I protested. "We have to take this side street!"

"No. Gadji outsmart them crowds. Watch." He didn't look nearly as panicked as I felt. Perhaps because he wasn't *Inglaize*.

About halfway between the main street and the dead end, Gadji stopped the donkey. "Get off," he said.

"What?" Was he abandoning me to my fate? I'd be completely helpless—a sitting duck!

"Do you wish Gadji should risk his neck for you or no?"

"Why would you help me against your own people?"

Gadji shrugged. "Effendi miss is paying me. And they is not my peoples. Now, hurry."

As I swung my legs around and prepared to dismount, he reached a grubby hand out to stop me. "Gadji get big tip for this, right, miss? Saving miss's skin much harder than steering dumb donkey."

"Yes, yes. Of course. Please let me down." The sounds of the mob were quite close by now. Surely they would be rounding the corner at any moment.

I dropped to the ground, ready to ask, *Now what?* but the words froze in my throat at the donkey boy's antics. He had bent over at the waist, as if he was going to be sick, and was pulling at the back collar of his robe. I watched in horror as the hump on his back began to gyrate and wiggle. Thinking it rude to witness his physical struggles, I turned away, only to jerk back around at the sound of high-pitched scolding *chatter*. There really was no other word for it.

My mouth dropped open in shock as I saw that the hump on his back was gone, and on his shoulder sat a small, scrunch-faced monkey. It was he who was chattering.

"Sefu will help," the donkey boy said, then lifted the monkey up into the saddle I had just vacated. "Your jacket, miss."

Quickly grasping his plan, I started to peel off my jacket, stopped by the wretched reticule. With a sigh of frustration, I took it from my wrist, hung it on the saddle horn for a moment, then slipped all the way out of my jacket.

There was the sound of breaking glass from just around the corner. "Hurry!" Gadji said, and I threw the jacket to him. He quickly draped it around the monkey. Of course, it was far too large and lay in a puddle around the small creature, but in a pinch it might look as if I was just leaning in low to avoid any thrown objects. "Here," I said in a burst of inspiration, and took my hat from my head and plopped it onto the monkey's. Gadji muttered some words in Arabic, then slapped the donkey's hindquarters.

The creature brayed and bucked, then lurched forward in a jolting trot, the monkey crouched low.

As the monkey steered the donkey toward the tiny little back street, the boy grabbed my hand and pulled me into a recessed doorway. If we squashed very close together and sucked in our stomachs, we would—just barely—be hidden from view.

And none too soon. The sound of pounding feet and the angry roar of the mob reached the mouth of the alleyway. I closed my eyes and pretended I was nothing but a dilapidated wooden door, a trick I'd learned to help minimize my life force when dealing with angry *mut* and *ahku* in our museum at home.

A single shout went up from the crowd as someone spotted the donkey. *"Inglaize!"*

There was an answering roar, then the pounding of feet as the mob set off in pursuit. I kept my eyes closed and my breathing shallow for several more tense moments. Finally, I dared to open one eye and peek over at Gadji. His eyes were closed, and I briefly wondered if he knew the same trick I did about trying to disappear.

His eyes popped open and he smiled cheerfully. "Gadji's plan work."

I nodded. "It wouldn't hurt to check and be sure they didn't leave someone behind to act as a spotter."

"Good idea." Gadji poked his head out from the doorway. He gave a quick grin, then stepped fully into the alley. "Is all clear now, effendi miss," he said, spreading his arms wide.

Some of the tension left my body, but I peeked around the lintel to see with my own eyes before stepping out.

Gadji's face fell. "Effendi miss not trust Gadji?"

"No, no," I said. "I have just learned to be very, very cautious about some things. Being chased, for example. Thank you very much for risking yourself on my behalf."

"Oh, Gadji is not risking anything. Crowd is not mad at

Gadji. I not *Inglaize*." Then he smiled mischievously and held out his hand, rubbing his fingers together.

The promised tip. "Er, I haven't got any money on me," I said, reaching for—"My reticule!" I whispered, whipping my head around to where the donkey had disappeared.

"Is something being wrong, miss?"

"My purse. I left it on the donkey's saddle." There was a hollow, sick feeling deep in my stomach. "Where will the donkey go?"

"Back to his stable, miss."

I began heading toward the side street the donkey had taken. "Can we catch up to him, do you think?"

Gadji gave me an incredulous look. "No, miss. Donkey is being much too fast."

"You don't understand," I told him. "I have to at least try. There is something very important in my reticule."

"Is effendi miss forgetting the crowd?"

Er, yes. In my panic over the orb, I actually had.

"It is not safe for effendi miss to travel now."

But it was even less safe for the orb to fall into the wrong hands. "Very well. Do you think you could fetch my reticule and return it to me? I'm staying at the Shepheard Hotel. I'll be there until tomorrow morning, when we'll be catching the nine o'clock train to Luxor."

Gadji shook his head. "Gadji is not going back to stables, miss."

I nearly stomped my foot in frustration. "Why not?"

"He would receive beating for abandoning his donkey."

I gawped at him. Saving me had cost him his job? "Why did you risk so very much for me?"

Gadji rose to his full height, an almost imperious look coming over his face. "I am miss's guide. I am taking my duties most seriously."

"And so do I," I muttered. I simply *had* to retrieve the orb. "Tell me how to get to the stable and I'll go and speak to the stable owner myself. I'll explain everything to him and get my purse back."

Gadji burst out in great big guffaws, slapping at his knee. "Miss is making a funny joke."

"I'm not joking. I am quite serious."

Gadji stopped laughing and shook his head. "Any moneys in that purse now belong to donkey master."

"But it is mine!" I protested.

Gadji shrugged. "It is how you say: find it, keep it."

"Finders, keepers, you mean."

"That's it," he said, repeating it to himself for good measure. "But do not look so sad, miss. Gadji is still saving you."

"No, you don't understand. I must get the purse back! It doesn't just contain money, but something very valuable. I'll be in loads of trouble if I lose it." I reached out and grabbed his thin shoulders. "You have to tell me where this stable is."

Gadji shrugged. "It is in the old quarter, the seventh street, behind the carpet seller. But miss will not be finding it unless I am with you."

"Then you must come with me," I said.

"Very well. But I am only taking you there, not talking to stable owner. I am not wanting a beating."

"No, of course not," I assured him. But his words made me uneasy. What chance would I have of reasoning with the stable master?

We left our hiding place and retraced our steps to the main street. My pulse was still racing and I could feel panic nipping at my heels, urging me to hurry. The crowd was much thinner now, which gave me hope that we might catch up to the donkey, or at least reach the stables before he did. Gadji paused and put a hand out to stop me. A man riding a donkey was heading our way. I wondered briefly if I could talk him into letting me borrow his mount, then noticed his long limbs nearly sweeping the street beneath his feet.

"It's Mr. Bing!" My initial relief at no longer being lost quickly evaporated when I realized I'd just lost my chance to go after the orb. I thought briefly about stepping back into the alley, but it was too late. Mr. Bing had seen me.

He sat up in his saddle and waved. He urged his donkey

to a bone-jarring trot that made my teeth ache to watch. I quickly turned to Gadji. "Say nothing about losing my purse." He gave me a startled look, and then Bing's donkey rattled to a stop in front of us. Mr. Bing lowered his legs to the ground and stepped off. "Miss Theodosia! I am so glad to have found you! Your mother is quite frantic with worry. As was I."

The donkey boy stepped forward and tapped himself on the chest. "Gadji is keeping miss safe. Not let anything happen to her."

Mr. Bing looked down his nose. "Who are you, precisely?"

"He is the donkey boy," I reminded him. "He used his donkey as a decoy to keep the mob from finding me. I owe him my safety."

"Oh. Very well done, then," Bing said, nodding awkwardly at Gadji.

"I, er, promised him a tip," I said, feeling awkward. Now that he had no job to return to, it was even more important that he not be left penniless.

"Ah." A look of cynical understanding appeared on Bing's face. "Did it for the money, did you?" He narrowed his eyes and studied Gadji more closely. "How do I know you weren't in on it? That it wasn't all part of some grand plan to extract ransom for the girl?"

"It wasn't like that!" I said, horrified.

"I don't expect you to understand how they are, miss. But I have a few coins I can spare."

Again, Gadji drew himself up to his full height, a surprising nobility descending over his features. "Do not be bothering yourself, effendi. If the safety of the effendi miss is not worth a small gift, then I will make a gift to you of her safety." He bowed formally, then turned and retreated down the alley, his small shoulders stiff with pride. I wanted to run after him, to apologize for Bing's blundering ham-handedness and insist he take the money now that he had no job.

"Come now, miss," Bing said gently. "Let's get you safely to your mother."

I longed to confide in Mr. Bing, tell him of losing the orb, but I wasn't absolutely sure I could trust him. The shock of almost being nabbed by Carruthers, then coming face-to-face with von Braggenschnott at the museum this morning had planted rather significant doubts about Bing's trustworthiness. If my suspicions were unfounded and he was trustworthy, he would surely think very poorly of me for having lost the orb. He would most likely tell the other Chosen Keepers, and I could hardly bear the shame of all of them knowing of my mistake. I would just have to figure something out on my own.

CHAPTER SEVEN
TO LUXOR WE WILL GO

THE ONLY GOOD THING TO COME of Mr. Bing's rescue was that I was able to tell him about von Braggenschnott as Bing escorted me back to Mother. He seemed genuinely horrified and could not wait to deposit Mother and me at the hotel, then return to the museum and try to apprehend the man. I, however, was convinced von Braggenschnott would be long gone. His mission was accomplished, after all: to let me know in no uncertain terms just how intimately he knew of my every move.

Perhaps it was just as well I had taken Quillings's weapons, I thought.

When the stately entrance and elegant patio of the Shepheard Hotel came into view, I nearly wept with relief. The hawking vendors and street entertainers began to swarm, but honestly, these people had nothing on the seething masses from which I'd just come. I ignored them and dragged myself up the front steps behind Mother. I was shaky and weak and wanted nothing more than to lie down, but of course I couldn't. I had to come up with a plan to retrieve the missing orb. Especially with the Serpents of Chaos skulking nearby. I shuddered to think what would happen if it fell into their hands. I could only hope that they didn't know how to properly activate it.

Once back in our rooms, Mother decided we should rest until it was time to dress for dinner. That sounded lovely to me. I closed my room door, then leaned against it and took a deep breath. I gave myself exactly one minute to collect myself, then pushed away from the door. "Did anything exciting happen while I was gone?" I asked Isis.

She meowed, then hopped gracefully off the bed and came over to rub her head on my ankle.

"I'll take that as a no." I glanced over my shoulder to be certain I'd closed the door, then went to the wicker basket. I lifted Isis's cushion from the bottom, then stopped. Best to be cautious.

I hopped up, grabbed a pillow from the bed, and stuffed it along the bottom of the door to seal it. Then I went to the window and pulled the drapes shut. When I was certain no hint of the tablet's magic or power would leak from the room, I reached in and removed the false bottom that Wigmere had built for me, relieved when I saw the piece of old newspaper. However, after my disaster with the orb, I wanted to be absolutely certain. I unwrapped the layers of newspaper, then the thin lead sheet that kept the tablet's magic from leaking out and being detected. I sighed in relief at the dull green stone. The Emerald Tablet, something for which occultists and alchemists had been searching for centuries. And, by a bizarre twist of fate, had ended up in our museum's basement. But it held far more than alchemical secrets. It was actually a coded map that led to a cache of artifacts that had once belonged to the Egyptian gods and still held unimaginable power. Power that would be terrible and deadly if it fell into the wrong hands—the hands of the Serpents of Chaos, say.

I gave the tablet a little pat, then carefully rewrapped it. "Good work," I told Isis as I put the false bottom back, then replaced the cushion. "I, however, have botched things horribly." She came over and nudged my ankle. Only too happy to cuddle for a moment, I picked her up and buried my face in her soft black fur. When I felt strong enough to go on, I

lifted my head and stared into her bright green eyes and confessed every horrid detail of my afternoon.

When I got to the part about losing the orb, she stopped
kneading at me with her claws and looked up. Was it just my
imagination, or did her golden green gaze hold a hint of re-
proach? "It wasn't really my fault," I told her. "I was in danger, and everything was happening at once. It could have
happened to anyone."

She blinked, then went back to her kneading.

"I don't suppose you can slip out into the city and hunt it
down for me, can you?"

There was no response.

Nearly sick with regret, I went to the door, retrieved the
pillow, and put it back on the bed, then went to look out the
window.

Gadji had given me the stable address, such as it was, but
honestly! It would be like trying to find a needle in a
haystack, I thought as I looked out over the rooftops of the
city. How on earth was I to find the old quarter, and if I did,
there had to be at least a hundred carpet sellers in Cairo.
Which one was the stable behind? The sheer enormity of my
blunder made my throat tighten with panic. Perhaps I ought
to lie down just for a moment to collect myself.

While I lay staring at the ceiling, petting Isis, there was a
soft rap on my door. "Yes?" I called out.

"Are you dressed for dinner, dear?" Mother asked. "It's almost time to go down."

"No, Mother. I don't think I want dinner this evening."

I heard the door open, then the rustle of skirts as Mother made her way over to the bed where I lay. She peered down at me, her lovely eyebrows drawn together in concern. "What's wrong, dear? Are you ill?"

As I stared up into her worried brown eyes, I was overcome with a desire to tell her everything—the whole sordid mess. I was so tired of keeping secrets! They made my head ache.

I'd spent the entire afternoon trying to think of a way to explain to her just whom she'd had tea with at the Antiquities Service, but it was, quite simply, impossible. While she knew of von Braggenschnott from his work as a slightly shady antiquities dealer, she had no idea who he *really* was. And if I tried to alert her, she would wonder how I had come to know him. And of course there was no explanation for that, not without explaining everything. Something I'd sworn not to do.

"I have a bit of a headache," I said. "Perhaps from too much sun."

Her frown deepened. "Well, that doesn't bode well for you working on the excavation."

Bother! I wasn't about to risk the only pleasant thing

about this entire trip. "Well, perhaps not the sun so much as the crowd this afternoon. It was a bit unsettling."

Mother's face grew pale. "Indeed. You must be very careful not to let anything else like that happen again, do you understand? This is not like our own neighborhood, where you can be allowed some freedom. The streets of Cairo are very different from the streets of London."

I thought it was beastly unfair of her to blame that on me.

"You gave me quite a fright, Theo." Her voice softened. "I would never forgive myself if something happened to you." She placed her hand on my cheek. I closed my eyes and let myself soak in the comfort she was offering.

"I'm sorry, Mother. I didn't mean for that to happen. The crowd was just so big and confusing, and people were pushing and shoving . . ."

"Shh. I know, dear. Everything's fine now. Here, let me get you a cool cloth." She went over to the basin and wet a linen cloth, then wrung it out. When she put it on my forehead, it smelled faintly of lilacs. "When I return, I'll have them send up some light broth and toast. How would that be?"

"Lovely. Thank you."

She leaned down and kissed my cheek, then headed for the door.

"Oh, and Mother?"

"Yes, dear?"

"Could you have them send up some sardines for Isis?"

There was a long pause. "Very well. Broth, toast, and *sardines*." Then she closed the door behind her, and I was alone.

However, I'd wallowed in self-pity long enough. It was time to come up with a plan. A course of action that would allow me to . . . well, a *plan* would be good. I didn't like having to give up on the orb, but I didn't see that I had much choice at this point. The tablet was the bigger priority. While the orb was a hugely powerful artifact, the Emerald Tablet could lead the Serpents of Chaos to an entire cache full of artifacts, all of them as powerful as the orb, if not more so. Best to cut my losses and focus on keeping the tablet out of Chaos's hands.

Wigmere and I had discussed the possibility that the Serpents of Chaos would learn of my whereabouts. He'd done his best to create diversions for them far away from Egypt, but it looked as though they hadn't taken the bait.

I needed to keep them at bay long enough to hand off the tablet to the wedjadeen. Once it was no longer in my possession, Chaos would have no reason to hound me.

Well, except for the small matter of revenge. But honestly, an organization like that should have much bigger fish to fry than getting even with one eleven-year-old girl!

The next morning we were up and packed bright and early. We were scheduled to be on the nine o'clock express to Luxor, but I dragged my feet so that we managed to miss it. Mother was rather put out, but honestly! Just because Chaos knew our every move didn't mean I had to make it easy for them.

Mother had ordered a carriage. ("No more donkeys for us for a while," she'd said.) When it arrived, the hotel's porter bundled all our trunks and bags into it, and then we set off for the train station.

The streets were much quieter, just the normal hustle and bustle of the people of Cairo going about their business. I kept my eyes peeled for any signs that we were being followed, but as best I could tell, we weren't. Well, except for the men wanting to sell us sweetmeats or lemonade and a handful of scraggly children crying for baksheesh.

The station, too, was much less chaotic today. For one, there was no public speaking going on nearby and no crowd of angry men with raised fists and loud voices. As we disembarked from our carriage, I eyed the nearby donkey boys, looking in vain for the boy who had helped me.

Unfortunately, he was not among them, and I worried about what might have happened to him with no job to return to and no money.

"Theodosia?"

I pulled my attention away from the donkey boys. "Yes, Mother?"

"You stay here with the luggage while I make certain our seats on the ten o'clock train are confirmed."

I winced as she threw me one of her *I have still not forgiven you for that* looks. With a sigh, I set my satchel and Isis's basket down on the ground, then perched myself on the edge of Mother's steamer trunk. A quick glance assured me that no one in the station looked like a member of Chaos, so I relaxed and allowed myself to watch the other travelers.

A light tap on my shoulder had me nearly jumping out of my skin. I whirled around to find Gadji standing right behind me, his odd little monkey perched on his shoulder.

"Greetings, miss."

"Hello!" I said, my hopes soaring. "Did you make it back to the stables yesterday?"

Gadji frowned. "No, Gadji told you. Is not wanting great big beating that waits for me there."

"Of course." My shoulders slumped as my hopes were dashed. I quickly glanced over at Mother, not sure how she'd react to finding me chatting with one of the locals. Fortunately, she was still deep in conversation with the man behind the counter. I turned back to Gadji. "Even so, I am glad to see you again. I wanted to thank you properly." His fate had haunted me ever since he'd confessed he'd be out of a job on my account. "I'd promised you a big tip," I re-minded him as I fumbled in my skirt pocket.

Gadji grinned. "Very good of miss to remember."

"Here." I pulled out a few coins and thrust them at him. I glanced over at the ticket counter, where Mother was just finishing up her business. "You have to go before my mother returns," I told him. "Good luck!" I said brightly. "And thank you!" Then I gave him a gentle nudge to get him moving. If I wasn't careful, Mum was going to have me sequestered under lock and key during my entire stay in Egypt.

"But miss—"

"You know how much trouble you would have been in if you'd returned to your master without the donkey? That's how much trouble I'll be in if my mother finds me talking to strangers. Now, please go. I really do appreciate all that you've done for me."

Gadji threw an understanding look in my mother's direction, nodded his head once, then slipped silently into the crowd of milling passengers.

And just in time. Mother arrived with a porter in tow. "Theo, who was that you were talking to?"

"No one, Mother."

"I distinctly saw you speaking with a young Egyptian boy."

"Oh, that." I waved my hand. "He was asking for baksheesh."

Her face cleared. "Very well, but you need to be cautious of whom you mingle with. If I can't be assured of your co-operation and safety—"

"You can, Mother! I told him no and sent him on his way immediately."

She gave a crisp nod of her head. "Excellent. Now let's get on this train before it leaves without us, too."

We climbed on board and made our way to our traveling car. It was quite luxurious and felt more like a drawing room than a compartment on a train. As we settled comfortably into the seat, Mother took out her notes and began reading. I pulled Isis's basket closer to me. "May I take her—"

"No. Absolutely not," Mother said without looking up.

I sighed loudly, then put my face down next to the basket. "Sorry, Isis. Mother says no." I wanted to be certain she knew exactly who was keeping her cramped up in there. I watched Mother. Did she plan to spend the entire trip reading and writing in her journals? That would be quite boring, indeed. I craned my neck, trying to see what she was writing. "Mother," I asked casually, "do you keep a journal for all of your excavations?"

"Yes, dear," she said absently. "Every one."

"Even the one on which I was born?"

Her pen stilled. "I-I'm not sure if I had begun that habit back then." She kept her eyes on the journal and I had the most distinct sensation that she was not being wholly truthful.

"Will we be passing the temple in which I was born on the way to Luxor? Will I be able to see it from the train?"

Mother's answer was a clipped "No, I'm afraid not."

As I turned to look out into the aisle, I nearly squealed when I saw a small figure standing outside our car, staring at me with his nose pressed up against the glass. It took me a moment to realize it was Gadji.

I glanced over at Mother, but she was thoroughly engrossed in her notes. I turned back to the window and mouthed, *What?*

He motioned for me to get up and meet him out in the corridor.

I shook my head no, then jerked my thumb in Mother's direction to let him know she was the reason.

"Theo, do stop fidgeting," she murmured.

"Yes, Mother," I said, my eyes still on Gadji. As I watched, he reached under the folds of his gown, then pulled something out. He lifted it in front of the glass, and I had to bite back a gasp of surprise.

My reticule!

Before I could do anything, a conductor spied Gadji and hurried over to shoo the boy away. Mother looked up at the commotion.

"Mother, this is the boy that I'd promised baksheesh to. I told him I'd ask you for a few coins. Do you think we could spare some?"

"Giving in to their demands only encourages poor behavior, Theo. It's not a good idea."

I made my eyes as big and round as possible. "Please! He reminds me a bit of Henry, and I would hate to think of Henry, all alone in a huge train station, having to beg for a living—"

"Oh for goodness sake, Theo! There is no chance of that happening to your brother. You do let your imagination run away with you. But here, give him this so he can be on his way and we can be on ours." She opened her pocketbook, pulled a few coins from it, and dropped them into my outstretched palm.

"Thank you, Mother!" I popped up, kissed her on the cheek, then darted out the door to the corridor where the conductor was scolding Gadji in blistering Arabic.

"It's okay!" I said, diving into the fray. "He's with me."

The conductor stopped talking and frowned. "With you, miss?"

"Yes, I told him to come find me on the train. He . . . he has something of mine. He's returning it."

"Very well," the conductor said. "But be quick. The train

leaves in minutes." With one last skeptical glance at Gadji, the conductor moved on down to the next compartment.

When he was out of earshot, I turned back to Gadji and nearly hugged him. "However did you find it?" I asked.

Gadji smiled. "Sefu. When he returns to me that afternoon, he is dragging this with him." He held the reticule out to me and I quickly took it back, relieved to feel the familiar weight. Wanting to make sure it hadn't been substituted for an orange or something, I quickly peeked inside. The orb sparkled back.

"Thank you," I said. "You've no idea how badly I needed this."

"Why is effendi miss carrying such a valuable Egyptian *antikah*?" he asked suspiciously.

"My mother is an archaeologist. That's her job, finding the lost treasure of the ancients."

Gadji frowned. "But they are our ancients, no? Should not the treasure be ours, then?"

Well. He certainly had a point. "I suppose they should," I said slowly. "But I don't make the rules. Neither does my mother. But here." I handed him the coins Mother had given me. "As a reward for returning my purse."

Just as his grubby hand closed round the coins, the train whistled, then lurched forward.

"Quick! You must get off!"

Gadji looked unconcerned. "I do not think so. Maybe I stay on this train and visit Luxor."

"But your family? Won't they be frantic with worry?"

Gadji shrugged. "No one but angry owner of donkeys back there. Besides, Gadji's family is from Luxor. Perhaps I will return and search for them. You," he said, his face brightening, "is giving me the means to do so." He gave me a nod of thanks. "Until Luxor," he said, then bowed and began making his way back to the third-class cars. Still trying to understand what just happened, I returned to our compartment, relishing the familiar *thump-bump* of the reticule now that it had been returned to me.

INTRODUCTIONS

IT IS A LONG TRAIN RIDE from Cairo to Luxor. Twenty hours or more, depending on the conditions. I could not help but be wildly grateful for our deluxe traveling compartment and thought often of poor Gadji, standing hip to jowl with scores of other travelers in third class. Try as I might, however, I could not come up with any reason to give Mother as to why an Egyptian boy she'd never met should travel with us. She had been unhappy enough about a cat.

"Theo, have you got all your things?"

"Yes, Mother," I said, wrapping the reticule string twice around my wrist for extra security. I gripped my satchel in one hand and Isis's wicker basket in the other and followed

Mother off the train. Luckily, this station wasn't nearly as big—or as crowded—as the Cairo station. Nor was there a Nationalist demonstration going on just outside. Even better, Mother's dragoman, Nabir, was waiting for us, his dark face creased in smiles as he greeted Mother with a bow. "Welcome back, madams."

"It's wonderful to be back, Nabir," Mother said. "And you remember my daughter, Theodosia?"

His smile dimmed ever so slightly. "But of course." He bowed to me and I thought I detected a flicker of panic cross his face. I could not imagine why. Nabir and I had gotten on quite well last time, although I'd had to strong-arm him a time or two in order to carry on with my business. Surely he didn't hold that against me.

"Have you assembled all the workmen?" Mother asked.

"Most all, madams." He and Mother began walking toward the baggage car, discussing archaeological business. I hung back a bit, hoping to find Gadji. Score after score of dusty Arabs disembarked the train, but they were all adult size. Finally, a small figure appeared in the doorway, a monkey clinging to his shoulder.

As Gadji stepped onto the platform, I cast one more glance in Mother's direction, but she was still occupied with the luggage. Good.

"You made it," I said.

He gave me an odd look. "Of course Gadji makes it. Why would I not?"

"No reason. Do you have someplace to stay here in Luxor?"

Gadji shrugged. "Not yet."

"I thought you had family here?"

"Gadji used to have familys here," he corrected. "I am not knowing if they are still here until I look for them."

"Where will you spend the night?"

"I will find someplace. A barn, a doorway. If all else fails, I will sleep under the stars and let Nut watch over me."

I couldn't decide whether to be impressed by his trust in Nut, the Egyptian goddess of the sky, or horrified by his casual disregard for his circumstance. Horrified won. "But that's not safe, is it? How will you eat?"

Gadji shrugged again. "I will beg." He nudged Sefu and the little imp scampered under the collar of Gadji's robe and settled onto his back, making him appear misshapen.

"I don't think that's a good idea. Maybe you should come with us?" I suggested.

Gadji flicked a glance over in Mother's direction with a look of scorn. "You think she is being pleased with that?"

"I'll come up with some excuse," I explained, but before I could elaborate, Nabir spotted us and hurried over. He erupted into a quick spate of Arabic and tried to shoo Gadji away. Honestly, he wasn't a fly! Why did everyone insist on treating him so? Gadji flashed me a look as if to say, *See, I told you so.*

"It's okay, Nabir. He's with me."

Nabir's words stumbled to a halt, a look of wariness on his face. "What is he doing with you, miss?"

He had me there. I grabbed the first explanation I could think of. "I had promised that I would hire him to carry my things once we arrived in Luxor. Here." I shoved my satchel at Gadji.

Thinking quickly, he reached out and took it. Then he held out his other hand for Isis's basket. I hesitated. Conscious of Nabir's suspicious stare, I had no choice but to hand it over. "Do be careful not to jostle the basket," I told Gadji. "It contains very precious cargo."

He gave a surprisingly regal little bow. "I am carrying it most carefully, effendi miss," he said just as Mother joined our little group.

"What is going on, Theo?" she asked with a small frown. "Is he one of yours, Nabir?"

I jumped in before the dragoman could say anything. "No, Mother. He's the boy on the train. Remember? I'd promised to give him baksheesh, but you said that wasn't a good idea since it only encouraged poor behavior. So I took your suggestion and offered him a job carrying my luggage instead."

I smiled brightly, as if this was the most brilliant idea she'd ever had.

"That was my idea?" she asked faintly.

"Yes, and it *is* much better than begging, Mother. You said so yourself."

"I suppose I did," she muttered. "Very well. Come along, then. Do we have everything, Nabir?"

"More than enough, madams." He threw an annoyed look at Gadji, then began herding us all toward the exit.

With both my arms empty except for the reticule, I couldn't help but feel as though I was forgetting something. I turned around to be sure I hadn't dropped anything and caught a flash of movement out of the corner of my eye. A black-cloaked figure quickly stepped back behind a column. I sighed. With Mother having unwittingly told the Serpents of Chaos of our every planned move, of course they would be following us already.

That just meant we'd have to come up with some *un*-planned moves.

As I stepped out into the streets of Luxor, I braced myself for the impact of the magic that surely ran rampant in the city's streets. So close to the ancient monuments, it would be nearly overwhelming. Awi Bubu had warned me that this trip would be different from my first. On that first trip, I'd been wearing the powerful Heart of Egypt amulet, which had protected me from the worst of the old, powerful magic that hung over the land. This time, I had nothing but a few measly homemade amulets protecting me.

I needn't have worried. The unseen *heka* sat like an invisible haze over the city and prickled against my skin with a faint fizz and pop, much like the bubbles off ginger beer, but it wasn't dark or oppressive. Odd, that. I wondered if it was because the ancient monuments themselves were so close by and so steeped with centuries' and centuries' worth of good worshiping-type magic that it canceled out the darker kind?

The house Nabir had secured for us was a large sun-baked bungalow that sat up against a slight hill, looking back down on the village of Luxor. There was a small husk of a stable, and the yard was mostly hard-packed dirt with a lone, valiant vine doing its best to earn its status as a garden.

A figure swathed in black from head to toe—with only her eyes exposed—met us at the front door and bowed low. "This is Habiba," Nabir said by way of introduction. "Your new housekeeper. She is my wife's cousin and is very skilled in the ways of keeping a house." She looked rather like a tall, slender tent with eyes, I thought. She also looked unbearably hot in all those layers of black. Her dark eyes widened when she saw Gadji behind me and she sent a questioning glance at Nabir. His answer in Arabic put a scowl on her face and Gadji's. For one brief moment, I was afraid the donkey boy was going to kick the dragoman, but Habiba bustled us all into the house and the moment passed.

She pointed Gadji and me down a short, narrow hallway, then disappeared in the opposite direction to take Mother to the master suite.

My small room was stark and spare—a narrow bed, a rickety washstand, and a small chest of drawers. There wasn't even a desk.

A low, impatient warble emerged from the basket. Gadji dropped it and leaped back.

"Don't be silly," I said, hurrying over. "It's only my cat." I knelt and unlatched the basket. Isis came up out of its depths with a mad howl, going straight for the monkey who had emerged from Gadji's robe.

Gadji and Sefu both squealed. Gadji ducked, but the monkey leaped away onto the top of the screen that covered my window. Isis prowled over to sit below and emit warning howls from deep in her throat.

"What is being wrong with your cat, miss?" Gadji asked, sounding deeply offended.

"I don't think she likes Sefu."

The monkey, sensing it was out of harm's way, waggled its fingers at Isis and made a series of ugly little faces at her. She abruptly leaped up onto the windowsill, surprising the monkey. It screeched and leaped back onto Gadji's shoulder. Isis glanced at it, then hopped out into the garden, dismissing Sefu with a disdainful flick of her tail.

When she'd left, the little monkey began chattering excitedly. Gadji said a few comforting words to the creature in Arabic, then turned his attention back to me. "I think we will be going now."

"Will you stay here?"

"No, I will look for my peoples. Someone might know where they have gone."

"When was the last time you saw them?"

"Five years ago."

Curiosity won out over politeness. "How did you get separated from your family?" I asked, but my question was drowned out by a scream from somewhere near the kitchen, followed by Mother's voice. "Theodosia Elizabeth Throckmorton! Come get this cat! At once!"

"We is definitely going now." Gadji hurried to the window and hoisted himself up onto the sill.

"You can use the door," I said.

He flashed a grin. "This is being quicker," he said, then disappeared.

"Theodosia!"

"Coming, Mother!" I called back, then hurried to retrieve Isis from whomever she was terrorizing.

The next morning after breakfast, Mother set out for the British consul office to check in with the Inspector of Upper Egypt. Nabir was off finalizing the work crew, and Habiba was doing something in the small, hot kitchen. I had assured Mother I would be happy to entertain myself, without actually specifying *how*. But of course, I had a visit of my own to pay, to Major Harriman Grindle, Supervisor of Security in Upper Egypt and my Brotherhood of the Chosen Keepers contact here in Luxor.

But first things first. I studied my room carefully, trying to decide where on earth to hide the Emerald Tablet. Now that the Serpents of Chaos knew of our every move, I had to assume our rooms could be searched during the long hours we were away. But there were simply no good hiding spots. In a drawer or under the mattress was too obvious. Anyone would find it within seconds. And I simply did not see how I could carry it with me every day. I could never dream up an explanation that would satisfy Mother.

A sound at the window pulled me from my quandary and I found Isis up on the sill, needing to go outside.

And then I got a great big wonderful idea.

"Wait just one minute," I told her. I left her looking slightly put out and slipped into the spare room where all our supplies were stored. Just as I'd hoped, I found a flat, short-sided lid to one of the larger boxes. I snagged that and a spare canvas sack. Back in my room, I removed the tablet from the bottom of Isis's carrying basket, wrapped a layer of oiled cloth around the newspapers that currently hid it from view, then placed the well-protected tablet in the shallow box. Isis came over to inspect what I was doing. "Two seconds, I promise," I told her.

I grabbed the sack and went to the window. Nobody was outside in the sad little yard. Perfect. I sat on the windowsill, swung my feet around, then dropped to the ground, careful to close the window right behind me. I kept near the wall, hopefully out of sight as I filled the sack with dirt. When it was full, I set it on the sill, opened the window once more, and climbed back into my room. I quickly shut the window, almost catching Isis's nose as she tried to get out. "I'm sorry! Two more seconds, I promise!" The poor thing was practically crossing her legs at this point.

I dumped all the dirt into the box, then stood back. "All yours," I told Isis.

Curious, she came over and sniffed, then climbed in and began scratching around, doing what all cats do when presented with a box of dirt or sand. "Good girl," I told her when she was finished. Because, of course, it was perfect! No one would think to search there. Besides, ancient Egyptian magic believed that Underworld demons were especially fond of such things as Isis had just deposited in the box. Anyone who knew enough about the tablet to understand its value would also know that and steer well clear.

Of course, I was grubby now and had to have my second wash of the morning, but that was quickly done. When I was finished, I secured the reticule around my wrist and grabbed my pith helmet. I left Isis standing guard and went to find my Chosen Keeper contact here in Luxor.

CHAPTER NINE
MAJOR HARRIMAN GRINDLE,
AT YOUR SERVICE

ONCE OUTSIDE, I REALIZED I had only the vaguest sense of where I might find Major Grindle's quarters. Intent on protecting the tablet from discovery and escaping undetected, I had forgotten that I had no idea where I was going. I glanced back at the house. Should I ask Habiba? Would she want to know where I was going or, worse, tell Mother?

Just as I decided I'd have to risk it, a shape darted out in front of me. I leaped back, then relaxed when I saw it was only Gadji's monkey, rather than a small demon, which is what it had looked like at first. That meant Gadji must be nearby, and *he* had lived in Luxor. Maybe he knew his way around.

Almost as if reading my thoughts, Sefu turned and scampered back the way he had come, pausing once to be certain I was following.

He stopped in front of a ratty abandoned shack with a pile of rags in the doorway. Except the pile of rags turned out to be Gadji. The small, sleeping boy tugged at my heart. It wasn't just that I was grateful to him for having helped me at such great cost to himself. It was more than that. With a niggle of surprise, I realized that I'd told Mother the truth; something about him made me homesick for my younger brother, Henry. Gadji was smaller and younger than Henry, but his outlook seemed older. Probably from having to live on the streets and make his own way. I imagine that would mature a person right up. But while Gadji was clever and shrewd, he was also remarkably cheerful for someone in his position. I found that most admirable.

Sefu pinched Gadji and woke him. Gadji rubbed his eyes and sat up, then leaped to his feet when he saw me standing over him.

"Good morning," I said, politely ignoring the fact that he'd been sound asleep.

"Good mornings," he replied somewhat stiffly, no doubt feeling embarrassed about having been sound asleep.

"No luck finding your family?" I asked.

He scowled ferociously at me. "Not yet."

"I could help you if you'd like," I offered.

He thrust his chin out. "I am not needing your help."

Talk about waking up on the wrong side of the bed! Or doorway, I amended. Ah, perhaps that was the problem. Or maybe he was hungry. Henry is always grumpy when he is hungry.

"Would you like some breakfast?" I fumbled in my pocket for the small snack I had brought along for lunch.

He recoiled from the food. "Gadji is no beggar, miss."

Hadn't he just said yesterday that he would beg if he had to? Maybe it was easier to beg from those you didn't know. Thinking fast, I said, "But I have a job for you and I have nothing else to pay you with."

That caught his attention. "What sort of job?"

"You used to live in Luxor, right? Do you still remember your way around?"

Gadji nodded and eyed the small packet more hopefully.

"Well, I need someone to act as my guide around town."

Gadji nodded. "I will guide you, and for this thing I will accept your inadequate payment—"

Inadequate? I thought I was doing him a favor.

"—and then you are owing me," he finished brightly, grinning broadly as his good humor returned. He snatched the food from my hand and demolished it in about thirty seconds. Then he was ready to go. "This way, miss." The monkey leaped up onto his shoulder, and we were off.

As he led me down the dusty streets, I nearly sprained my neck trying to take in all the sights. It turned out, I needn't have bothered. Luxor itself was basically a small village with a handful of grand hotels.

The only area that gave me pause was a small cluster of streets just off the main thoroughfare. Gadji tried to hurry by, but I called him back. "What's down here?"

He frowned. "Gadji not sure, but very bad. No place for effendi miss."

"How do you know that if you're not certain what's down there?"

His frown turned to a perplexed scowl. "Gadji just knows this thing, miss."

The truth was, I could feel a foul, roiling miasma emanating from the alley. Could he? Was that how he knew it was very bad?

"*Antikahs,*" he said at last. "No good, very bad *antikahs.* Not like miss's."

Did he mean a black market in antiques? Or something more ominous, such as horribly cursed artifacts? I made a mental note to ask my Chosen Keeper contact about it and let Gadji lead me away.

Major Harriman Grindle lived in a small box-shaped house by the British consulate offices near one of the large hotels.

"I wait out here so I can show you the way back." Gadji gave a snappy salute, then slipped away to settle in at the foot of a dusty palm tree that provided a small sliver of shade.

I squared my shoulders and rapped smartly on the door. It opened immediately and I found myself staring into a large, broad chest covered in a rough goatskin tunic. Baggy black trousers were tucked into red leather boots, and a red cap with a rolled edge sat low on the man's brow. He wore a wicked-looking dagger at his hip. I looked up—and up, an impossibly long way—into a face not any darker than mine and a pair of eyes that were the color of aquamarines. He said nothing—not even hello—so I cleared my throat and spoke. "Um, is Major Harriman Grindle in?"

The man gave a silent nod, then opened the door all the way, indicating that I should enter. It was cool and dark inside, and I had to blink a number of times so my eyes could adjust.

"Follow me." His deep voice reverberated throughout the hall. He led me down a corridor, which descended in a series of steps and landings until we came to a closed door, which he opened to reveal a study of some sort. He ushered me inside. "Sahib will be with you shortly," he said, and then he shut the door behind him. I was alone in the cramped, dimly lit room.

Or so I thought, for there was no one sitting at the desk. However, I had the distinct sensation of being watched. It wasn't quite the same feeling as when a curse was nearby. That was more of a beetles-marching-up-the-spine sensation. This was more like a few ants pirouetting along my shoulders—an entirely different feeling. Even so, it unnerved me, and I quickly turned around to see who was there.

And nearly screamed when I came face-to-face with a small shrunken head. Three of them, to be precise. They were hanging from a brass hat rack. I took a quick step back and nearly tripped on the enormous leopard skin on the floor. I squealed and stepped back again, bumping into a large brass urn with ostrich plumes sprouting out the top. I grabbed for it, trying to keep the entire thing from tipping over.

Completely unnerved, I closed my eyes and took a few deep breaths to steady myself. When my heart had quit racing, I slowly opened my eyes and tried again.

The entire room was full of all manner of curiosities and oddities, like a macabre museum. Strange things, marvelous things, and some truly frightening things were tucked on shelves that ran all the way around the room, as if the room itself were one giant closet. Petrified crocodile eggs were displayed on a small table. Next to it on the floor was an

enormous snakeskin. The table next to that held dried scorpions (although they were so lifelike that I held my breath for a full minute, trying to decide if they were alive).

But it was the shelves that drew my attention. Some of the things were easily dismissed as junk: a battered yellow turban, a severed goat's foot (ew!), three sharp teeth, a brace of black feathers, and a battered old brass lamp such as you'd find in any Egyptian bazaar.

Except, I realized, the lamp wasn't quite as harmless as it first appeared. Something—not quite a curse, but something dark—lurked within that brass lamp. Or maybe that sensation was coming from the leering bronze mask next to it. Honestly, it could have been coming from any of the strange things on the shelf. Rings of bone, the large horn of a bull that disturbed me whenever my eyes fell on it . . . There was an ancient-looking bronze trumpet, and while it didn't feel cursed, exactly, it felt powerful in some way I couldn't put my finger on.

I glanced at the door, glad that it was still closed and Major Grindle hadn't arrived yet. It seemed to me that a man's shelves said an awful lot about him, and Major Grindle was shaping up to be very interesting, indeed.

The room also held the most astonishing collection of exotic weapons I had ever seen, surpassing our weapons room back at the museum in London. Henry would have been green with envy! There were thrusting daggers and chakrams, long knives and short swords, strange pointed weapons with a use I could not even guess. There was a deck of ancient tarot cards that had a faint malevolent feel to it, a winged frog, samurai war masks, and dried scarab husks. In the midst of all that strangeness sat a crumbling mud brick. What kind of brick would have earned a place among all these oddities, I wondered? I peered closer, not surprised to see strange carvings and glyphs upon it.

"What do you think of my cabinet of curiosities, Miss Throckmorton?"

I whirled around, surprised that I hadn't heard the Major come in. He stood tall and erect, his shoulders thrown back as if he was constantly at attention. He wore a bright red jacket bedecked with all manner of medals and brass. His thick white muttonchop whiskers covered the lower half of his face and met with the mustache that flourished atop his very stiff upper lip. His beak of a nose looked permanently sunburned, and his eyes were squinty, as if used to peering into the distance in search of danger. "Y-your what?"

"My cabinet of curiosities." He gestured with his hands, indicating the whole of the room. "Mementos of a life spent searching out the mysteries of the world."

"Very impressive, sir." I glanced over at the shelves, then back to the major. "But I do have one question . . ."

He gave a crisp nod. "Fire away."

"Why do you have these things when it is the Brotherhood's mission to remove curses from ancient artifacts?"

His blue eyes studied me intently. "You believe they are cursed?"

"Yes, sir. Some of them, anyway."

"Very good, Miss Throckmorton, if not completely accurate. Show me which ones you have questions about."

"Well, that bronze mask, for one."

"Not cursed, I'm afraid. It did, however, belong to a sorcerer from the Sichuan province in China. Perhaps you sense the vestiges of his power."

His words sent me reeling, for if I understood him, and I am fairly certain that I did, then it was not only Egyptian artifacts that still held power in this world. Nor were my unique abilities confined to Egyptian magic.

"What else?" he asked.

"That thrusting knife." I pointed to a wickedly sharp blade with an elaborate handle.

"My *katar*, a Hindu thrusting dagger. Again, not cursed, but it has taken a number of men's souls from them and those souls are said to linger in the blade."

His answers were not the least bit comforting. "What about those black feathers, there?" They didn't feel cursed, but I was hugely curious about them.

"Found among John Dee's possessions. Do you know who John Dee is, Miss Throckmorton?"

I swallowed. "Yes, sir." John Dee had been a scholar and one-time tutor to Queen Elizabeth I. He was said to have searched long and hard for ways to communicate with the angels.

"Then you no doubt understand the significance of that wing."

I stared at the small brace of feathers, unable to believe what he was implying. My glance fell on a chisel next to the feathers. It was ancient, possibly from the Old Kingdom, and some sort of power rose up from it, but it was too mixed with the remnants of the others' for me to be able to tell what it was. "What about that chisel?"

"Not cursed, exactly, but it does hold some power."

Taking a leap of faith, and perhaps wanting to give him a test of my own, I asked, "Is it an artifact of the gods?"

His gaze sharpened. "What do you know of the artifacts of the gods, child?"

"Quite a lot, actually."

He smiled then. "Come, let us have a seat and you can tell me what you know."

I settled myself on one of the chairs facing his desk. "How much has Lord Wigmere told you about me?" I asked.

"Quite a lot, actually," he said with a smile. "But apparently not everything."

"That's what I'm here to do, sir. Return an artifact of the gods."

There was a knock on the door just then and Major Grindle held a finger up to his lips in warning. "Come in," he barked out.

His servant entered, carrying a tea tray. He set it on the desk, then bowed.

"Thank you. I'll do the pouring," Major Grindle said.

Looking oddly disappointed, the man left the room. Major Grindle waited until his footsteps had disappeared down the hall, then got up and took the teapot from the tray. Then he did the oddest thing (which was saying a lot, considering how odd the morning had been). He carried the teapot to the window and dumped its entire contents out.

At my astonished look, he winked. "My factotum is trying to poison me. I saved his life in a battle, and his tribe's customs force him to save mine in return. We haven't been near any battles recently, so he is trying to kill me himself. Then he can save me and his debt will be repaid."

Major Grindle set the teapot down, went over to the urn, and lifted the ostrich plumes from it. He shoved his arm deep down, rooted around for a bit, then produced two somewhat dusty bottles. "Ginger beer," he announced triumphantly.

He replaced the plumes, then brought the bottles to the table. "I prefer it to tea, anyway, don't you?"

"Quite," I said, taking a bottle from him.

"Now, let's get down to business, shall we?"

That, I thought, *would be lovely.* I took a sip of ginger beer, then set the bottle down on the table.

"Wigmere said you had some item of great import that needed to be returned at once and I am to lend you any and every assistance that is in my power to lend." He paused a moment, then added, "He appears to be rather fond of you." He sounded puzzled by this, but whether because Wigmere didn't normally form attachments or because he did not think me fond-worthy, I couldn't tell. He leaned forward, his blue eyes bright as flames as he glanced at the reticule dangling from my wrist. "Is the artifact you are returning in there?"

How had he known, I wondered? Had he sensed it? "Er, yes."

He leaned even closer. "May I see it?"

I hesitated. Wigmere had assured me that the major was absolutely trustworthy. (*I'd trust the man with my life* were his exact words.) Even so, I was reluctant to flash the orb in the full light of day.

Sensing my hesitation, Major Grindle winked, then rose

to his feet. He closed the wooden shutters behind him, then hurried over to the door, and kicked the carpet up to cover the crack between it and the floor. "Better?" he asked.

"I suppose so." While I appreciated his caution, I was still hesitant. However, there was no reason I shouldn't show it to him, so I untangled the cords from my wrist, opened the reticule, and withdrew the small, golden Orb of Ra.

Major Grindle leaned forward, a hungry look on his face. "May I?" he asked, holding out his hand.

I did not know if my reluctance to show it to him was due to the fact that we'd just met, or some hidden character trait in him that I could not identify. Or perhaps the orb, being an artifact of great power, was exerting some sort of influence over me. Reluctantly, I handed it to him.

"Amazing," he breathed, his face bathed in the soft golden glow thrown off by the orb.

"Do be careful," I warned. "It appears to be able to be used as a sort of bomb or mortar."

"How extraordinary." With his free hand, Major Grindle fished on his desk for a pair of spectacles. He placed them on his nose, then peered even more closely at the hieroglyphs etched into the orb's surface.

"Yes, it was, rather," I said, remembering how Awi Bubu had tapped out some unknown pattern on the orb's symbols and created a blast that had knocked five grown men onto their backsides. I had been quite uneasy about carrying it, until Awi Bubu had assured me that one needed to know the proper sequence in order to activate it.

"So"—the major straightened and handed the orb back to me—"that is what must be returned, eh?"

"Yes." I busied myself putting the orb back into the reticule so he couldn't see my face. I am a fairly good liar, but something told me that the major was an excellent reader of men, and I had promised to tell no one of the Emerald Tablet.

"How can I help?"

I breathed a sigh of relief. I so appreciate an adult who is ready, willing, and able to take orders from an almost twelve-year-old girl. I hadn't known if a soldier would be able to do that. "I can handle the returning-it part, but what I really need help with is the Serpents of Chaos."

He straightened like a foxhound who had just spied a fox. "Chaos? Are they here?"

"If they aren't yet, they will be soon. There was a nasty surprise waiting for us at the Antiquities Service in Cairo." I proceeded to tell him of finding von Braggenschnott in Maspero's office. "So you see, sir, Chaos now knows all of my mother's plans. And consequently, a number of mine."

"If you tell me your plans for the next few days, I'll arrange for some additional security."

"Mother is visiting with the inspector even as we speak.

She'll also be interviewing a few last men to include in her work party. After that, I should think we'll be heading over to the Valley of the Kings to begin documenting Thutmose III's tomb."

"Very well. I shall get some men right on it."

"Thank you, sir."

"I am glad to see you wearing Professor Quillings's Homing Beacon and Curse-Repelling Device. He has sent me the tracking mechanism, should the need to track you arise."

"About Professor Quillings, sir," I began, glad for the opening. "I have some things I would like you to return to him." I reached into my pocket, retrieved the fountain pen and the compact, then placed them on Major Grindle's desk.

The major raised an eyebrow in question. "You might need those, Miss Throckmorton."

I eyed him warily. "You know what they do?"

"Of course."

"And you are comfortable with that? With me carrying around the sorts of curses the Brotherhood is supposed to remove from artifacts?"

Major Grindle leaned back in his chair. "What precisely has Wigmere told you about the Brotherhood?"

"That the Brotherhood exists in order to protect the innocent against the black magic and curses that still cling to ancient artifacts found in museums and private collections."

"Well, that is partly correct." Major Grindle studied me, as if weighing something in his own mind. "But not the whole of it."

It felt as if the bottom dropped out of my stomach. "It's not?"

"No," he said, and I had the most horrible feeling that I almost didn't want to know what he was going to say next. "Perhaps if Wigmere hadn't wanted me to know, it's better that I don't?" I said.

"Is that what you really believe, Miss Throckmorton?"

"No," I said miserably. The truth was, I was crushed that Wigmere hadn't told me the entire story, whatever it might end up being.

"It is not the Chosen Keepers' job to simply remove curses and protect the innocent from their effects," the major said. "We have a much greater task than that." He took a deep breath. "The Chosen Keepers are descendants of the ancient librarians of the Royal Library of Alexandria—the few, the proud, and the learned. We have sworn an oath to seek out and replace all the ancient knowledge that was lost when our great library was destroyed by Emperor Theodosius. Our goal is to reignite the flame of knowledge and restore it to mankind."

I gaped at him.

"Wigmere oversees one branch of our organization, a last

line of defense. His branch is the last bastion that can stop the artifacts with dark magic from coming into the country when they get by us. A fallback position, if you will. But our greater mission is to search out the artifacts and extract their knowledge so we can reconstruct all the wisdom and learning once held in the library. Then we remove the magic and curses from the artifacts so they can go into museums and private collections."

My head began to spin. "But surely some of that magic shouldn't be reintroduced to mankind."

"Agreed. But nor should it be lost for all eternity, either. There is a secret vault in which we store that sort of information. It is quite full, as you can imagine. But even more important is that we seek out and acquire that information before other organizations who wish to use that knowledge for the wrong reasons do."

"The Serpents of Chaos," I murmured.

"Exactly."

"But sir, why are you telling me all this?" Normally, I was quite fond of answers, of knowing things, but for some reason this revelation unsettled me.

Major Grindle studied me for a long moment, as if taking my full measure. "You need to know the truth," he said at last. "Because the blood of the Chosen Keepers of Alexandria flows in your veins."

CHAPTER TEN
A HIDDEN HERITAGE

I BOLTED UPRIGHT IN MY CHAIR. "What do you mean?"

He sighed, a deep, heavy sound full of sorrow and disappointment. "Has no one spoken to you of your grandfather Throckmorton?"

"No," I whispered, suddenly feeling as brittle and fragile as spun glass.

Major Grindle's intense blue eyes never left my face. "No one told you he was in the Brotherhood? That he was a Chosen Keeper, too?"

His words brought me up out of my chair. "My grandfather was a Chosen Keeper?" This went beyond anything I could ever have imagined.

"Oh, I'm not surprised your family didn't tell you. But Wigmere, now. I would have expected him to explain it to you. After all, they were great friends, Wigmere and your grandfather. You look like him, you know."

"I do?" I plopped back into my chair as all the air went out of me in a whoosh.

"Very much. The eyes in particular. And you have the same stubborn chin."

"But sir . . . are you certain my family knew? My grandmother hates anything to do with archaeology." My words dribbled to a stop as I realized the implications. Perhaps she hated it *because* he had been involved.

"She knew, up to a point. Although I suspect she knew more than she ought. And at the end, well, there was almost no way she couldn't have known."

I looked up sharply. "At the end?"

"It killed him, in the end." He turned and looked to his cabinet full of oddities, collected from a lifetime of dealing with magical remnants and artifacts. "But not before everyone thought he'd lost his mind and gone off the deep end. It was a tragic end to a great man."

A heavy, solemn silence filled the room, and in that silence, realization began pinging through my mind like bolts of lightning. Grandmother's aversion to all that heathenish knowledge. Father's fear that I was exhibiting signs of impending lunacy. All of that stemmed from a grandfather I'd never met. Slowly, I looked up to meet the major's patient, understanding gaze. "Did my father know?"

"He was invited to join us when he was of age. He declined. Told Wigmere in no uncertain terms that he didn't want to be involved with a group that dabbled in fringe beliefs."

That sounded like Father. Grindle had given me a gift—a painful, horrible gift. And he knew it.

He rose to his feet and went over to the shelves against the wall. "I feel certain your grandfather would want you to have this," he said. "And it wouldn't hurt for you to carry a piece of it with you in your current circumstances." He reached out, lifted one of the crumbled corners from the old mud brick, and held it out to me. "It was the last thing your grandfather was working on before he died. He was certain he had located the foundation stones of the Tower of Babel just south of the ancient city of Ur."

I stared at it with a combination of disbelief and fascination. "Er, thank you."

His mustache twitched. "Be advised that it is not any old brick, Miss Throckmorton. You hold in your hand a sliver of the Tower of Babel itself." He leaned forward and lowered his voice. "It works. When you hold that in your hand, you can understand any language spoken by man."

My jaw dropped open and I stared at the small piece of brick with new appreciation.

"Keep it, Miss Throckmorton. Other than memories, it is all I can give you of your grandfather."

I could feel Major Grindle's servant watching me as I started down the narrow road that led from the bungalow. His intent gaze made my neck itch. I did not even pretend to understand the relationship between Major Grindle and his strange servant.

I finally felt him look away, then heard the faint clunk of the door closing behind him.

I found Gadji squatting beneath the small scrubby palm tree, picking fleas off his monkey. When he saw me, he leaped to his feet and saluted. Not sure what else to do, I saluted back, nearly clobbering myself in the face with the weight of the orb. Gadji glanced at the reticule, then back at me. "Miss is not leaving the *antikah* with the *antikah* man?"

I sharpened my gaze. "Who says he is an *antikah* man?" I asked.

Gadji shrugged. "Why else are you going to him?"

I relaxed slightly. "Right. Exactly so. That is exactly why I visited him."

He gave me an odd look, then led me back to the house,

careful this time to avoid the dark street I'd been so curious about. Which reminded me: I'd forgotten to ask the major about that. Bother.

My thoughts were in such a tangle that I could hardly manage to put one foot in front of the other. Grindle's revelations haunted me. I was angry with my entire family for keeping such an enormous secret from me. I was also filled with a deep sense of having been cheated by never having met my grandfather. Oh, the conversations we could have had! The things he could have explained to me!

Mother wasn't back from her errands yet, and try as I might, I found no signs of Nabir anywhere. That left only Habiba to get around. I had no idea if she'd noticed I was gone or if that was even a part of her duties. Even so, I have learned it is best to tread cautiously.

Motioning for Gadji to stay back by the road, I crept forward to the window near the kitchen. Satisfied at the sound of crockery and splashing water, I motioned for Gadji to follow. I'd had another corker of an idea on the way home and I couldn't wait to share it with him. "I have a business arrangement for you," I said. Then I took a deep breath and began to tiptoe my way through the proposition. "I will need a guide here in Luxor. Not all the time, because I will be working with Mother mostly. But I have a few, er, side jaunts that I will need to make and would dearly love a guide to show me the way. Someone whom I can trust—and I feel I can trust you."

"Effendi miss can trust Gadji. Sefu, too," he said.

"Excellent. Then in exchange for your services as a guide, I can provide you with a place to sleep. Would that be acceptable?"

Gadji folded his arms across his chest, a shrewd glint in his eyes. "And foods," he said.

"And food," I agreed. "And you should still have plenty of time to look for your family. Deal?" I held out my hand for him to shake. Instead, Gadji spat on his palm, then, before I could retract my arm, placed his palm against mine and held it in a strange manner—almost as if he meant to arm-wrestle—and gave it a firm squeeze. "Deal," he said.

"Excellent," I said, trying not to think about what now coated my glove. "Let me show you where you'll sleep." Skulking past the main house, I quickly led him to the un-used stable. "Will this work?" I asked, nervous about the old dusty straw and the general abandoned feel of the place.

"This do very nice," Gadji said, ever cheerful. "Look!" he said. "It even has blanket."

Honestly, the rag hardly lived up to the word. It was faded, dirty, and moth eaten, but he held it up like a treasure. I felt a horrible twinge of conscience for not being able to offer him the spare bedroom. But I could absolutely do better than that filthy rag. "I'll get you a better blanket," I assured him. "And a few supplies. I'll be right back." I left him clearing the worst of the debris out of the biggest stall and hurried to the house.

I went first to my room, where Isis was waiting for me. "I'm back," I told her, then went to lift the sandbox, pleased to feel the weight of the tablet still there. "You can go out now." Happy to hear this, she jumped up onto the windowsill and waited patiently for me to open the shutter. When I had done so, she took off like a streak of black lightning for parts unknown.

I stripped off my gloves, fished a fresh pair from my suitcase, then quickly washed my hands. I snagged an extra blanket from the trunk at the foot of my bed and tried to think what else Gadji might need.

Water for drinking at least, if not washing. Somehow, I didn't think he performed that last chore very often. Food. And a change of clothes would be nice, but we did not have any extra boy-size robes lying about.

I went into the supply room and rooted around until I

found a canteen. I filled it with water from the pitcher in my room, then set that on my bed next to the blanket and went to find some lunch.

Habiba was still busy in the kitchen. She was so absorbed in her task that she didn't hear me in the doorway. When I cleared my throat, she jumped nearly a foot.

"I'm so sorry, Habiba. I didn't mean to startle you."

She glared at me and her fingers twitched. Either that or she was making the sign of the evil eye. I pretended not to notice and grabbed two figs and a handful of sticky dates (ruining yet another pair of gloves) from a bowl on the table. When Habiba turned back to the stove, I slipped one of the freshly made pieces of flatbread into my pocket.

Halfway back to the stable, I heard an unholy racket rise up. *Now what?* I thought, then broke into a run.

Inside the stable, Isis and Sefu circled each other like two pugilists, growling and hissing. The monkey bared his teeth and erupted with a spate of angry chatter. Isis flicked her tail disdainfully and hissed. Gadji was sucking on his hand.

"What happened?" I asked Gadji.

He removed his hand from his mouth and I saw three angry scratches along the back of it. "This black demon of the Underworld fall from the skies and tries to eat my monkey!" he shouted, nearly as worked up as Sefu.

"I already told you," I explained. "That's my cat."

This seemed to enrage the monkey even further. He jumped up and down, and his scolding reached earsplitting levels. "Gadji! Make him stop or the racket will bring somebody and we'll be found out."

Gadji shook his head. "Not want the demon should curse me, effendi miss."

"Oh, honestly! She's just a cat. Here, watch." I went over to Isis and picked her up, careful to grasp her paws with my gloved hands so she wouldn't shred me to ribbons. In spite of what I'd told Gadji, she had been a bit demonic ever since her unfortunate incident with the cursed Bastet statue back at our museum in London. Her low growl rumbled along my arms, but to my great relief she did not scratch or try to claw her way free. "Relax," I whispered in her ear. "It's only a silly monkey." Louder, I said to Gadji, "Now make yours be quiet."

His eyes full of newfound respect, he said something to the monkey in Arabic. Sefu shut his mouth with a snap, then scampered up onto Gadji's shoulder. With one last grimace of protest in Isis's direction, he dove under Gadji's robes and settled himself along the boy's back.

And none too soon. From outside I heard the clop of hooves and raised voices. I held my finger to my lips and went to the stable door to see who—or what—was coming.

It was Nabir and Mother, both astride donkeys and leading nearly a dozen more. It looked as if our stables were going to be populated after all.

Mother saw me standing in the doorway and gave a cheerful wave. "Look, darling! We've our own means of transportation! Aren't they dear?"

"They're lovely!" I called back, trying to sound equally
cheerful, even though they had just destroyed my plan for
Gadji's lodgings.

"I hope she is not paying too much for them," Gadji said
from behind the doorway where he hid. "They are not so
very by Jove as all that."

I glanced at him. But of course! I grabbed his arm and
pulled him into the doorway with me. "How perfect, Mother,
for I have found us a donkey boy!"

CHAPTER ELEVEN
THE NECROPOLIS

THE NEXT MORNING we were up before the sun, wanting to arrive at the Valley of the Kings in the coolest part of the day. I vowed to put all my secret-mission intrigue behind me for now and concentrate on the unspeakable thrill of being on an official excavation team. I was quite sure I was the first eleven-year-old to be in such a position.

The Valley of the Kings doesn't look like much, truth be told. It is the most barren, dry, desolate collection of sandstone cliffs and ravines imaginable. However, the atmosphere of the place is nearly overwhelming. As we entered the necropolis, the air grew thick with the weight of old souls and lingering *mut* and *akhu*, remaining long after the bodies were gone. In spite of the near-blinding glare of the sun, the valley felt dark to me, as if the tunnels that peppered the desolate cliffs reached down to the Underworld itself and allowed the darkness there to seep back up through the earth's crust.

I shivered. Even the lone guard who patrolled the entrance to the valley seemed touched by the dark forces. He was rude and surly and almost wouldn't let us pass.

Mother kept a sharp lookout for the gentleman who owned the right to dig in the valley. It was highly unusual for us to be allowed back in, but since my parents had laid an earlier claim to the tomb of Thutmose III and had managed to convince the rights-holder that we were there for recording purposes only, the Antiquities Service had allowed the exception.

The tomb we were looking for was at the very end of the valley. A small crowd of men in black robes and white turbans waited for us at the base of the cliff. There were two Europeans with them. One was a thin whippet of a man, and the other put me more in mind of a bear. A bear who had just very unhappily awakened from his winter hibernation. Mother introduced him as Kazimerz Jadwiga of the Polish Institute. He had a thick brown mustache that drooped mournfully, and his eyes were kind but sad, as if he expected to have his heart broken at least twice before luncheon. I liked him immediately and vowed to think of some way to cheer him up.

The whippet fellow was Gunter Rumpf of the Berlin Archaeological Society, a pale, intense man who stood extremely erect. He had thin lips and flared nostrils. His hair, which he wore longer than was fashionable, was straight as straw and swept straight back. Instead of offering me his hand as Jadwiga had done, he peered at me over his small gold-rimmed spectacles, as if he did not quite believe what he was seeing. However, before I could decide whether or not to be offended, Mother called us all to work.

The access to Thutmose III's tomb was particularly tricky, as it sat high off the ground, perched atop a cliff between two pillarlike formations of rock. Just looking at the small entrance made my heart beat faster—and not simply due to excitement, although there was plenty of that. I felt some trepidation as well. The last time I had been there, I had come face-to-face with some of the most ruthless Serpents of Chaos in a deadly showdown. Even now, if I half closed my eyes, I could hear von Braggenschnott's cruel laughter echoing out from the tomb's shadowy depths.

Nonsense. I'd seen von Braggenschnott myself in Maspero's office back in Cairo.

Unless he'd managed to beat us here. I glanced nervously up at the tomb entrance.

We settled our donkeys at the base of the cliff and dismounted. The men got busy getting out the tools and equipment we'd need, and soon we were ready to enter Thutmose III's burial chamber. Fortunately, I would not be the one who would enter first. That honor was Mother's.

I watched her climb the crumbling set of steps that had been set into the rock, then cross the last distance on a rickety ladder. Next up was the Polish fellow, Jadwiga. He was such a broad, solid man that I was afraid the ladder would crumble under his weight. He was, too, if the doleful look on his face was any indication. However, the ladder proved to be much stronger than it looked and he made it to the top in one piece.

When it was my turn, I stepped carefully on the crumbling steps, not wanting to send a shower of scree onto the fellow below me. Although his turban was so thick and padded that I'm not sure he would have felt a thing.

I had planned ahead this time and brought a pair of Henry's trousers with me to wear under my skirts so I wouldn't have to worry about anyone seeing my knickers. It is surprising how much confidence one gains when all one's limbs are thoroughly covered.

The ladder was downright wobbly and I tried not to think

of the hard rock below. There was a bad moment at the top when the ladder didn't quite reach the ledge outside the tomb opening. Much to my relief, Jadwiga was there, holding a hand out to me.

"Thank you," I said, when I was safely on the cliff ledge.

"*Ja*," he said in his glum voice. "Wouldn't want you to tumble to your death before we'd even set foot in the tomb."

We really had to do something about his dour outlook.

Mother's men unpacked the electric torches she'd brought and handed them around, and then Mother came over to me and gave me a bright smile. "Are you ready, dear?"

I smiled back, thrilled to be included as an equal on this dig. "Ready!" She took my hand in hers, then frowned.

"Tell me you didn't bring that wretched reticule with you."

"Er, yes," I said, whipping my hand with its heavy weight away and hiding it behind my back. "Still practicing," I said, then ducked around to her other side and grabbed her right hand with my left.

She sighed and shook her head, as if I was a great trial to her, and then together we approached the mouth of the tomb.

At the threshold, I felt the ancient magic swirling in the dark, just past the daylight, the pressure of it throbbing against my skin, like the beat of a drum. Or a heart.

"I love this part," Mum confessed in a whisper. "That moment when we step into the past and all the wonders that it holds."

Together, we went inside.

I shuddered violently as the flood of *mut* and *heka* washed over me. I took slow, deep breaths and hoped that Mother hadn't noticed.

"It is a bit chilly in here after the sunlight," Mother said. I looked at her sharply. Did that mean she had actually felt something similar to what I felt but merely dismissed it as a chill? However, she looked thoroughly unperturbed. Drat. For a moment there I had had a flicker of hope that she, too, had an ability to detect curses and black magic, albeit a latent one.

We proceeded down the corridor to the first stairway. The others followed. I felt as if I were wading through a stream of sinister, shadowy things with power that plucked at my flesh, wanting to find a way in. There was the heavy presence of old souls, pressing down on me, wanting to chase me from this place. My fingers crept up to my throat, where I wore three amulets of protection. As my hand closed around them, the sensation lightened somewhat. I sent a silent plea up to whatever Egyptian gods might be listening to please forgive us for trespassing on their sacred space.

I gripped the electric torch more tightly, grateful for its solid feel in my hand. If the gods or spirits were watching, I couldn't help but wonder what they might think of such a technological advance. Would they see it as magic, perhaps? My heart gave a tiny leap of excitement. *Were* electric torches magic? Was science simply magic explained? I grew a little dizzy with the thought.

A big, thick hand reached out and grabbed my arm, jerking me back. I looked around to find Jadwiga shaking his massive head at me. "Be careful, *ja*? You are too young to tumble to your death."

I glanced back to see that I had nearly plowed right into the ritual shaft, a gaping hole that spanned for yards, then plunged downward for who knew how far. Perhaps right down to the Underworld itself. "Thank you, Mr. Jadwiga," I said, vowing to keep my mind on matters at hand and not on philosophical questions.

When we reached the vestibule, Jadwiga and Rumpf gave murmurs of exclamation and hurried to examine the walls. As they marveled over the entire text of the Book of the Dead painted there, I took the opportunity to try to acclimate myself to the thick sea of magic that filled the room, rushing up against me in waves. I'd had no idea how much the powerful Heart of Egypt had protected me during my first visit. Trying not to think about all the corrosive magic swirling about, I concentrated on Mother's voice as she described for Jadwiga and Rumpf how Father had found Thutmose III's tomb back in 1899 when Loretti had been in charge of the Antiquities Service and how Loretti had claimed the find for himself. (She managed to keep her bitterness to a minimum, which I thought quite sporting of her.) As we proceeded into the main burial chamber, she continued with the story of how Father had deciphered some texts that led him to believe that Thutmose's war minister, Amenemhab, had been buried near Thutmose himself.

"I still say that makes no sense," Rumpf said. "Amenemhab is most likely buried in the Valley of the Nobles with the other high officials."

"I do admit that it is inconsistent with other pharaonic burial practices," Mother said. "But Mr. Throckmorton's research did bear rich fruit, even if we haven't deciphered what it all means yet. That is why we are here, gentlemen. We have come across further translations that indicate our initial understanding of the situation may have been incorrect. This was further highlighted when our daughter located a secret annex last year that we have yet to explore in depth. Which leads us to today's expedition."

Interesting, I thought, that she did not tell them we were

looking for indications of a possible location for a temple dedicated to Thutmose or Mantu, the god of war. Did she not fully trust them, I wondered? Or was she simply hesitant to put forward such a theory only to be proved wrong?

Mother led the way into the main burial chamber, with Jadwiga and Rumpf hard on her heels, eager to see what new wonders awaited them. As I crossed the portal into the burial chamber, a loud rustling whooshed by me, as if an entire flock of pigeons had taken flight nearby.

But of course, it wasn't pigeons; it was all the invocations and curses and blessings laid down by priests thousands of years ago to watch over the dead pharaoh. With luck, perhaps they would recognize me from my previous visit and remember that I bade them no ill, nor had any thieving plans for the items they were preserving for the pharaoh in the afterlife.

The workers put their equipment down in the main burial chamber and began setting up for operations. Jadwiga and Rumpf began exploring the room, their excitement clear. Honestly, they were like children in a sweetshop!

And I couldn't blame them. Even though I had been here once before, my heart beat faster and I felt tingly all over. Four thousand years ago, ancient Egyptians had worked in here, creating these carvings and fashioning this majestic sarcophagus. I held myself very still and closed my eyes, wondering if perhaps I could hear the echo of their ancient voices, feel the scrape of their ancient tools. Then I remembered the sliver of brick in my pocket. I hesitated, then thrust my hand into the pocket and closed my fingers around the brick.

My ears popped, as if I had just yawned, and the whispering voices altered slightly. If I listened carefully, I could just make out the words.

"I am the Benu bird, the soul of Re, who guides the gods to the Duat when they go forth."

". . . they have raised up tumult; they have done wrong . . ."

"They have reduced what was great to what was little."

"Hail to Him who dwells in His shrine, who rises and shines . . ."

"Theodosia?"

I jumped at the sound of Mother's voice, and the whispering receded. "Yes, Mother?"

"Did you want to lead the way to your portion of the tomb?"

A small wave of pride swept through me, followed quickly by embarrassment as I felt everyone turn to look at me. I never thought professional admiration would feel so awkward.

Trying to hold myself casually, as if this were nothing out of the ordinary, I walked toward the annex.

The thick wall of black magic in front of the annex was so vile that I stumbled and gasped out loud. When I regained my balance, I glanced quickly over at Mother, but she was too busy talking to Rumpf to have seen. Jadwiga, on the other hand, sent me a mournful look, as if he expected me to drop dead any minute.

Gritting my teeth against the sensation, I continued forward. Honestly, the air was so heavy with the weight of all the magic—how could the others not feel it? Or smell it, I thought, wrinkling my nose against the slight stench of sulfur. The walls here were covered with grisly scenes of war and the pharaoh crushing his enemies. Even though the red paint they had used had faded over the centuries, it still looked like spilled blood.

As I stared at the walls around me, I couldn't help but look at them with eyes opened by the newest interpretation of the stele we had deciphered over the past few months. Was this just the tomb of the minister of war? Or was it a mortuary temple giving thanks to the Egyptian god of war, Mantu, for all of Thutmose's victories?

Or did it hold vital clues to an as-yet-undiscovered temple of Thutmose III, which is what I had convinced my parents of?

"We'll need a way to get down," I told Mother.

"Yes, dear. We brought one." She stepped aside and Nabir came forward carrying a wooden ladder. He carefully set it in place, making sure the foot was secure on the level below, then went down to hold it for the rest of us.

I descended quickly, followed by Mother and the others, and went down the short corridor to the tomb proper. Caution warred with eagerness, and I thrust my electric torch out in front of me to illuminate the annex, then gasped. "What did you do with all the things that were in here?" I asked.

Mother frowned. "What things, dear?"

I waved my hand frantically. "The artifacts, the treasure—those things."

Mother glanced uneasily at the others and lowered her voice. "There was nothing in here when your father came back. But it is still a wonderful discovery," she rushed to add.

I turned away from her, feeling sick. For there had been treasure. Loads of it. Which meant that the Serpents of Chaos had found the time to remove it before Father had returned after taking me to a doctor.

Almost afraid to look, I raised my eyes to the far end of the chamber, which sported a huge image of Thutmose III carved in bas-relief. On his chest sat the Heart of Egypt. The last time I had seen it, von Braggenschnott had clung to the wall, his hand caught in the dark magic that had sealed the amulet to the wall. I was immeasurably relieved to discover his hand was not still there, a useless, shriveled limb.

"Why, look at that!" Mother said, drawing closer and raising her electric torch. "It looks just like the Heart of Egypt."

It *was* the Heart of Egypt, but I didn't explain that to her. Best if she thought her artifact had been stolen by a clever thief rather than learn it had been returned to its rightful resting place by her own daughter.

CHAPTER TWELVE
WHERE FOR ART THOU, O TEMPLE

NEARLY THREE HOURS LATER, my eyes were crossed and I had a beastly headache. We had decided to break up into groups, each one taking a different portion of the multisectioned tomb. That way we could cover the most ground initially, then crosscheck one another's work if we didn't stumble upon what we were hoping for. But honestly, didn't they ever stop for lunch?

I turned away from the carvings in front of me to ask Mother that very question, only to find I was alone in the chamber. They had better not have broken off for luncheon and not told me!

Or worse, have left without me, I thought when I didn't hear any other voices nearby. Which meant I was quite alone in the secret annex I had discovered. Drawn by some unseen hand, I found myself moving toward the far wall and the huge carving of Thutmose III. When I had first seen it, his face had been grim and terrible, a portrait of gruesome retribution. But once I had returned the Heart of Egypt to its place on the wall, all that had changed. Whatever magic had allowed the amulet to become a part of the carving had also shifted Thutmose back into a mighty yet beneficent ruler.

There was absolutely no sign of von Braggenschnott's hand. Not so much as a scrap of flesh or a fingernail to be seen. How had they gotten it out, I wondered? Had they cut it out? Or used magic? I leaned in closer to inspect the Heart of Egypt. It was well and truly fused with the wall now. When they had named it the *Heart* of Egypt, they had been quite literal, indeed.

I froze. That was it—a literal interpretation!

We had found many references to a temple of Thutmose III, and the way it was mentioned made it clear that it wasn't simply a temple here in the tomb. What if all the inscriptions about Thutmose being no longer content to stand in Hatshepsut's shadow and wanting to stand above her were a literal observation rather than a comment on her usurping his reign?

What if the inscriptions were directions to an actual location?

Perhaps we should begin looking at all the monuments and buildings that Hatshepsut had erected.

As soon as the thought formed in my head, it was followed by an image I had seen early that morning on the way to the valley—the mortuary temple of Hatshepsut built directly into the cliffs at Deir el-Bahri. I snapped my fingers. "That's it!"

"What's it, dear?" Mother's voice came from directly behind me. "Are you ready for lunch?"

Too excited now to even think of food, I whirled around to face Mother. "Hatshepsut's temple at Deir el-Bahri. That's where we should begin looking."

"Why there?"

I quickly explained all the references to temples that I had seen on the tomb walls that morning and my new belief that they were to be taken literally.

"Eureka!" Mother said, beaming at the wall.

"Eureka?" I asked.

"Well, it's what they shout when they find gold, and this is better than gold! Oh, you are brilliant, my daughter!" She flung her arms around me and gave me a giant hug that sent all the air whooshing from my lungs. I was so thrilled that she thought me brilliant that I didn't mind a bit.

I could only hope that brilliant made up for peculiar.

As we rode back through the valley toward home that evening, I almost didn't need my donkey. It felt as if the thrill of my discovery had given wings to my feet. I had forgotten my hunger, and my headache had disappeared, and I was certain I could have worked all night.

However, the others needed rest. And I had to admit, as we drew closer to home, my euphoria began to seep away, leaving only a deeply satisfying exhaustion behind.

When we reached the house, Gadji came out to greet us and take our donkeys. I raised my eyebrows in question, and he gave a quick shake of his head.

As Mother and Nabir left for the house, I lingered behind. "No luck?" I asked.

He shook his head. "They is all gone. No signs of them left anywhere. Big *Inglaize* hotels where family used to be."

"I'm so sorry." I thought for a moment. "What about shops? Did your family do their shopping at one place? Maybe they still shop there even though they changed houses?"

Gadji's face cleared. "Indeed, by Jove. I will try there next."

That settled, I made my way to the house, anxious for a quick wash before supper. I went immediately to my room.

And nearly shouted in surprise. The entire room had been ransacked. My bedcovers had been scattered and thrown to the floor, my traveling chest turned upside down, the drawers pulled open and everything topsy-turvy. Even Isis's carrying basket had been dumped upside down. My gaze flew to the sandbox, which had been scooted over a few inches, but all the contents seemed to be intact. Needing to be absolutely sure, I went over and knelt by the box. I hesitated a moment, almost afraid to know. If it had been taken, then what?

I took a deep breath, gripped the side of the box, and lifted it an inch. It was still heavy with the tablet. Wanting to be extra certain, I picked up one of the pencils that had fallen to the floor and poked around in the dirt until I felt the tablet itself.

Nearly weak with relief, I turned back to the room. "Isis?" I called softly, for she was nowhere to be seen.

There was a faint warble, and then her sleek black head poked out from under the bed. "Isis," I said, joy running through me. I hurried over to the bed, picked her up, and held her close to my chest. "I'm so sorry!" I said, leaning in to touch my nose to hers. Still holding her, I sat down on my bed and stared at the mess around me. Who had done this?

Isis wriggled in my arms, wanting down. I gently placed her on the floor, and she hurried over to the window. I opened it to let her out. As I watched her, I found myself wishing desperately that she could talk. Leaving the window open, I returned my attention to the room. Best to get it cleaned up before Mother saw it.

That thought lit a fire under me and I began scooping up the scattered clothes and returning them to their proper places. As I worked, I tried to puzzle out who the searchers might have been. My first assumption was Chaos, but that was just a guess. There was no evidence that it was, except my deep and abiding distrust of them. I grunted as I set my trunk back to rights.

Could Gadji have done this? I actually knew very little about him. Perhaps he thought I had money or valuables hidden away in here. One could hardly blame him. He had so little. Being a beggar must be wearing on the soul.

Or what about Habiba? She skulked around here like a dark, silent shadow. Hmm—it was nearly dinnertime. Perhaps I would go to the kitchen for something to eat. That would give me a chance to further observe our mysterious housekeeper.

As I drew near the kitchen, delicious smells met me in the corridor. I found myself hoping it wasn't Habiba who'd searched my room. It would be a shame to lose such a good cook. Especially since Mother couldn't be counted on to fill in if push came to shove.

When I stepped into the kitchen, Habiba looked up from the counter, where she was chopping something with an exceedingly sharp knife. I swallowed. Maybe this wasn't such a very good idea, after all.

A flicker of something moved in her dark eyes when she saw it was me. "Miss Effendi need something?" she asked.

"Yes," I said. "I'm a bit hungry and thought I would check on how long till dinner."

"Not long now." She turned back to her chopping, her hands wielding the knife in quick, precise movements.

"Have you had a busy day?" I asked.

"Oh, very busy. I cook and clean and cook some more." She looked up and met my eyes again, and I cursed the veil that hid most of her face. It wouldn't hurt to keep a more careful eye on our housekeeper.

Today had been close. Too close. Someone had known we would be gone and had taken full advantage of our absence. I needed to get rid of the tablet before it fell into the wrong hands.

CHAPTER THIRTEEN

The Agony and the Ecstasy

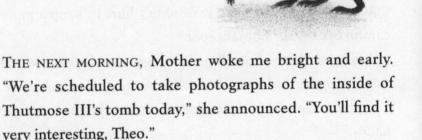

THE NEXT MORNING, Mother woke me bright and early. "We're scheduled to take photographs of the inside of Thutmose III's tomb today," she announced. "You'll find it very interesting, Theo."

I knew I would, but there was something else I had to do before allowing myself to return to the excavation site. "I'm afraid I don't feel well, Mother. I think I should stay home today and rest."

"What's wrong, dear?" She hurried to my bed and placed her cool hand on my forehead.

"Perhaps I took too much sun?"

She frowned. "You were inside the tomb all day," she pointed out.

Bother. "Perhaps it was the heat, then? Or maybe I just got overexcited."

She smiled. "It was a rather exciting day, I'll grant you that."

"I think it would do me good to stay home and rest. I'm sure I'll be right as rain in a day or two."

Her face fell. "Well, if you really think so. I'll miss you on the dig. You're a huge help, you know. Besides, I can hardly wait to see what you'll discover next! You definitely have a knack for this work, Theo."

Her words were music to my ears! Music I had waited years to hear from my mother's lips. But duty—and deathbed promises—called. Completely unaware of the agony I was going through, Mother smiled. "I suppose we can manage without you this once. I'll tell Habiba." And with that, she got up and left the room, leaving me alone with my horrid promises to Awi Bubu and Lord Wigmere.

Clearly it had been only sheer chance that whoever had searched my room hadn't found the Emerald Tablet. But they would keep searching, of that I was certain.

I would have liked to pay my visit to the Luxor temple in the cool of the morning, but I knew the tourists would be out in full force then. Best if as few people as possible were there when I left my message to request a meeting with the wedjadeen. Consequently, I spent a long, slow morning in my room, brooding about the grandfather I never knew. I could still hardly stomach my family's perfidy. That they would have kept so much from me! How could I ever trust them again? Not to mention that the weight of their disapproval had suffocated me for years. How comforting it would have been to know that I had had a grandfather just like myself.

Although, after what had happened to him, that realization might not have been as comforting as one would hope. My grandfather (how odd that sounds!) had been a grown man, and look how badly things had turned out for him. What chance did I, an almost twelve-year-old girl, have to do any better?

The truth was, I couldn't wait to return the orb and the tablet to the wedjadeen so I could concentrate wholly on being an unpeculiar archaeologist.

By the time the afternoon rolled around, I was not in the best of moods. When Quillings's hideous watch contraption told me it was one o'clock, I was only too glad to get moving. I dressed quickly, made my bed, and left a lump of my old clothes carefully concealed under the covers. *There,* I thought, with one last prod at the decoy. That should look as though I were fast asleep to the casual observer. And hopefully, that was what Habiba was—a casual observer. It occurred to me that she could be a well-placed spy on behalf of Chaos, but Arab women led such sheltered and secluded lives that I didn't see how that could be the case.

Habiba was busy in the kitchen, so it was easy enough to sneak out to the stable, which was empty. Gadji and Sefu must have been off looking for Gadji's family. A sharp slice of regret cut through me and I was filled with a nearly overwhelming desire to have Sticky Will at my back for this adventure. But, of course, that was impossible, since he was an entire continent away. I gave myself a mental rap on the head and told myself to get on with it. How hard could it be to find the Luxor temple, anyway? Surely a landmark so popular with tourists and scholars would be easy enough to find.

I quickly discovered that finding it wasn't the problem—it was making my way through the small army of shopkeepers trying to sell post cards or ostrich feather fans or dragomen trying to talk me into hiring them. There was a small army of donkey boys, all shouting the virtues of their beasts at the top of their lungs, as well as men hawking *antikahs* and children begging for baksheesh. Finally, out of sheer self-defense, I hired one of the older children to act as my guide and lead me through the din and clamor to the temple.

It worked. Dodging and ducking around the clusters of locals, he led me through a maze of streets lined with shops and bazaars until we at last came upon the temple. It sat, solemn and majestic, spreading out for as far as the eye could see.

I paid the boy his coin and, in spite of his desire to stay and show me the temple, sent him on his way. I wanted to experience this ancient wonder without the constant chatter of my guide.

As the padding of his footsteps disappeared, I stared up at the marvel in front of me and felt as if I had been transported back to the days of the pharaohs. This was the place where the essence of the gods had lived. They had been worshiped here, housed, fed, clothed, and celebrated. There was no hint of dark magic or curses coming from anywhere nearby. Only a sense of unearthly power wafted across my skin, a faint breeze of sensation that felt both hushed and holy. There was also something just the tiniest bit familiar. With a flutter of recognition, I realized I'd felt a similar trickle of power coming off the artifacts of the gods that I'd handled. Now that I'd spent time in Egypt, so close to the source of all these magics, I was able to better distinguish the nuances between them.

A single obelisk rose up against the brilliant blue sky, and two rows of sphinxes guarded the entrance to the temple. Two colossal statues of Ramses II sat on either side of the entrance, imposing guardians of this once-sacred place.

No, it was *still* sacred, I thought.

I straightened my shoulders and tightened my grip on the reticule, then made my way down the procession of sphinxes. They were just statues, I reminded myself, even if it did feel as if they were watching me.

Luckily, most of the tourists had returned to their hotels and the temple appeared deserted. It was eerie, really, and if I hadn't needed to conduct my business in utmost secrecy, I would have been slightly unnerved.

The thick walls of the temple were covered in carvings, scenes of a battle of some sort. My hands itched to trace them so I could study them later, but there would be time enough for that once my promises had been kept.

I passed through the pylon, a shiver dancing along my shoulders as I did so, and entered the Court of Nectanebo II, the last true Egyptian pharaoh. On the left was a mosque, built much later, but on the right was the triple-barque shrine constructed by the great builder pharaoh, Ramses II. Yet another ancient marvel I had no time for this afternoon. I forced myself to cross the courtyard to the great papyrus-styled columns that lined the path to the inner sanctuaries of the temple. The truth was, it was physically painful to be among all these ancient wonders and have no time to examine them properly. In the end, I made myself stop looking and hurried through with my head down.

When I finally reached the altar, I paused a moment, letting the weight of the ages press down upon me. As reverently as possible, I removed from my pocket the small scroll that Awi Bubu had given me and laid it as an offering on the stone altar just as he had instructed. I said a little prayer, entreating whoever was listening to let the wedjadeen know I came in peace and in an effort to return what was rightfully theirs.

I felt a sense of well-being come over me. I was doing the right thing, returning the tablet and the sacred knowledge to the people who had guarded it for centuries. A faint breeze picked up and fluttered through my hair. I remembered Awi Bubu's insistence that even Shu, the god of air, had ears to hear us. Perhaps even now he took my message to the Eyes of Horus.

My hand slipped inside my pocket and searched for the sliver of brick. As my fingers closed around the rough surface, I listened carefully, wondering if the Babel stone would allow me to make out the words of an actual god.

The faint whooshing of the wind grew louder, and I fancied it almost sounded like a whispering voice. I closed my eyes and concentrated even harder, trying to make out the words. The rustling of the wind rose, then fell, grew louder, then softened, sounding remarkably like a far-off conversation. But alas, not one with words I could understand.

With a sigh of disappointment, I turned and began making my way back through the columns, my steps already feeling lighter. I was so close to handing off this suffocating burden and being able to get on with my life. Not to mention all the discoveries that were practically begging me to find them. As Mother said, I did seem to have a talent for that sort of thing. Just think of how much progress I could make if I wasn't constantly being pulled in another, decidedly dangerous direction!

There was a scrape along the dusty stone floor of the temple. The sort of scrape a footstep might make.

My gaze flew to the shadows among the small army of colonnades. Nothing. No, wait. There. A flutter of movement behind one of the Ramses statues. As my eyes zeroed in on it, the shadow came forward and formed itself into the shape of a very old wizened little man.

He was hardly any taller than I was. His head was large and bald. Except for being thinner and more shriveled, he could have been Awi Bubu's twin brother.

But probably most astonishing, he wore the robes of an ancient Egyptian *sem* priest—a white linen tunic draped over one shoulder, embellished by a leopard skin. "Hello?" I said.

"Greetings," he said in heavily accented English. "How may I help you?"

I glanced back at my little offering on the altar. That had

been fast. "I am looking for the Eyes of Horus. I have business to conduct with them."

The priest's eyebrows rose. "Who may I say is looking for them?"

"My name's Theodosia. Awi Bubu sent me."

At the sound of the magician's name, the priest stilled. "Indeed. If that is the case, we must send for them." He lifted two fingers to his lips and gave a short, piercing whistle. Within seconds, a dark shape appeared overhead in the sky. A falcon! It dipped low, flying in our direction and coming to land on the priest's outstretched arm. The priest whispered something to the falcon, who watched me with fiercely intelligent eyes. When the priest finished talking, he threw his arm up, launching the bird back into the sky. In silence, we watched the bird fly away.

"Now what?" I asked.

"Now we wait," he said.

"You mean they'll come right away?"

He nodded, lowered himself to the ground in front of one of the colonnades, and sat down. Not knowing quite what else was expected of me, I did the same.

After a while (half an hour, according to Quillings's watch), I heard the sound of hoofbeats in the distance. The priest smiled at me. "And here they are," he said.

Minutes later, three men strode into the courtyard. They wore long, flowing black robes and head cloths secured with green and gold cords. "You have called us, Baruti?"

"I did not call you, Khalfani. It is she who has left an offering for you." The priest pointed in my direction.

Khalfani spun on his heel and speared me with a fierce, dark gaze that reminded me of the falcon's. A wave of power bumped up against me, far stronger than anything Awi Bubu had ever tried to exert over me. When I steeled myself against it, Khalfani narrowed his eyes and strode over to the altar. He retrieved my note and read it in silence. When he was done, he looked up at me, his face giving none of his thoughts away. "How did you know how to summon us?"

"Awi Bubu told me."

A moment's stunned silence was followed by everyone talking at once. As unobtrusively as possible, I slipped my hand into my pocket and touched the sliver of Babel stone.

"Is Awi Bubu here?"

"Why did he not come himself?"

"What do you know of He Who Is Dead to Us?" This last was said in English and directed at me.

"He Who Is Dead . . . oh! You mean Awi Bubu?" Honestly! You'd think none of them had ever made a mistake. "I know he is very sorry for whatever it is he did. And it is he who sent me because I have something he thought you'd want rather badly. In fact, what I have is so important that he hoped returning it to you would earn him his way back into your good graces."

Another eruption, this time accompanied by outrage.

Finally, the priest hushed everyone. "Perhaps we should see what the girl has brought us before we judge and condemn Awi Bubu yet again."

I swallowed. "I have brought the Emerald Tablet to return to you."

Khalfani stepped forward, his eyes searching me for signs of the tablet. "Where is it? You do not have this thing on you."

"No," I admitted. "I needed to be certain I could reach you before I started lugging it all over town. It isn't the sort of thing one ought to leave lying out in the open."

"How do we know you are speaking the truth?"

"What possible reason would I have for lying?" I countered.

The man looked down at the note in his hand. "He says also that you carry with you a sign of good faith."

"I do. Here." I thrust the soiled, tattered reticule in his direction. "Proof that I mean what I say."

We eyed each other suspiciously, and then Khalfani

stepped forward and took the reticule from me. He returned to his men, who crowded around to watch. When he opened the purse, he drew back in surprise. "The Orb of Ra!" They began speaking to one another in soft whispers.

The leader shifted his attention back to me. "How did you come by it?" he asked.

I stared at the shiny gold artifact, glinting in the afternoon sun. If these wedjadeen were anything like Awi Bubu, they could smell a lie at twenty paces. Best stick with the truth, but the absolute minimum of the truth. "It was in my parents' museum," I confessed.

The man to Khalfani's right spoke, still in Arabic. The leader nodded, then repeated the question to me. "Did you find the orb alone?"

I shifted slightly on my feet. "No," I admitted. "I found it with a staff. The Staff of Osiris."

That got their full attention. "Where is the staff, then?" the leader asked, taking a step toward me.

Honestly! Did he think I was hiding it under my skirt? "I left it in London. With the Brotherhoo—er, a very wise man. He felt it was too risky to keep them together. Especially when traveling."

The wedjadeen nodded. "He was right to think so. No man should ever wield that kind of power."

Oh good. Something we agreed upon at last.

Khalfani's hand tightened around the orb. "Even so, it belongs to us. It should be returned as well."

"I'm sure he'll get right on that, sir." No wonder Awi Bubu ran away from these people. They were impossible to deal with.

"Why did this wise man of yours not bring it himself? What manner of coward is he that he hides behind a child's skirts?"

That did it. I put my hands on my hips and glared at them. "I thought you were supposed to be the Eyes of Horus, not some schoolyard bullies. Wig—the wise man didn't come himself because Awi Bubu told us that if a grown man approached you, you would most likely kill him on sight. He thought I, at least, would have a chance of being allowed to speak."

The look on the leader's face let me know I had scored a direct hit.

"Plus, he has a bad leg and can't get around well." The truth. "But more important, it was my task to complete; I had promised Awi Bubu on his deathbed that I would do this thing. And he promised you would not harm me."

The old priest's brows knit together in concern. "Awi Bubu is dead, then?"

"No. He lives. But he has been badly injured and his injuries are not healing well. That is why he was not able to come himself." I glared at the man who had asked that original question.

This caused a small flurry of rapid Arabic. Even holding the chip of Babel, I could barely make out what they were saying.

". . . just take the orb and be done."

"Why not just take this orb, silence her, then retrieve the other treasure from its hiding place?"

"No, I say let us honor Awi Bubu's wishes, at least at first. We can always change our minds later."

At last the leader motioned for the others to be quiet. "The orb has been used. How did you know how to use it?"

He could tell that by looking at it? "It was Awi Bubu who used it, against some very evil men. That's when he was horribly injured—while saving my life. So I owed him, you see, and when he thought he was dying, he made me promise to return this to you." The Egyptian magician could just as easily have left me in the hands of the Serpents of Chaos, but he hadn't and so had set this whole chain of events in motion.

"Very well," Khalfani said at last. "We will accept this orb as a gesture of good faith and will wait for you to bring the tablet to us. How quickly can you get back here?"

"It won't be today!" I protested.

"Tomorrow at sunrise, then." His will bumped into mine again, trying to ensure I would do exactly what he wanted.

It didn't work. "Do you have any idea how hard it is for me to get away? My mother knows nothing about this and I'd like to keep it that way. I had to pretend I was ill just so she would allow me to stay home today."

Khalfani shrugged. "Pretend you are sick again."

I nearly stomped my foot in frustration. "Have you ever had a mother? Because if you had, you'd know that if you're sick for more than a day, they expect a fever, or spots, or throwing up. They need proof. And while I am good at pretending, I am not *that* good."

After a long moment during which he had a very odd look on his face, he finally asked, "When *can* you get away again?"

"I could probably do it the day after tomorrow. I'll most likely be out in the sun all day and can then tell her I'm suffering from the heat."

"Weak *Inglaize*," one of them muttered.

"I am faking, remember?"

"Enough! We will return the day after tomorrow. What time is good for you?" Khalfani inquired mockingly.

CHAPTER FOURTEEN
DEIR EL-BAHRI

THE GOOD NEWS WAS that I made it home before Mother and Nabir with fifteen minutes to spare. The bad news was that Mother fussed over me a bit, wanting to be sure I was feeling better. And of course I was, since I had never been sick. Consequently, I made a special effort to slump and drag my feet. I also tried to look appropriately mopey. It was a tricky balance, however, because while I wanted to show that I had been sick, I also needed to demonstrate I was well enough to return to the dig tomorrow. Especially once I'd learned they planned on scouting out the area near Deir el-Bahri and Hatshepsut's temple. She couldn't honestly expect me to stay home while they pursued my ideas, could she?

Besides, I would have to play sick again the following day in order to meet the wedjadeen and hand off the Emerald Tablet. I didn't think I could stand to miss three days of archaeological discovery.

Morning's first light saw us on our way to the hills of western Thebes. I don't know about the others, but I had an entire swarm of butterflies in my stomach. What if I was proved right? How magnificent would it be to have two discoveries under my belt before I was even twelve?

Of course, I could also be proved wrong, which would be most embarrassing. Not wanting to think about that possibility, I turned my attention back to the red ocher hills rising up before us. They were said to be sacred to Hathor, the goddess of love, music, and motherhood. If so, surely she must be pleased with the monument Hatshepsut had built there. It was an architectural marvel, the temple and landscape fused together by the skill of the ancient builders so that they became one. It completely dwarfed the older temple of Mentuhotep II, which shared the valley with it.

Mother leaned over on her donkey. "Naville has done a magnificent job restoring the mortuary temple, hasn't he?"

I didn't know who Naville was, but the mortuary temple was certainly in excellent shape.

"Ja," Jadwiga agreed. "He is so meticulous, it seems hard to believe he would have missed an entire temple."

Mother raised her chin a bit. "People miss things all the time."

"Plus, the ancient Egyptians thought children brought good luck," Gunter Rumpf added. "Perhaps your daughter will bring us the same." He smiled at me, clearly a gesture he'd not had much practice with. Even so, I appreciated the effort and smiled back.

As we drew closer to the temple, Mother glanced around for any signs of other archaeologists. "Now, remember," she said. "If anyone else shows up, we're just here to see the sights and have a picnic."

"Do you British always bring your picks and shovels with you on your picnics?" Jadwiga asked in his woebegone voice.

Mother ignored him and turned her attention to the incredible edifice before us. A long ascending ramp led up to a series of broad, raised terraces, built into the actual cliff one atop another like a fancy cake. A series of columns supported each level. Hatshepsut's temple was enormous. I closed my eyes and tried to imagine it full of people: priests and officials, commoners come to make offerings to the mortuary cult of Hatshepsut. I also tried to determine if there was any *beka* emanating from the monument. It had been built to glorify the pharaoh Hatshepsut and connect her to her "father," the god Amun. His presence was heavy here, as was Hathor's. But there was no sense of the dark forces of magic or curses swirling nearby. Or at least none that could be felt from where we stood. "Can we go inside?" I asked Mother.

"Er, not today," she said.

So much for sightseeing!

"Let's tie up the donkeys over here." Mother led us to a spot in between the two temples, a place that was partially hidden by the southwest corner of the temple terrace. I glanced back the way we'd come. Our mounts would be hidden from any passersby.

While the men organized the equipment we'd need, I lifted the wicker basket from the back of my donkey and set it on the ground. Mother thought I was being peculiar again, insisting on bringing Isis, and perhaps I was, although not in the way she thought. This peculiarity had a very specific purpose. I had almost lost the Emerald Tablet two days ago; I didn't dare take any more such risks now, not when I was scheduled to hand it off tomorrow.

After looking to be certain everyone else was busy, I opened the lid. "Come out, Isis. No one is watching." As sleek and silent as death itself, Isis crept out of the basket. "Make yourself at home," I told her. With a quick flick of her tail, she slunk off and quickly lost herself among the shadows of the rocks. I breathed a little easier. It never hurt to have access to her excellent cat senses.

I went to join Mother, who kept looking nervously over her shoulder. "You did get permission to be here," I asked, keeping my voice low, "didn't you?"

She got very busy unloading her tools from her donkey. "There was no one to ask, really. Weigall was out in the field, and when his assistant kindly explained Naville wasn't going to be working here this season, I decided surely no one would mind if we had a quick look around."

Honestly! I'd never seen this side of my mother before. I had no idea she was so ruthless. This could end up being a problem, especially if we *did* find something. It would be so disheartening to have one's first major discovery be disputed.

"Now, Theo," Mother said. "What exactly did that translation say again?"

She was just trying to distract me. I knew she had memorized it, just like I had. *"For Thutmose sits in no one's shadow. He alone is most beloved of the gods and sits above the right shoulder of his forebears.*

"Which would be right about . . . there." I pointed to an enormous pile of rubble and scree.

"There?" Mother frowned.

"Well, it is between the two temples, so any temple Thutmose III had built would be staring down at Hatshepsut, and he would in effect be above her," I explained.

"*Ja*, but it looks like all the excavators in the valley have dumped their unwanted debris until they created a mountain of junk," Jadwiga pointed out.

"True," I said, my enthusiasm waning somewhat.

"Well, that's why we brought shovels, isn't it?" Rumpf asked, handing one to Jadwiga and Nabir. "The sooner we start, the sooner we'll know." And with that, he strode over to the tower of rocky debris and began digging.

The rest of us followed, albeit less zealously.

We dug—and dug—our shovels making nothing but a small dent in the enormous pile. In fact, we dug the entire morning. I quickly realized that doing excavation of *this* sort is far less satisfying than just stumbling onto a hidden annex.

Just past noon, we took a short break for a quick lunch. Everyone else took a seat in the shade from an outcrop of the third terrace of Hatshepsut's temple. I, however, looked for a place to sit a small ways away. All this digging was discouraging enough that I was afraid I'd catch a case of Jadwiga's doldrums if I sat too close to him. He was so downcast that his poor mustache nearly drooped to the ground.

Although I had to admit I would be, too, if I did very much of this and never found anything.

Isis had been poking and sniffing around all morning and now sat perched at the base of a particularly steep section of debris. After looking at it closely to be certain it wouldn't all come tumbling down, I laid my handkerchief on the ground and sat down on it with my back to the hill, almost like a chair. As I unwrapped my sandwich, Isis came over to see what I was eating.

"You probably shouldn't sit there, *ja?*" Jadwiga intoned. "The whole mountain might fall down on your head."

We had to find something today, if only to cheer him up. "I'll be fine," I chirped, putting as much cheer into my voice as I could. "I checked it before I sat down." I reached out and patted the mound of dirt behind me, which let loose with a small shower of debris. Bother. That was not the reassurance I had been looking for. Luckily for me, however, Jadwiga's attention was drawn by something else at the moment.

"Here comes the frosting on the cakes," he said with a deep, sad sigh. "They have found us out and will now drag us to jail."

"What?" Mother hopped to her feet and spun around to see who was approaching. "Quick," she said over her shoulder. "Hide those shovels."

I shielded my eyes from the bright sun and peered at the figure riding toward us. The rider was a tall man with military bearing wearing unrelieved black, except for the little red fez perched atop his head. As he drew closer, I saw the glint of gold-rimmed glasses and a fat black mustache.

Oh no! I thought, glancing to see where I'd set Isis's case. It was back by the donkeys, where, hopefully, he wouldn't be able to get a good look at it.

When the rider had drawn close enough that we could make out his face, it confirmed my worst fears. "Mr. Borscht!" Mother said, sailing forward.

My heart skipped a beat at the sight of him and it was all I could do to keep from running in the opposite direction. Mr. Borscht—von Braggenschnott—halted his horse in front of us, stepped off the beast, and bowed low to Mother. "Good day, Madame Throckmorton," he said. "I had reason to come to Luxor this week and thought I'd check in on you. Although"—he smiled—"I had thought to find you at the Valley of the Kings, as we had discussed."

"I'm so glad to see you again," Mother said. "We've been enjoying a little picnic today and seeing the sights." Her voice was a bit loud, as if she could make up with volume what she lacked in honesty.

Mr. Borscht gave a friendly chuckle. He glanced good-naturedly at the partially concealed shovels. "So I see, Madame Throckmorton, so I see."

Eager to turn the conversation to other things, Mother asked, "Have you met my assistants?" As she introduced Mr. Rumpf to von Braggenschnott, a horrid thought occurred to me. What if Mr. Rumpf was working for Chaos, too? He was very intense, a trait that nearly all Serpents of Chaos seemed to possess. He was also German, like von Braggenschnott, and he even wore the same glasses.

But Awi Bubu had recommended the man himself, hadn't he? Or had he recommended Jadwiga? My gaze darted back and forth between the two, trying to determine which looked like someone Awi Bubu might have recommended.

"And how is your lovely daughter enjoying Luxor?" Von Braggenschnott's voice interrupted my escalating suspicions. "Is your education progressing nicely, fräulein?"

"Quite nicely," I said stiffly.

"Have you spotted any more vermin, I wonder?" he asked.

I narrowed my eyes. "A few." My words were clipped, and he laughed. Mother looked a bit perplexed but laughed politely.

"Do be careful, fräulein," von Braggenschnott added.

"Be careful of what?" Gunter Rumpf asked. He, at least, could sense the undercurrent between Borscht and me, even if he didn't know what it meant. Which made me feel horridly guilty for my suspicions.

Von Braggenschnott leaned forward. "There are many hidden dangers in the valley," he said. "Black-market antiquities dealers, cutthroat collectors who are not above knocking heads around and taking what they want. Unstable conditions," he added, with a glance at the shifting pile of rubble behind us. One can never be too careful," he said, looking pointedly in my direction.

"If any of you need anything, Madame Throckmorton, anything at all, you let me know," he added.

"Excellent. Thank you so much for stopping by."

"My pleasure, Madame Throckmorton." He bowed at Mother. "Miss Throckmorton." When he bowed at me, I felt faint. This whole visit had been designed to let me know that he was here and he was watching me. No matter if we changed our plans or not, he would always be one step ahead of us.

As he rode away, Mother said, "See, Mr. Jadwiga, there was nothing to worry about." She was trying to cheer up the poor man. When she is happy, she likes everyone to be happy.

"Ja," he said, picking up his shovel. "Or maybe he is just trying to lull us into a false sense of security."

Could the man *be* any more of a wet blanket?

Depressed enough on my own, I returned to my lunch spot before he could infect me with even more melancholy. I dropped to the ground, my mind awhirl with the implications of von Braggenschnott's visit. I would have to get word to Major Grindle. And what about my meeting with the wedjadeen tomorrow? How would I keep von Braggenschnott from finding out about that?

I groaned and leaned back against the pile of rubble, my head clunking on a particularly large rock. "Ow." I turned to brush the rock aside, but there wasn't one. Just dirt. That was odd. I reached for my work gloves and slipped them on, then felt along the hillside where I'd just bumped my head.

It was hard as stone. I scowled at it, then began carefully brushing the dirt aside, grateful for something to focus on. The voices of the others faded into the distance, along with all thoughts of Chaos. It was just me and the dirt and whatever mystery might lie behind it. After a few moments, I'd gotten rid of enough dirt to see something dull white shining through. *A bone?* I wondered, with a faint jolt of horror. I hesitated then, not wanting to disturb the dead. Then I reasoned he was most likely already disturbed and continued brushing away the dirt.

A few seconds later, I realized that it wasn't a bone at all. It was much too big for that. It had a slightly rounded shape with vertical ridges running up and down. *Man-made, then,* I thought, a tiny thrill running through me. Using the greatest of care, I began scraping away the last of the excess dirt from around the object.

Like a hound on point, Rumpf bounded over to me, nearly quivering in his eagerness. "Have you found something?"

"I'm not sure . . ." I said, not wanting to spoil the surprise if I had. "Mother!" I called out. "Could you come check this out?"

She hurried over and dropped to her knees next to me in the dirt.

"Look," I said. "At first I thought it was round, and most rocks aren't perfectly round. But when I began to clear away the sand and debris, I realized it has a polygon shape to it."

Mother's hands joined mine on the hillside and within minutes we had brushed away the last of the dirt to reveal a short stub. Of a column. A polygonal column. The sort used in ancient Egyptian temple architecture. Which meant . . .

"Excellent work, Theodosia!" Mum beamed at me. "I think you've found the temple of Thutmose III!"

CHAPTER FIFTEEN
THE LIFE OF THE PARTY

IT WAS INDEED A COLUMN, a standing column. Another hour's work revealed one on either side of it, which meant it was at the very least a new section of Hatshepsut's temple and could quite possibly be the Thutmose temple we'd been hoping for. Mother had Rumpf carefully sketch out the exact location of the columns, then had the men re-cover them with the debris so no one else would find them. If I had been expecting Jadwiga to cheer up at this discovery, I was sadly mistaken. His mood went from mournful to glum, but that was all.

Mother invited both men over to the house for dinner that night to celebrate our discovery. Jadwiga and Rumpf gave us just enough time to wash and change before they showed up on our doorstep. Mother brought out a bottle of champagne to celebrate and gave it to Rumpf to open. The cork shot off and nearly hit Habiba, who was clearing the plates. She sniffed in disapproval and removed herself from the dining room.

Rumpf poured the sparkling champagne into the crystal flutes Mother had produced from somewhere. Honestly! How had she known to pack those? Had she been that certain we'd find something?

"Here, darling," she said, and handed me a glass with an inch of champagne in it. "It was your discovery, after all, so you must join in the celebration." Then she lifted her glass and said, "To great finds, gentlemen!"

"To great finds, and the children who find them!" Rumpf amended. Have I mentioned that he is growing on me?

Even Mr. Miseryguts lifted his glass and gave me a morose nod.

I lifted the flute to my mouth, fascinated as the tiny bubbles popped and fizzed off the surface. It smelled fruity. Cautiously, I lifted it to my lips and took a sip. It crackled on my tongue, an odd sensation, but I did not care for the taste at all, so quickly put it back down on the table.

"Your mother said you were the one who discovered the second annex to Thutmose's tomb," Mr. Rumpf said. "How did a young girl like yourself come to make such a spectacular discovery?"

I looked to Mother for permission. After a faint pause, she inclined her head.

"Well," I began, not sure where to start. "In January, when Mother had just returned from months and months in the field, she suddenly needed to return to the valley to . . ." I didn't want to tell them of the ruthless competitive streak that had propelled her halfway around the globe so soon after returning, nor could I tell them it was a setup so that I would have an excuse to tag along and return the powerful Heart of Egypt to its rightful resting place before it destroyed my country. I glanced up at Mother, who was studying her champagne glass as if the secrets of the pharaohs could be discerned in its depths. "I decided I'd had enough of being left behind and, er, stowed away—"

"Invited herself along!" Mother said over me, then took a gulp of champagne.

"Right. Invited myself along. Then, once we'd arrived in Luxor, I'm afraid my impatience got the better of me and I snuck out one morning when my parents were still asl—"

"Dealing with the paperwork!" Mother said loudly.

"Right. Dealing with the paperwork." Honestly, was she going to tell this story or was I?

"And?" Mr. Rumpf prompted.

"And," I said, picking my way carefully over this part, "while exploring the tomb, I tripped and fell—"

"Such an awkward age," Mother murmured into her champagne glass.

"—against the back wall," I finished, but my focus was directed at Mother. She was embarrassed of me. She was nearly squirming with discomfort. Suddenly, my enjoyment of this story—of this discovery itself—turned to dust in my mouth. "It gave way and I tumbled into the newest annex."

Rumpf leaned forward. "And it was full of artifacts? Treasure of all kinds?"

Bother. Heard that, had he? But before I could try to explain, Mother gave a little laugh. "I'm afraid my daughter is mistaken, gentlemen. She was a trifle overset when we found her."

Overset? *Overset!* I'd never been overset in my life.

"She fainted shortly after that, and her father and I think she must have bumped her head in the fall."

Oh, how I longed to argue! I had not been overset and I had not imagined anything. "But Mother," I said sweetly, "how do you explain the Was scepter I found?"

She looked blank for a moment, unable to come up with an answer for that. However, before I could make a fool of myself and shout, *"Ha!"* Jadwiga spoke up.

"It was most likely the tomb raiders, *ja*? They are like a swarm of flies on honey. They can clear a tomb overnight."

Mother looked relieved. "Yes, perhaps that was it." She gave me a condescending smile that telegraphed quite clearly that she still thought I had imagined it all. A complete stranger believed me more than my own mother did. This was a fine state of affairs.

She began questioning the others about earlier digs they had worked on, but I hardly heard. I was torn between wanting to fume and wanting to weep. She was quite happy to benefit from my peculiar behavior—when it led to fascinating discoveries, say—but wanted to hide it from the rest of the world, as if it was something of which she was ashamed.

"And you, Mrs. Throckmorton?" Jadwiga asked. "What other digs have benefited from your expertise?"

The question jerked me out of my fugue, and I looked up at Mother. Perhaps her answer would reveal the temple where I'd been born.

As if quite aware of my powerful curiosity, she waved her hand prettily in the air. "Oh, the usual. Saqqara, Edfu, Dendera," she rattled off, then turned the conversation to a safer subject.

Pah! That was three different temples. There was no clue hidden there.

Suddenly I was gripped by some dark, ugly desire to remind her that there were far more shameful and embarrassing members of our family.

At the next lull in the conversation, I spoke up. "Did either of you know my grandfather?" I asked. "He was an archaeologist also, wasn't he, Mother?"

"Theo! How did you know of that?" she asked.

"I overheard someone talking of it once, at the museum."

"Well." She laughed nervously. "I'm sure these two gentlemen are too young to have worked with your grandfather." Then she changed the subject once again. But not before I saw the flicker of recognition in Jadwiga's brown eyes. He had heard of my grandfather.

CHAPTER SIXTEEN

ANOTHER DECEPTION
OR TWO

I WOKE FAR TOO EARLY. I dreaded what I had to do and knew Mother would give me one of those looks I was beginning to fear. I'd slept so poorly that I had the beginnings of a headache. The only advantage was that when Mother came in to collect me, I looked pale and drawn.

"Good morning, darling," Mother trilled as she bustled into the room with a swish of skirts and lilac scent. She seemed cheerful enough, which meant she had most likely forgotten about my bringing up Grandfather at dinner last night. That was one hurdle behind me. "Morning, Mother," I mumbled back.

She stopped pulling my clothes from the drawer and

hurried to the bed. "Oh, Theo! Not again." She laid her cool hand on my forehead. "You're not feverish."

"No, but I have a beastly headache and my stomach hurts." Neither of which was a lie. My stomach was packed full of nerves and dread, so of course it hurt. "I never dreamed it would take so long to get used to the hot sun," I said, trying to push her thoughts in the direction that would bear the most fruit.

"Oh dear, we *were* out there a rather long time. I wish you would have said something, darling."

"I felt fine at the time, only a trifle warm."

"Well, I suppose another day of rest won't harm anything. Besides, what is there possibly left to find?" she asked with a laugh.

"Aren't you going to see Mr. Weigall this morning about permission to excavate there?"

She turned away from me and busied herself straightening the clothes I'd forgotten to put away last night. "I thought we'd wait until we were absolutely sure. I'd love to have something solid to present to him that would prove it wasn't merely an extension of Hatshepsut's temple, but an entirely separate one."

"That makes sense," I said, secretly glad. If she was to be at Deir el-Bahri all day, there was even less of a chance of my absence being discovered.

"I'll send Habiba in with some peppermint tea and dry toast. Between that and a little more rest, I'm sure you'll be good as new by tomorrow." She came over and planted a kiss on my forehead, then cupped my face in her hands. "I am so very proud of you, Theo. You really have an amazing calling as an archaeologist, my dear." Then she took her leave and I was left alone, staring at the ceiling.

For some reason, the words of praise I'd so longed to hear made me feel like crying, and I had no idea why. Sensing my distress, Isis hopped up from under the bed, where she'd disappeared when Mother had first entered the room, and began licking the tears from my face. I have found it is surprisingly difficult to remain sad when a cat is doing its level best to sandpaper one's cheeks. I sighed and petted Isis's soft black fur. "Hopefully, this will be the last time I have to lie to her," I whispered. Isis stopped licking and began purring, her paws finding their way into the crook of my neck and kneading at my hair.

We stayed like that until the door burst open and Habiba appeared, carrying a tray. She nearly shrieked when she saw the cat next to me and said something in rapid, indecipherable Arabic. Not liking her tone one bit, Isis leaped from the bed, shot over to the window, and hopped outside.

I glared at Habiba, and she glared back at me over her dark veil. Still muttering, she set the tray down with a thud, then turned and left the room. I gave a passing wish for the Babel brick, curious to know what she was saying, but I hadn't thought to keep it near me while I slept.

When she was gone, I swung my legs out of bed, grabbed the tea tray, and inhaled the toast. The truth was, I was starving. All the hard work in the field yesterday had made me rather hungry.

Once I'd eaten my breakfast, there was nothing to do but wait. And wait. And wait. We had set up the meeting time for late afternoon again, when most tourists would be out of the heat of the day. Meantime, there was little I could do. I didn't dare get dressed yet, in case Habiba came back. So instead, I lay in bed and let myself daydream of all the things I would do once I had finished my business with the wedjadeen. First, I would try to talk Mother into taking me to the temple where I was born. I was keen to see it for myself. I also wanted to start asking some questions about Grandfather Throckmorton. Jadwiga, at least, had reacted last night when I mentioned him—I was sure of it.

And why hadn't Wigmere said anything? What was it with grownups and their beastly secrets!

In the end, I fell asleep. When I woke up again, a quick glance at Quillings's watch told me that it was almost time to leave. Just as I threw off the covers and swung my feet out of bed, Isis arched her back and hissed at the door.

Someone was coming! I hurriedly pulled my feet back under the covers and lay down.

I felt rather than heard the door open a crack. Even with my eyes closed, I could sense someone watching me. I forced my mind to go blank, as it would if I were truly asleep, and concentrated on slow, deep breaths. After a harrowing, long moment, there was a faint snick as the door closed. Seconds later, I heard the sound of another door closing. I hopped out of bed and ran to the window. Habiba was hurrying down the road carrying a shopping basket.

I breathed a deep sigh of relief. Of course. She simply wanted to check in on me before she went shopping. And what perfect timing!

After I was dressed, I gingerly took Quillings's fountain pen and compact from my drawer and slipped them into my pocket. As much as I loathed the idea of them, I was enough of a realist to know that without backup, I needed some sort of plan B.

I left the dresser and went to my bed, where I quickly set up the decoy under my covers. Once that was out of the way, I turned to Isis's carrying case, then paused, overcome by a desire to see the tablet one last time. After this, it would disappear forever and I would never see it again.

I retrieved the sacred object, set it on the floor, and slowly unwrapped it, revealing the dull green stone of unpolished emerald. I stared at the figures carved in its surface: the falcon-headed Horus, the ibis-headed Thoth, the Chaldean glyphs. Even though there was no moonlight in which to see the even stranger glyphs hidden in the emerald itself, I could feel them buzzing lazily against my gloved hands—not trying to burrow their way into my skin like a curse would have, but more like a cat, bumping up against a person's leg in lazy affection.

I realized that as thrilled as I was to get this off my hands, I was also filled with regret that I would never discover its secrets. That realization gave me pause. Surely I shouldn't pine after something as dangerous and forbidden as the tablet. Nervous that perhaps the magic was having some influence over me, I quickly rewrapped the object and placed it in the false bottom of the wicker carrying case. Everyone had gotten quite used to my carrying Isis around. Seeing me with the basket now should raise no questions.

It did, however, mean I would need to ride a donkey to the temple, as the basket weighted down with the tablet was far too awkward and heavy to carry for long. With any luck, Gadji would be out looking for his family again and I could sneak out unnoticed.

My luck failed, and I hoped it wasn't going to be an omen. Gadji was in the stable, lying in the straw and scowling at the ceiling. "Good afternoon," I said, startling him. He jumped to his feet, his eyes going immediately to the carrying case.

"Where is effendi miss going?" he asked.

"On an errand. Could you please saddle up my donkey for me?" I loathed having to ask him, especially since he wasn't invited on the errand, but I didn't know how to do it myself.

"Effendi miss need Gadji to go with her?" His voice was full of hope and for a moment I was tempted. But it was too dangerous. I had no wish to drag anyone else into this tangle I'd found myself in.

"Not today," I said cheerfully. It was a trick I'd learned from Mother, delivering unwelcome news in the most jaunty tone possible.

He looked injured and hung his head dejectedly as he saddled the donkey.

"Have you had any more luck with your family?" I asked.

He shook his head. "No lucks. Old market is having new peoples in it. None of those peoples know mine."

No wonder he was so discouraged. "I'm sorry," I said. "But I want you to know you can stay here as long as you like."

He nodded. "It is right that you offer me this since I save your life. Miss is needing me to keep her safe," he said slyly.

"Just not today."

Once the donkey was saddled, I secured the basket on its back and made sure the straps were extra tight. Gadji silently offered to help me up onto the saddle, making me feel even worse for excluding him. "Look," I said, leaning down, "I do need you to do one thing for me."

His whole face brightened.

"If I am not back by dinnertime, I need you to go to the *antikah* man's house. Do you remember it?"

"Of course."

"Good. Go to that house and ask for Major Grindle and tell him that I haven't come back. He'll know what to do."

"Will he be knowing where effendi miss goes?"

He was a sharp one. "No, he won't. And if I tell you where I'm going, you need to promise not to follow. Can you do that?"

He nodded solemnly. "I promise to not follow you."

I checked to be sure his fingers weren't crossed. (Did Egyptians even know about that trick, I wondered?) "Very well. Tell him I went to the Luxor Temple."

Gadji nodded. "Yes, miss."

I slapped the reins. The donkey lurched forward and stumbled. Not the most auspicious beginning to my adventure, I thought.

It didn't take long before the temple came into view. Even from here, I could feel the great magic and power pulsing off the monument, like a giant heart beating. Only instead of pumping blood, it was pumping *heka*. But good *heka*, thank heavens.

Just before the temple, I slipped off the donkey, tied it up to a scrubby little palm tree, and hauled the basket from behind the saddle.

It seemed to have grown heavier during the ride.

As I walked down the row of sphinxes, the air stirred faintly, pale shadows and flickers of hieroglyphs swarming on the statues' surfaces. I blinked to clear my eyes, and when I looked again, the symbols were gone. I wondered if I'd just seen my first mirage. Somehow, I didn't think so.

The sphinxes were intended as guardians, I reminded myself. So as long as I didn't mean the temple or the gods any harm, I would be fine.

I circled around the walls of the temple and approached from the northeast side, until I reached the colonnade between the Great Court of Ramses II and the Great Court of Amenhotep II. Once inside the cover of the columns and hidden from all-seeing eyes, I felt a bit easier.

Eager to get things over with, I made my way to the innermost part of the temple. Even in the broad daylight, the place was thick with powerful magic.

The Court of Amenhotep echoed eerily as I crossed its broad expanse. I had only to set the offering on the altar, wait until the wedjadeen found it, then leave as quickly as possible. Then it would all be over.

But if that was the case, why did I feel so melancholy?

I must have caught it from Jadwiga.

CHAPTER SEVENTEEN
THE MOST PRECIOUS
OF ARTIFACTS

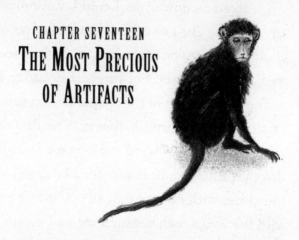

I HAD GOTTEN TO THE TEMPLE before the appointed time in order to avoid a surprise ambush. Consequently, I spent a long hour waiting among the colonnades in Hypostyle Hall. I tried to distract myself by watching the faint eddies of air shimmering around the columns, trying to see if any of the glyphs or symbols would be visible enough to recognize, but they weren't.

When I looked at my watch for the twenty-seventh time, it was five minutes to three o'clock. Close enough. A shot of adrenaline spurted through me, coupled with relief that I could finally get moving. I surged to my feet, gripped the basket, and began weaving through the columns toward the offering room.

I walked as quietly as I could, not only to avoid waking any sleeping gods or other creatures of power, but to see if I could detect anyone following me. I had seen no sign of the wedjadeen at all yet, but surely they had to be nearby?

The inner rooms of the chapel were much smaller than the great courtyards and hallways. The floor rose up and the ceiling sloped downward, making me feel as if I was walking through a long shaft. I did not like meeting in here. It was too close, with no way out. In essence, I would be trapped, with the wedjadeen between me and escape.

But I *was* giving them the tablet, so there shouldn't be any need to escape, I reminded myself.

I entered the offering chamber and, for a moment, allowed the thrill of being inside an ancient temple's holy of holies wash over me. To think of all the rituals that had once taken place here! Gods placated, prayers answered, souls weighed. The walls were covered with fascinating reliefs and images that I longed to examine, but now was not the time. Instead, I set the basket down on the floor, carefully removed the wrapped tablet, and carried it to the altar. Balancing the heavy tablet in one hand, I unwrapped the layers of linen so the wedjadeen would recognize the green stone as soon as they arrived.

As I laid the precious artifact on the altar, a boot scraped on the stone floor behind me. I whipped my head around. Half a dozen wedjadeen stood in the doorway. I recognized Khalfani and two others from our previous meeting, but the rest were new to me, except for the little priest. I was surprisingly happy to see him again.

They all stared at the Emerald Tablet on the altar.

"She has returned the tablet," Baruti, the priest, said. "She spoke the truth."

Khalfani turned his gaze to me. "But not the entire truth, I think."

"What do you mean?" I asked, thoroughly confused.

He took another step into the room. "You have in your possession another treasure we hold dear, dearer even than this tablet."

"I already gave you the Orb of Ra."

"Do not play games with us!"

"Honestly, I'm not! I don't know what you are talking about."

A look of uncertainty appeared on his face, then quickly passed. He took two giant strides into the room, eating up the space between us. He loomed over me. "Do not toy with me."

"I'm not. This is the only thing I have left to give you. I promise. The orb and the tablet. That was all."

"You lie! We have seen this treasure with our own eyes."

"You've been following me?" I asked.

He looked just the tiniest bit sheepish, and then the look vanished. "We were right to do so, it seems, for that is how we learned of this other treasure you possess."

"What treasure?" I asked, so frustrated I wanted to scream.

One of the men behind Khalfani pulled a long, thin knife from the sheath at his waist. "You would hide from us that which we seek. We have killed for less than that."

So much for Awi Bubu's assurances that they would treat a young girl gently. "Look," I said, unable to tear my eyes away from the point of the knife. "I have brought the Emerald Tablet in good faith. I don't know what else you are talking about."

Just then there was a rustle of sound. A small, quick figure jumped into the room and threw himself in front of me.

I blinked at Gadji in surprise. "I told you not to follow me!"

He grinned. "And I am telling you, you be needing my help."

As Gadji spoke, the wedjadeen did the most extraordinary thing. One by one, they bowed low before him.

"Young miss *did* bring us our treasure," Khalfani said when he rose to his feet. "She has not broken the trust between us."

"Him?" I asked. "He is your treasure? An orphaned donkey boy fresh off the streets of Cairo?"

"Me?" Gadji asked, the look on his face an odd mixture of suspicion and pleasure.

Khalfani shook his head. "He is no donkey boy. This child is descended from the most highly treasured bloodline in our history. This donkey boy, as you call him, is the last pharaoh of Egypt."

CHAPTER EIGHTEEN

The Last Pharaoh

I LOOKED FROM GADJI in his tattered rags to the wedjadeen's serious faces. They had to be joking. Didn't they? "Gadji," I said slowly. "Do you know these men?"

"No, miss. I never see them before."

"You see?" I told the wedjadeen. "There must be some mistake."

"Come," the man with the knife said. "It is not good to linger. We will take the girl with us and talk where it is safe."

As Khalfani nodded and motioned for someone to pick up the tablet, one of the wedjadeen bowed in front of Gadji and politely indicated that he should go first. Another wedjadeen grabbed my arm, rather roughly, I might add.

"Do not be harming her!" Gadji called over his shoulder, and the man relaxed his grip somewhat.

"Where is this safe place you would take us?" I asked.

"A day's ride from here," said the man holding my arm.

"I'm terribly sorry, but I can't be gone that long. I'll be missed."

A second wedjadeen took up position on my other side. "We cannot leave you here. You know too much."

"But that was our agreement," I protested. "I would give you the tablet and you would let me be. If Gadji wants to stay, that's up to him. We said nothing about your taking me with you."

The man put his head down close to mine so that we were practically nose to nose. "We said nothing about letting you go free, either."

I swallowed. No, they hadn't, come to think of it. I had just assumed that part.

The priest, Baruti, stepped closer. "She did keep her promise," he pointed out. "Are we not required to honor the agreement that Awi Bubu made with her?"

"*I* made no such agreement," the man with the knife said.

"Nevertheless," Baruti continued, "it is the word of a wedjadeen and we must honor it."

One of the other men said something in his own language, and then someone else spoke up. I slipped my free hand into my pocket and grasped the small sliver of Babel stone.

". . . we cannot leave her here. She knows too much about us."

"If we take her, there will be a huge hue and cry. The *Inglaize* will make all our people suffer until they find her."

Another man shrugged. "So we leave her but cut out her tongue."

"That won't work," I blurted out. "I'm perfectly able to write things down, you know."

Then Khalfani, who had been arguing on my behalf, threw me an aggrieved look. "You are not helping your own cause."

Honestly! They could hardly expect me to stand by quietly while they discussed mutilating me.

Khalfani frowned and tilted his head in question. "You speak Arabic?"

"Er, a little," I said, fingering the stone inside my pocket.

"Come," one of the others hissed. "We have tarried too long. We must leave."

We had reached Hypostyle Hall and I tried to see if there was anywhere to run to if I managed to break free. Perhaps I could hide among the columns.

Gadji was ahead of me, with only one wedjadeen in front of him, but he wasn't in any danger. They wanted to treat him like a king! But I had two testy men on either side of me, gripping my arms. The situation appeared hopeless. I couldn't even get to Quillings's fountain pen. So much for plan B.

A shout went up in front and a tall, red-jacketed figure stepped from behind one of the columns. Just as I recognized Major Grindle, he snagged Gadji from the guard, put him in a chokehold, and calmly slipped a knife up against his throat. "I'm so sorry to interrupt, gentlemen, but I'm afraid I must insist you let the girl go. Once you do, the boy here can go with you, but only if he wishes."

There was the ring of steel as every one of the wedjadeen drew a sword or knife. The men's grips on my arms tightened painfully.

"You will die for daring to lay hands on him."

Major Grindle tilted his head. "Funny, I feel precisely the same way about Miss Throckmorton. She is very special to my people, just as this boy here is very special to you. Which is why an even exchange works out so nicely, don't you think?"

The leader shouted something in Arabic and one of the men holding me answered back. A short argument ensued. Finally, with great reluctance, the men let go of me and the others parted so I could work my way up to Major Grindle and Gadji.

"You have the upper hand. For now," Khalfani said. "But we will not forget this insult."

"We'll cross that bridge when we come to it. Now, Gadji, do you wish to go with these men or return with us? It is your choice, but make it quickly, please."

Gadji did not hesitate. "I am returning with effendi miss."

His answer shocked me. "But why, Gadji? These men say you are a king."

Gadji shrugged. "Effendi miss be needing me, and I honor my debts."

"Very well. You will come with us, then," Major Grindle said.

The leader was furious. "We will follow you to the ends of the earth and hunt you down like the jackal you are."

"As I said, we'll deal with that at the proper time." Major Grindle drew Gadji and me close to his side, his eyes never leaving the wedjadeen. "Miss Throckmorton, would you be so kind as to adjust your watch?"

I stared at him blankly for a moment.

"It is three against eight. The odds are not in our favor without a little help," he said, glancing at my wrist.

Of course! Quillings's watch! I quickly reached down and twisted the dial so that it would create the curse-repelling field.

The major pulled a small jar from his jacket, shook it vigorously, then dashed it on the ground. It shattered, sending a maelstrom of stinging, burning sand and raging wind to engulf the wedjadeen.

"Come, Miss Throckmorton. *Move.*" Major Grindle shoved Gadji and me in front of him and put himself between us and the wedjadeen, who had all begun to shout and flail as the small sandstorm cut us a wide berth and consumed them.

We didn't stop running till we reached the outermost temple courtyard, where two horses waited. "Donkeys are not all that different from horses. I assume you can handle one?" Major Grindle asked Gadji.

Gadji nodded, and then the major lifted him and placed him in the saddle. Before I knew what was happening, I felt the major grasp my waist and toss me onto the other horse, then leap up and settle himself behind me. "All right then, let's go. At a gallop, I think."

At some command from him, the horses surged forward and we were away, riding like the wind itself.

We didn't stop until we reached the major's house. As we clattered into the courtyard, he called out to his factotum, who appeared in the doorway. "See to the horses," he said, swinging himself out of the saddle before lifting me down and gently setting me on my feet. "We'll be riding out again within the hour.

"I think a conversation is in order," Major Grindle said to us. "Let's retreat to the study, shall we?"

Gadji and I exchanged glances. While I had been very glad to see the major at the temple, I wasn't looking forward to facing his displeasure.

We followed him into his office and the riotous mix of strange magics was like a punch to my gut. Even Gadji's mouth dropped open as he stepped into the room. The major waited for us to file past, then firmly shut the door. Slowly, as if engaged in deep thinking, he made his way over to his desk. He did not sit down but merely stood with his hands behind his back, staring at the two of us.

Even though my knees were still weak from the close call at the Luxor Temple, I dared not sit, not with him standing. Gadji remained standing, too. When Major Grindle's stern blue eyes settled on me, I tried not to squirm.

"Would you care to explain what that was all about, Miss Throckmorton?" he asked.

"I was returning the artifact I had told you about, sir." Which was only partially a lie. I *was* returning an artifact, just not the one I had mentioned to him.

"Did it never occur to you to ask for backup?"

"No, sir." I wanted to hang my head in shame at having deceived him and just barely kept from doing so.

He stared at me a long moment, his eyes boring into me.

"Did Wigmere know what you were about? Or did you deceive him as well?"

"If you please, sir. It wasn't a question of deception," I rushed to explain. "Or not intentional deception, anyway. I had made a deathbed promise, sir, which I viewed as sacred. Part of that promise was not telling anyone else the details of the plan."

Major Grindle stared at me a few seconds longer, his brows beetled and mouth pursed. Finally, something shifted, something that gave me hope that all was not lost with him.

"Does the nature of that secret have to do with those men at the temple? For do not tell me they were Serpents of Chaos. I know that they were not."

I swallowed. "Yes, sir. The secret deathbed promise had to do with those men."

"Hmm," was all he said before turning the full weight of his regard to Gadji. "And you, young man. They seemed to be quite interested in you."

Gadji, who had been silent all this time, nodded his head, as if dazed. "They did most certainly," he said.

"Do you know why?"

Gadji snapped out of his trance and looked up to meet the major's gaze with a grin. "Because I am the last pharaoh, mister major."

The words fell into the room, a swell of silence growing

around them. I cleared my throat. "Is it true? Was your father a pharaoh?"

Gadji shrugged. "My father works in Valley of Kings. He moves stone and dirt for the *Inglaize,* as his father and his father before him."

"Is that the family you've been looking for all this time?"

Gadji shook his head. "Father dies in great accident."

"Oh, I'm sorry. What about your mother?"

Gadji shrugged again. "She die many years ago, while having baby. Baby die, too. Only sister is left. Safiya."

"Did you recognize any of those men?" Major Grindle asked.

"No."

"So you don't know who they are, then?"

"No, mister major. But . . ." his voice trailed off and we all waited.

"But what?" Major Grindle finally burst out.

"But something about them is being familiar. I do not know. Perhaps they are friends of my father?"

"Why doesn't everyone have a seat and we'll start at the beginning. Gadji, let's start with you."

Gadji, unused to sitting in front of important *Inglaize,* perched uneasily on the edge of his chair. "I is born in Luxor. But it is changing much since I saw it last." He scrunched up his nose. "Too many new buildings and tourists."

"Hear, hear," Major Grindle agreed.

"I live with my father and my older sister in the old quarter. But where our house used to be now stands a fancy *Inglaize* hotel."

My heart broke for him. Not only had he lost his family, but his entire home was gone.

"I have no memories of my mother. She dies when I was"—he paused and counted on his fingers—"three, I think. My sister takes care of the house then, and me, when our tutor is not there. I have many friends." He paused. "Then one day, there is big accident in valley. A tomb caves in. Everyone in uproar. Sister hurries to valley to see if our father is okay. When tutor arrives and finds her gone, he goes after her." He looked up and met Major Grindle's eyes. "That is the last time I see them."

"What happened after that?"

Gadji scrunched up his face again, trying to remember. "I got hungry. I remember that because I began eating the honey cakes Safiya made for dinner. I am afraid I will get in trouble, but I am so hungry I don't care. Then . . . then I remember nothing until my first train ride."

"First train ride?" Major Grindle asked sharply. "To where?"

"Cairo. Very long train ride. Hot and dusty. Stand up the whole time. My legs begin to ache, and I begin to cry." He paused as if embarrassed by this. "I am very young," he explained.

"Of course," Major Grindle said.

"The man next to me shakes me and tells me not to be a baby."

"Were you traveling with the man, or was he just a random passenger?" I asked.

Gadji paused, as if he had never thought of that. "I do not know, miss. But the womans next to us shoot him evil eye and make a nest for me at her feet. I sleep the rest of the way to Cairo. When we arrive, I slip away and follow womans home. I is not wanting to stay with men who pinch and shout."

"Then what?" I asked.

Gadji shrugged again. "The womans, she nice and feed me, but is not having enough for an extra mouth to feed. So Gadji live on streets. Until miss finds me."

Major Grindle leaned forward. "Now think, Gadji, because this is very important. Did the men traveling with you back then look anything like the ones you ran into today? Similar facial features, clothing, identifying marks or tattoos?"

"Oh no. Not at all. These mens, they were wearing Egyptian robes, but under their turbans, the faces, they were *Inglaize*."

A stunned silence followed that announcement. "English," Major Grindle repeated, leaning back in his chair. "Not French or German or American, but English?"

Gadji waved his hand. "All the same. Not Egyptians."

"And traveling in the third-class car meant for natives. That cannot have been a random coincidence, I think. What about this tutor of yours? Who was he? Did he have a name?"

"Oh yes, mister major. His name is Master Bubu."

CHAPTER NINETEEN
MUCH IS MADE CLEAR

I GASPED. I couldn't help it.

"You know this Master Bubu, I take it," Major Grindle said.

"Yes, sir. He was a magician performing in London when we first met him, but he turned out to be . . ." I waged an internal struggle, trying to decide how much to tell him. "Something much more than that. It was to him that I made the deathbed promise. He had been injured trying to protect me from the Serpents of Chaos."

Major Grindle raised an eyebrow but said nothing for a long moment. "Well, this is a Gordian knot if ever there was one. For the time being—"

"Sir?" I said, making up my mind.

"Yes, Theodosia?"

"This Master Bubu. He belonged to the same group of men we ran into at the temple today. They are a group, rather like the Brotherhood, who keeps an eye on sacred objects here in Egypt." I didn't feel quite as if I'd broken my promise to Awi Bubu. The cat was already out of the bag since Major Grindle had seen the wedjadeen with his own eyes.

"I see."

And I was very afraid that he did see. See everything I was not telling him. "Sir," I hastened to add, "I am not trying to keep things from you; it is just that promises were made—"

He held up a hand to stop me. "I understand. I would not expect you to break a promise, Miss Throckmorton."

"You wouldn't?" If not, he was certainly a rare exception among grownups. They are forever thinking that a child's promise should be easily broken if it makes *their* lives easier.

"No. However, now that you have kept those promises, let there be no more secrets between us." He gave me a meaningful look, and I nodded.

We were quiet for a long moment before I asked, "Sir, do you think Gadji *could* be the last pharaoh?"

"I don't know what to think. The pharaonic bloodline died out years ago. Nectanebo II was the last Egyptian-born pharaoh."

"Of record," I pointed out.

Major Grindle tilted his head to the side. "What makes you add that disclaimer?"

"Well, quite frankly, it seems as if we are always bumping up against things we didn't know about ancient Egypt and its magic. I don't see why the pharaohs should be any different."

"True enough," Major Grindle agreed. "But it seems to me that what is important right now is that others think he is the last pharaoh. That also works to our advantage somewhat, for they are reluctant to force him to do anything he doesn't want to do. We'll use that. For now. Where are you staying?" he asked Gadji.

"I work for effendi miss. As her donkey boy. I sleep in the stable."

"Very well. At least we'll be able to keep an eye on you. You, however," he said, turning his gimlet eyes on me, "will be in danger until these men get what they want. That means no more gallivanting about. Do not go anywhere unless you are with me or your mother. Do you understand, Miss Throckmorton?" Major Grindle leaned very far forward across his desk. "I will brook no argument on this. If you cannot comply with this one simple rule, then I need to know now so I can make other arrangements."

"No, sir. It won't be a problem. Now that my mission is accomplished, I have nothing left that Chaos wants. My only plans are to help Mother with her excavating." Why did that sound so flat all of a sudden?

The major gave me an odd look. "Don't forget the small matter of revenge."

Oh, yes. There was that. The Serpents of Chaos would like to repay me for having foiled their plans once too often.

"Now, let's get you back to your house before your absence is noticed and an alarm raised. I'll escort you myself."

With that, Gadji and I followed Major Grindle out of his study to where the horses waited in the late afternoon sun. We rode in silence for a ways, Gadji in the lead so Major Grindle could keep an eye on his safety as well as mine. Sefu had appeared from somewhere and now sat on the boy's shoulder, chattering softly in his ear and picking at his hair.

With Gadji's attention elsewhere, I gathered up my nerve to ask Major Grindle a question that had plagued me since we escaped the temple. "Sir," I said in a very low voice. "What sort of magic did you use back at the temple?" I turned my head around so I could see his face when he answered.

He kept his gaze fixed on the streets ahead of us. "It was much like the things Quillings gave you, Miss Throckmorton, only of a more ancient origin. But all of us in the Brotherhood use magic, Miss Throckmorton. I thought you knew that."

I shook my head. "Not like that, they don't. They only use

the principles of magic to remove curses. Or in Dr. Quillings's case, they harness the ancient magic. But that's not what you did, was it?"

Major Grindle gave me a look that was equal parts admiration and annoyance. "Not much gets by you, does it, girl? However, it was merely a bit of sand, that's all. Left over from when Sekhmet almost destroyed mankind."

The major returned his gaze to the horizon. Just when I was afraid that was all he was going to say, he began to speak again. "This is one area where Wigmere and I disagree. He feels magic should only be used to remove more harmful magic. However, that has not always been the case, and certainly not for those of us in the field. For many centuries the Brotherhood used its magical knowledge in offensive maneuvers as well, wielding it as a weapon in the fight against chaos. But mistakes were made. Occasionally operatives became corrupted through its use."

"Is that when you all started getting those tattoos, right here?" I tapped the top of my breastbone.

"He told you about that, did he?" For the first time, Major Grindle looked faintly shocked.

"He was trying to explain to me why someone I suspected of being guilty could not have been corrupted by magic."

He raised an eyebrow. "You wouldn't take his word for it?"

I squirmed in the saddle, suddenly aware of how very brazen that must seem. "No, sir."

"Eventually," Major Grindle continued, "it was decided that all our knowledge would only be used in defensive measures. However, those decisions were mostly made by men who spent their entire careers behind desks and not in the field. They were not actively involved in the fight against these darker forces and did not understand how badly not using the magic was crippling us. My own feeling is that we cannot truly defeat these forces without being willing to wield this magic as it was meant to be wielded. It is a tool, a weapon like any other, and can be used as such.

"Of course," he added, "with such great power comes great responsibility."

"You aren't worried about becoming corrupted?"

"I take precautions," he said, then glanced at me. His voice softened. "Wigmere is a good man and an old friend, but he is very attached to reason in a field that has none. Now look, I believe this is your house."

He had stopped at the foot of the road that led up to our bungalow, well out of sight of anyone who might be inside. He did not dismount but instead helped me slide down. I went over and held the reins of Gadji's horse while he dismounted, then handed them to the major. "Be safe, you two.

We'll talk again tomorrow. I'll wait here until you reach the house."

"Thank you, sir. For everything," I said, then turned and began the long walk up to the house with Gadji at my side. When we were well away from the major, Gadji sent me a cautious glance. "Miss?"

"What?"

"It was not just by accident that you chose me that day."

"Of course it was, Gadji! I had no idea who you were. How could I?"

He shook his head. "No, no. That's not what I mean. I mean, it was not *you* who picked *me*."

I turned and stared at him, my steps slowing. "What do you mean?"

He motioned for me to keep walking. "It is a small trick, one my tutor taught me. I can, sometimes, nudge people to do what I want, using my mind."

Well, that cinched it. He was definitely connected in some way to Awi Bubu. "But why? Why would you use that power on me?"

Gadji shrugged. "Because you . . . glowed," he said. "The light of the gods shone around you, like heat rising up from the desert sand."

I gaped at him. "How are you able to see this . . . power?"

I asked. Awi Bubu was the only person I had ever met who could do that. "Did Awi Bubu teach you?"

Gadji shrugged. "I do not know. Maybe it is because I am a pharaoh!" He grinned.

His words launched a flood of brief memories, odd things that I hadn't noticed at the time. How Gadji had referred to Nut, one of the old Egyptian gods, when very few native Egyptians remembered them anymore. His pride, sometimes verging on arrogance, even when facing English officials like Mr. Bing.

We had reached the house, so I waved to Major Grindle, who gave a brief nod of goodbye and began riding back. When Gadji and I reached the stable door, I peeked in and saw his little pile of straw and hand-me-down blanket. "Gadji?"

"Yes, effendi miss?"

"Why didn't you want to go with those men? Aren't you the least bit intrigued by their claim? Don't you want to know what being a pharaoh means? I'm sure they'll give you more than a pile of straw and a secondhand blanket."

He looked up at me, his face small and vulnerable. "Does effendi miss want me to leave?"

"No, no! It's just—this isn't much of a life here in our stable. If it were me, I'd be sick with curiosity."

Gadji's face cleared. "Effendi miss has very curious nature. Perhaps that is why you glowed?"

I rolled my eyes. "Just think about it, would you? You can stay here as long as you like, but Mother and I won't be in Luxor forever. I think those men would take very good care of you."

He merely sniffed in reply.

"I'll be back with some dinner later," I assured him, then headed for the house.

None of the donkeys had been in the stable, which meant Mother and the others were still out at the dig. I had only to worry about Habiba.

I opened the back door a crack and peeked in. I could hear nothing from the kitchen, nor any other part of the house, so I slipped inside and made my way to my room. I paused at the hall leading to the kitchen and listened again. It was as quiet as a grave. Relieved at this good fortune, I hurried to my room and opened the door.

Everything was exactly as it had been. Even better, Isis was curled up on my bed, waiting for me. Perfect. Nothing aided my thinking processes like petting my cat, and this day had certainly given me lots to think about. I stretched out next to Isis and began petting her.

Could Gadji be descended from the great pharaohs of ancient Egypt? I tried to remember all that Awi Bubu had told me about the wedjadeen and their place in Egyptian history. He had claimed that, due to the wedjadeen's help, Nectanebo II had been the secret father of Alexander the Great. What if Nectanebo II had fathered other children? If the wedjadeen could watch over and guard the artifacts of the gods for thousands of years, why not an ancient, royal bloodline?

There was also something else. A vague, unformed memory that had niggled at me in Major Grindle's office now began to take shape.

Awi Bubu claimed he was exiled because of something precious he had lost. What if that something precious had been Egypt's last pharaoh? The thought nearly took my breath away.

Under my hand, Isis stiffened and raised her head. At first, I thought she'd somehow intuited what I was thinking, but then I realized she was merely staring at the wall in that way cats do, as if they can see through them. I cocked my head and listened just in time to hear the faint whisper of a door closing. Habiba must be back. Mother wouldn't sneak in like that.

I waited for a few minutes, wondering if she would come check on me, and tried to imagine what sort of secret business could she possibly have.

Of course, I didn't really know it was secret business—it might just seem that way. It's hard not to appear intriguing and mysterious when one is draped in black from head to toe.

When no one came to check on me, I relaxed and resumed petting Isis. I bet *she* knew what Habiba did all day. Too bad she couldn't talk. My hand stilled as a great big shocking idea came to me. Would Major Grindle's Babel stone work on animals?

Eager to try, I fumbled in my pockets for the thin sliver of stone. I grasped it tightly in my left hand while I continued petting Isis with my right. Now to get her to talk.

I took my hand away. After a second, she lifted her head and stared at me, wanting me to get on with it. I withheld my hand, waiting for her to give a meow of complaint. Instead, she just watched me steadily with her brilliant green eyes. After a long moment, she uncurled herself from my side and stretched out her neck to sniff the stone in my hand. With one last reproachful glance at me, she jumped down from the bed and hopped up onto the windowsill, then disappeared into the growing dusk. Bother. That experiment had failed on all counts.

Before I could decide what to do next, I heard the clatter of hooves in the courtyard. Mother was home! I cast all thoughts of ancient bloodlines and centuries-old secrets aside and went to hear how the day's excavation had progressed.

I met Mother just as she was coming in the door. "Hello, darling!" she said, stripping off her gloves. "How are you feeling?"

Oh. Right. "Better," I said. "Much better, actually. Spending the entire day in a cool room seems to have taken care of it. I'm sure I'll be able to go with you tomorrow."

"Excellent!" She reached out and kissed my cheek. When she pulled away, Habiba was standing in the doorway, watching us. "Oh, Habiba," Mother said. "I'm famished. Let me just wash up and then I think we'll have dinner."

Habiba nodded, then disappeared back down the hallway. Even though I had already washed, I was not anxious to be alone with Habiba in case she tried to ask me any questions. "I'll go wash up, too, then meet you in the dining room," I told Mother.

Ten minutes later, Mother and I sat down to a dinner of spicy lamb stew. "So?" I asked. "Did you find any more columns? Anything to indicate it's not just an outbuilding belonging to Hatshepsut's temple?"

"We did! We found at least twelve more columns, and probably more than that. It appears as if the temple is in very good shape; it's just completely buried under piles of dirt and rubble. The cliffs overhead must have collapsed long ago and buried it. Being buried in rubble might well have helped to aid preservation."

"Excellent!" I said, trying to scrounge up some excitement. Surely it would feel different when I was back on the dig with them, I assured myself. "So what's on the schedule for tomorrow?"

"More digging. We think we can clear out the first terrace by the end of the week if we keep at it. We'll know much more then about what we've truly discovered."

"Wonderful!" I said. "I can't wait to get started." Which reminded me. "Mother?"

"Yes, dear."

"Since we have so very much digging to do, what do you think about having Gadji, the donkey boy, come work with us? There aren't any donkeys for him to tend to during the day, and it would teach him a skill he could use to better himself." And that way I could keep an eye on his safety.

"That is an excellent idea, Theo. The more people we have digging, the sooner we'll learn what we have found."

Habiba came in just then, her dark, heavy presence causing my mouth to snap shut. I avoided looking at her as she moved around the table, setting new dishes down and clearing the old ones. I wondered if she knew I had left the house today. Unable to help myself, I slowly looked up, not surprised when I found her eyes above her veil watching me.

She gave the faintest of nods, then glanced briefly at Mother. When Habiba saw that Mother was not watching us, she held her finger to her lips, so briefly that I almost missed it. I nearly dropped my fork in surprise. Before I could respond, she left to carry the dishes back to the kitchen, pausing once in the doorway to look over her shoulder. Honestly! What did she mean by that? That I should keep her secrets? Or that she would keep mine?

I loathe hand signals. They are harder to decipher than hieroglyphs.

CHAPTER TWENTY

FACING THE GODDESS

THE NEXT MORNING I felt a tad nervous about seeing Gadji. It felt wrong to have the last pharaoh saddling my donkey. But as it turned out, he was nowhere to be seen. Before I could worry over much I saw Sefu hiding up in the rafters, which meant Gadji was somewhere nearby. And while I was sorry not to be able to tell him that I'd found him a new job, I refused to let it ruin my day—the first day of nothing but pure archaeology with no beastly intrigue.

Nabir grumbled a bit about Gadji's absence, but the donkeys had already been saddled so it wasn't too much of an inconvenience. We mounted the beasts and rode out into the morning. "I have a wonderful feeling about what today might hold," I told Mother.

She smiled at me. "If you could pull something else out of your hat, that would be absolutely brilliant!"

I frowned slightly. I had meant only that I was looking forward to being back on the dig with her and the others, but now it appeared that she expected me to find something else, something even more remarkable. I'd been working so hard at keeping my spirits high that morning, but with one careless remark, Mother had taken all the wind from my sails.

We spent a hot, dusty morning up to our elbows in dirt and rubble. It was hard work, horribly hot and painstakingly tedious. Even so, it was the true work of an archaeologist, with no intrigue or power-hungry secret societies in sight. I should have been happier. Even Jadwiga, for all his depressing bluster, seemed to have moved up a notch in mood from desolate to merely dispirited.

I did begin to wonder, though, just how happy Gadji would be when he learned what I'd signed him up for. Mucking around in dust and rubble couldn't hold a candle to being a pharaoh.

Was that where Gadji was? I stopped digging. Had he decided to return to the wedjadeen? No, Sefu had still been there and Gadji would never have gone anywhere without that monkey.

Of course, thinking of Gadji quickly had me wondering about the wedjadeen and their plans, but I pushed those thoughts away. They were no longer my concern; my obligations had been met, I reminded myself. Although really, what one is supposed to think about while sifting through desert sand is a bit of a mystery. I never realized that archaeology required so little actual thinking and so very much digging.

Jadwiga and Rumpf hovered nearby all day. Every time I turned around, I nearly tripped over one of them. "Honestly!" I finally said in exasperation. "There is nothing left for me to find!"

I could not have been more wrong.

I had decided to dig in the most boring, least promising spot, hoping that Mother's two assistants would leave me in peace. Which worked. However, it did not turn out to be a boring spot.

As I cleared away a patch of rubble, I saw a small hole behind it. Curious—and excited—I began working faster until I had uncovered a small, narrow shaft. The rubble had covered only the mouth—the shaft itself appeared to be intact.

The mysterious dark passageway beckoned. I got on my knees and poked my head in far enough that I could shine my torch light inside. There were solid walls on either side and a closed ceiling up above. Even better, the ceiling didn't appear to have any ominous cracks or gaps.

I felt something move against my arm, nearly shouting in alarm as visions of scorpions danced in my head, but it was only Isis. "Do not *do* that," I told her. "You about gave me apoplexy."

She peered into the tunnel. "What do you think?" I asked. In answer, she twitched her tail and entered the shaft, her black shape quickly melding into the shadows. "Is it safe?" I called out.

She padded back to where I waited and touched her nose to mine, then turned around and disappeared down the shaft. "I'm thinking that was a yes," I mumbled. I glanced over my shoulder. Mother, Jadwiga, and Rumpf all had their heads close together discussing something. Perfect. I made sure my pith helmet was secure, gripped my torch, and crawled inside. I could stand as soon as I crossed the threshold.

Within seconds, I was enveloped in darkness, the opening behind me nothing more than a little square of light, none of which penetrated very deeply into the shadows. I paused a moment and shined my torch on the walls. Elaborate carvings decorated the passageway, the colors surprisingly bright for being thousands of years old.

It showed an offering ritual, I realized, with carvings of the pharaoh (and it *was* Thutmose III!) walking alternately with the gods Amun and Mantu, preparing offerings to both.

Amun was leading Thutmose in one, and in the next carving, Mantu embraced him.

I was so intent on learning what the walls had to tell me that I wasn't paying enough attention to my feet and cracked my toe on a large piece of rock.

"Ow!" I hissed, hopping up and down, making enough racket that Isis came back to see what was going on. She waited patiently for me to stop howling, looking a trifle smug about her ability to see in the dark.

When the pain in my toe finally dulled to a mere throb, I began walking again, using my torch on the floors. Isis deigned to assist me by always staying just within my sights.

The tunnel went on forever, growing smaller and smaller as the ceiling slanted downward and the floor sloped up, until it became so small that I had to get down on my hands and knees. Just when I feared I would have to give up and scoot out backwards, a dark opening loomed ahead. Isis paused and waited for me to catch up. When I had, she flicked her tail and leaped through the opening. I hesitated. The others might have missed me by now, I thought, then gave a short grunt. Whom was I fooling? No one ever missed me. Every time I hurried back, terrified they'd noticed my absence, they'd never even known I'd been gone.

Angered by that realization, I gripped the torch more

firmly and crawled over the pile of rubble into the chamber, then blinked.

Long pale fingers of sunlight drifted down from cracks in the ceiling, illuminating a small inner shrine. Images of Hathor decorated the north and south walls, while images of Isis decorated the east and west walls. The inner shrine of the goddess, then.

Dust motes danced in the sunlight. Wait! I peered more closely. Those were no ordinary dust motes but pale floating symbols of power and ancient hieroglyphs swirling lazily through the air.

As I stepped more fully into the room, it felt like wading into a warm tub of faintly moving water, only the water was soft and dry rather than wet. I held my hand away from my body and felt the warm currents push lazily against it. Not probing, like the power from a curse, but soft, like a gentle, playful breeze.

The quiet of the chamber stole over me, quieter and more peaceful than any other place I'd ever been in. I felt completely and utterly safe. And in that quiet safety, I was finally able to face how heartsick I was. How hungry for comfort. I carried anger and a sense of betrayal deep inside me like a heavy, ugly rock. Not to mention the huge gaping hole in my life where I now realized my grandfather should have been.

All the days of nerve-racking travel and sneaking around, trying to take care of everyone: Gadji, Mother, Awi Bubu, even Jadwiga's dour self. Without any warning a sob hiccupped in my throat, and before I had a chance to tamp it back down, I began to cry.

I cried for Gadji, who missed his sister so badly that he'd attached himself to me and passed up a chance to live as a king. I cried for Awi Bubu, who'd wanted nothing more than to be forgiven for his crimes by the unforgiving wedjadeen. I cried for Major Grindle, who I was afraid had sacrificed some vital part of himself in his unrestrained use of magic. I cried for my grandmother, who had had to watch the man she loved grow mad, and my father, who was so traumatized by it that he closed his heart and mind to the wonders right in front of his nose. I even cried for Jadwiga, just because he was so wretchedly sad all the time.

But mostly I cried for myself. I was tired of living a double life, tired of always having to be pleasing or brilliant for fear my parents would leave me behind. I cried for want of a grandfather who could have assured me I wasn't a freak and I did indeed belong to this family.

Eventually, I ran out of tears. Even so, I kept my head down on my knees, savoring the feeling of being absolutely empty. And as I savored that feeling, a sense of peace washed over me, as warm and real as if someone had just run a loving hand over my head. I gasped and lifted my cheek from my knees, but there was no one there. No one but my cat.

And the mysterious dust motes. The angle of the sun had shifted as I'd sat there blubbering like a baby, and it now fell across the left side of my body. Along that entire side I could see the ethereal symbols gliding and shimmying in the air about me.

As I wiped my eyes and fumbled for a handkerchief. I tried to remember the last time I had cried. It had been years, I suspected. But it felt safe in here. I could cry without risk of anyone seeing me or thinking me a silly child. I took a deep breath, as if I could drink in that sense of safety and carry it with me. In here, I could be peculiar or brilliant or nothing at all. I could be brilliantly peculiar, if I wanted.

Suddenly, I found myself on my feet, arms thrown out at my sides. Closing my eyes, I raised my face so that I could feel the rays of the sun upon it. "I am peculiar," I said out loud.

Nothing happened. The ground didn't shake, nor the shaft crumble. "I am peculiar!" I said again, only this time I shouted it.

I grew warm, and when I opened my eyes to look, I saw the magical dust motes dancing against my skin like a swarm of giddy butterflies.

I felt a bump against my ankle and looked down to see Isis

rubbing against me. "You don't mind if I'm odd, do you?" I murmured. In answer, she began to purr.

And that's when I realized something else. All my friends, my true friends—such as Sticky Will, Stilton, and Gadji—all liked me precisely because I *was* peculiar. Even Henry had come to cautiously admire that part of me.

The thing was, the part of myself that everyone else found so peculiar was the very part I liked the best.

"Theodosia?" From far away I heard someone calling my name. "Theo, dear, where are you?"

Bother. They were looking for me. I turned and looked at that magical place, reluctant to leave its four walls. With a shock, I realized I didn't even want to tell Mother about it. I didn't want to take a place of living magic and turn it into an empty husk, like the other monuments I'd visited. For that was the difference, I realized. They were empty of their true magic, while this place was still alive with it.

And I was not going to jeopardize that simply for a pat on the head from Mother.

I scrambled back along the narrow shaft, relieved when it finally grew big enough for me to stand. I was able to move along much more quickly then, reaching the opening in a matter of minutes. Determined that the others not find this

secret passageway, I knelt down and peered out, waiting to
be certain no one was around.

"Theodosia?" I heard once again, but it was coming from
over to the left, from Hatshepsut's temple. I quickly scrambled out, then ran around to the opposite side of the rubble.
"Mother? Is that you? Are you calling me?"

"Theodosia!" Mother poked her head out from behind one
of the colonnades in Hatshepsut's temple. "Where have you
been?" she asked, hurrying toward me. She was frowning, I
saw, but whether in annoyance or concern, I couldn't tell.

"I fell asleep, back over there in the shade beside the donkeys."

I waited for her to ask if I felt all right or was getting ill
again. At the very least to put her hand on my forehead and
see if I was getting sick. But all she did was cluck her tongue
at me and call out to the others that she had found me.

My tired spirits rose when our house came into view, but
when I halted the donkey just outside the stable, no Gadji
appeared to take the reins while I dismounted. With a sigh
of exasperation, I managed to dismount on my own (thank
heavens donkeys are so close to the ground!). By this time,
Mother and Nabir had drawn up behind me.

"Where is that no good donkey boy?" Nabir muttered, striding over to the stable. "Boy!" he hollered inside. "Get out here." There was a long moment of silence, and still Gadji didn't appear.

Muttering in Arabic, Nabir unsaddled Mother's donkey. Worried now, I went into the stable to peek into the stall that Gadji used. All his things were still there, but there was no sign of him. Or Sefu.

"Excuse me, miss," Nabir said, and I had to leap out of the way as he strode past carrying a saddle.

"Here, I'll help," I told the dragoman. "It was my suggestion to hire Gadji in the first place." But mostly I wanted an excuse to hang around the stable longer. Gadji's absence was beginning to worry me. *Had* he taken the wedjadeen up on their offer, then?

"No, no!" Nabir was scandalized. "Missy not help. Missy go in house with Mother."

"Nonsense," I said firmly, then went to remove the saddle from my own donkey. Only I hadn't realized how beastly heavy saddles were! With a grunt, I tried to lift it from the donkey but only succeeded in getting it halfway off. The donkey, no doubt tired and hungry and hot, had no patience for my fumbling and started to trot into the stable with me hanging on to the partially removed saddle.

Before I could so much as squeak out a "Help!" Nabir was at my side, grabbing hold of the runaway donkey and taking the saddle from me.

"I'm sorry," I said in a small, defeated voice. "I was only trying to help."

"I know. Missy has kind heart, but Nabir will do it. It is easier that way."

Frustrated in my attempt to be able to wait until Nabir was finished with the donkeys, I vowed to come back after dinner and see if I could find any hint of where Gadji had gone.

The house was cool and dark, a welcome relief after the blinding heat of the day. I walked into my room, then froze. There was a note on my bed.

On my pillow, to be exact.

A chill of foreboding ran through me, as well as a sense of violation. I was getting heartily sick of people tramping through my room without permission.

With trembling hands I plucked the note from my pillow, cracked the black wax seal, and began to read.

If you wish to see the young pharaoh alive, you must bring the Emerald Tablet to the altar of Khons in the Seti Chapel at Karnak by midnight tonight.

There was no signature, just a picture of a black coiling snake.

CHAPTER TWENTY-ONE
A RESCUE IS BEING THOUGHT OF

MY HANDS BEGAN TO SHAKE. The Serpents of Chaos had Gadji. But how had they even *known* about him?

"Theo!" Mother called through the door, making me jump. "Some of us are quite hungry. Do hurry."

"Yes, Mother," I said automatically. I washed in record time and threw on a clean frock as my mind raced in a thousand different directions.

Mother was already waiting at the table when I arrived. She gave Habiba the signal to begin serving.

"You look all fresh and clean, dear," Mother said, taking a sip from her goblet.

"Um, yes. It felt good to get rid of the day's dust," I said, settling into my chair.

Habiba put plates in front of Mother and me, then withdrew. Fear for Gadji's safety had taken up residence in my stomach and there was no room for anything else. I had no idea how I was going to manage to eat a bite.

Mother, however, was famished and plowed through her plate like a drayman, making small talk all the while. I tried to pay attention and answer in the right places, but I failed miserably.

"Theo," Mother finally said a bit sharply.

"Yes?"

"Are you not feeling well again? You've hardly touched your supper. And look, your hands are trembling."

I quickly set the fork down and placed my hands in my lap, out of sight. "My arms are just tired, that's all."

"But you're flushed," she exclaimed.

I desperately needed some excuse for my condition, which meant I had no choice but to claim illness. "Well, perhaps I am feeling a trifle off."

"Oh, really, Theo!" Mother's voice was filled with equal parts concern and exasperation. "This isn't going to work at all if you're going to get sunstroke every time I take you to the dig." She frowned. "You were wearing your hat the whole time, weren't you?"

Feeling wretched, I said, "Yes, Mother. I was. I'm terribly sorry. I'm sure it's just a matter of me getting used to the change in weather. A good night's sleep will put me right as rain." I forced a fake yawn, just for good measure. "In fact, may I please be excused? I'd like to turn in early for the night so I will be fully rested for tomorrow."

"Very well," Mother said with a sigh. "I need to write down my notes for today's work, anyway." We got up and left the dining room together. She turned down the hallway to her room, but I did not go immediately to mine. It was time for me and Habiba to have a little talk.

I found Habiba in the kitchen. Her black sleeves were rolled up and she was washing up the supper dishes. The small room was hot and stifling and her face above her veil was damp and red with heat. I felt a pang of sympathy for her but pushed it aside. Gadji's life could be at stake. "Who do you work for, Habiba?" I asked.

She gave me a sidelong look. "I work for young miss's mother."

"Then where do you sneak off to all the time?"

The small bit of skin that showed turned pale, then red again. "Young miss does not know what she is talking about," she said, her voice strained.

I decided to try to catch her off-guard. "What have you done with Gadji?"

"Who?"

"The donkey boy in the stable. What have you done with him?"

She looked mortally offended. "I? I have done nothing with him. Who says I have?"

"He is missing, Habiba, and I think you told some very bad men he was staying here and they came and took him away."

"No! This is not true!" Her eyes grew worried.

"Then tell me where you go when you leave here, because otherwise I'll have to assume you are meeting those very bad men."

I felt horrid, almost as though I were bullying the poor woman, but she was the only clue I had.

She glanced toward the doorway.

"Mother's gone back to her room," I told her. "She can't hear you."

Habiba nodded. "Very well. But young miss has secrets of her own, does she not?"

"I do," I said, "but they do not involve kidnapping any-one."

"Neither do mine! No, no. I do not nap the kid, as you say. I am merely going to meetings, that is all."

A vision of my meetings with the Arcane Order of the

Black Sun flashed immediately to mind. "What sort of meetings?" I asked.

"Meetings of Egyptians," she said softly. "Meetings where we talk, but that is all, young miss. We just talk."

"What do you talk about?" I asked.

She glanced around the room once more, then back to me. Her black eyes were filled with worry. "Young miss must not tell anyone—not her mother, no one. Understand?"

"Well, I most likely won't tell my mother," I said, "if that makes you feel any better." I was hoping she wouldn't notice how I had evaded the part about not telling *anyone*.

"I go to the meeting where we talk of Egyptians being in charge of our own land. Where we talk of being in charge of our own selves. I meet with those who would have Egyptians rule over Egyptians so that we are no longer lap dogs of you *Inglaize*."

I blinked in surprise. I had been expecting a confession that she worked for von Braggenschnott. Or that she was possibly a sleeper agent for the wedjadeen. "You mean you are attending meetings of the Egyptian nationalist movement?"

"Shh! Yes, yes, exactly so. This is the meetings I go to, nothing more."

I found I believed her. It explained so much, and not just

about her comings and goings, but about the small knots of Egyptians I'd seen huddling here and there, talking in low voices and watching me with great suspicion. "But why?" I asked, genuinely curious. "We do not hurt you in any way, do we?"

Seeing that I believed her, she appeared to relax a little. "Why does young miss sneak away and do things on her own?"

Not sure where she was going with this, I said, "Well, there are things I need to do that my mother disagrees with."

"Young miss does not like having her mother make all her decisions for her, no? Telling her where she can go and when. Who she can see and for how long. Does young miss like having no control over her own life? How she lives it and what she does with it?"

"Well, no, of course not!"

"And that is how it is with the *Inglaize* in charge of our country. They are always making the important decisions— how much, how long, who has power over what. And you can be sure that us Egyptians are never on the good side of that trade. No, we are to take what we are given and be grateful, no matter that you *Inglaize* take from our country what you like."

Honestly, when she put it like that, how could one *not* belong to the nationalist movement? "I see what you mean,

Habiba. It's not fair that you should have to be a child in your own country."

She blinked at me in surprise. "Young miss will not tell her mother? Most *Inglaize* do not like us to talk so."

"I will not tell my mother. But did you by any chance see the donkey boy today?"

She shook her head. "No, young miss. I did not see him at all."

"Very well. Thank you. And, er, good luck with your meetings."

Once back in the privacy of my own room, I let my shoulders slump as I gave in to the despair I felt. I looked immediately to the bed, my heart lifting when I saw that Isis had returned and was curled up near my pillow. I threw myself down next to her, earning a disgruntled look as my movement jounced her a bit.

"Don't be angry with me," I told her. "I've got quite a lot on my plate, thank you very much." She gave me a bored look and began washing herself. Well, honestly. I knew Gadji and Sefu hadn't been her favorite people, but really. She could at least pretend to care. For my sake.

As I saw it, I had no choice but to go to Major Grindle for help. However, he had told me in no uncertain terms that I was not to travel through the city alone. But how was I to get a message to him? We hadn't talked about that. Or maybe he'd assumed I'd use Gadji.

There was no other choice. I would simply have to risk the major's wrath and hope he'd understand.

Thus resolved, I changed into sturdier clothes for my journey and used the rest of my wardrobe to create a decoy shape in my bed again. If Mother thought I was ill, she might decide to check on me during the night. If the lights were off and she didn't come all the way into the room to feel my forehead, this deception would work. If not, well, the fat would really be in the fire then.

Just as I was putting the finishing touches on the covers, Isis arched her back and hissed at the window.

Already jumpy, I whirled around as a small creature catapulted through the shutters with an unholy screech. I got my arms up in front of my face just in time for them to catch the brunt of the creature's assault. I braced myself for the bite of teeth and the rending of flesh. Instead, I was subjected to clinging little hands with surprisingly strong fingers and a wrinkled little face poking into mine, scolding and chattering loud enough to wake the dead.

Sefu! I nearly laughed with relief.

He was nearly beside himself with agitation. "Shh. Calm

down," I whispered, as Isis circled my feet, looking up at Sefu and hissing periodically.

The monkey seemed to understand and managed to lower his chattering. He didn't stop plucking at my sleeve, though, and kept looking back toward the window. "Do you know where he is?" I asked.

Sefu bobbed his head up and down.

"Really? You understand me?"

He chattered and plucked at my sleeve again, then leaped back onto the windowsill and waited. "All right. I'm coming. But I need to make a side trip first. I'm going to need some help."

He screeched and flailed his arms at me.

"I mean, help other than what you can offer me," I quickly explained. Annoyed that I was paying so much attention to this miserable creature, Isis leaped toward the window, feinting a swipe in the monkey's direction. "Stop that," I scolded. "Wait a minute! How would you like to go on an outing?" I asked her. "A midnight outing?"

Isis turned away from Sefu, looked at me, then flicked her tail. Perfect. I would not be traveling through the city alone after all.

Isis did not take kindly to being put on a leash. However, once I explained to her that she would not be able to protect me if she was in her wicker basket, she submitted to the long sash I had hastily fashioned.

Sefu, on the other hand, wouldn't even come to me, much less let me carry him. He scampered around my room in his agitated state, anxious for us to get moving. He was not going to be happy when he discovered I wasn't planning on following him right away.

It was too risky to try to sneak out through the door, so instead I lifted Isis to the windowsill and climbed up next to her. Holding her safely in my arms, I dropped the few feet to the dirt below, grateful that the only sound was a faint crunch beneath my boots.

With every nerve on edge and my stomach coiled tightly with fear for Gadji, I began making my way through the darkened streets of Luxor to Major Grindle's bungalow.

Luxor was an entirely different place in the dark; all traces of charm and quaintness were chased away by darkness and shadows. Faraway laughter sounded sinister, and the squat, tattered buildings took on a threatening aspect, as if they were haunted. Isis carefully steered me away from groups of reveling British tourists enjoying the sights at night as well as the group of local men who watched them with ill-disguised hostility. But that wasn't even the worst part.

During the daylight hours, I had only been aware of the beneficent power of the gods that lingered in the ancient ruins. But at night, in the dark, those same ruins gave off something else entirely. Now they pulsed with several millennia's worth of accumulated dark magic and fragments of curses. They themselves weren't cursed, but rather, it appeared they acted as a lodestone for all the malevolent forces that lingered in the city. Perhaps pieces or bits of ancient curses from the artifacts that passed through, or the lingering *mut* or *akhu* from so many nearby ancient tombs. Either way, it was a distinctly unnerving sensation.

Sefu didn't help at all by scampering on ahead, then doubling back to be certain we were following. Every time he disappeared, I feared I'd never see him again. Then whenever he did reappear, it made my heart stutter.

In the end, he became quite distraught when he realized we weren't going to keep following him and pitched a raucous fit in the middle of the street. Dark, curious gazes turned in our direction. "Shh!" I told him. "I can't help Gadji alone. We'll need help."

He either understood or gave up, because he stopped making his racket and fell into step (more or less) beside me.

By the time we reached the major's bungalow, I was damp with perspiration and beginning to wonder just how much trouble I'd be in with him. All the lights were off save one toward the back, which I guessed to be his study. Squaring my shoulders, I knocked softly on the front door.

There was a long moment of silence, and then finally I heard the faint sound of footfalls coming from the back of the house. The door opened, and there stood Major Grindle himself, holding a lantern.

"Miss Throckmorton!" he exclaimed, scowling ferociously when he saw I was alone. "I distinctly remember telling you that you were not to move about this city alone."

"You did, sir." I bravely met his eye. "But I had no way to get a message to you, and it is rather urgent that we speak. Plus, I brought Isis with me. She can be surprisingly effective as a deterrent." I lifted the leash in my hand and the major's gaze followed it to the ground, where it was tied around Isis's neck.

"A cat is *not* protection."

"You don't know Isis, sir," I muttered. "Besides, Awi Bubu thought there was more to her than a simple feline. Not," I hurried to add, "that any feline can truly be called simple."

The major still looked highly skeptical.

"I assure you, sir, once you hear my reason for coming, you'll understand. May I come in?" I asked in a small voice.

"Yes, yes, of course. I am interested in knowing what is so important that you must risk life and limb to tell me." He moved aside to let me pass. Just as he started to close the door behind me, a small, scampering shape darted through and disappeared down the darkened hallway. "What, in the name of all that is holy, was that?"

"Gadji's monkey, sir. You see, that's why I've come. I'm afraid Gadji's been kidnapped."

Built behind him a small, stamping shape darted through and disappeared down the dark and hallway. What, in the name of all that is holy was that?

"Really, we'd better — I'm trying — I'm afraid I can't —

CHAPTER TWENTY-TWO
MAJOR GRINDLE'S MAGIC STUDY

MAJOR GRINDLE GOT VERY SERIOUS, very quickly. "How do you know this?"

I fished in my pocket and handed him the ransom note. "They left this on my pillow."

He raised his eyebrows but said nothing as he took the note from me. After reading it, he gave a brisk nod. "Chaos, of course. But what is this Emerald Tablet they are demanding?"

"Perhaps we should sit down, sir. It's rather a long story."

"Very well. We might as well get comfortable. I suspect we've a long night ahead of us."

As I entered his study, I shuddered as the wave of riotous,

jumbled magics assailed me. Isis paused in the doorway, every hair on her body standing on end, while Sefu leaped up into the air as if he'd been bitten. He landed on Major Grindle's desk, shaking his head and clacking his teeth.

"What's wrong with him?" Major Grindle asked.

"I don't think he cares for the otherworldly atmosphere in the room, sir." I tugged Isis gently into the room, then settled myself on one of the chairs facing the major's desk. "Do you mind if I unleash Isis? She's not terribly fond of the restraint."

He waved his hand to indicate for me to do as I pleased, then leaned back in his own chair. I unfastened the leash from around Isis's neck, and she began prowling cautiously around the room.

"The tablet?" Major Grindle prompted.

"Well, yes. You see, that was the item I was returning to the men you met at the Luxor Temple."

He raised a grizzled eyebrow at me. "Part of that deathbed promise, Miss Throckmorton?"

I swallowed. "Yes, sir."

"They did not seem very happy to have it back," he pointed out.

I frowned. "They were, actually. It was only that they got sidetracked with wanting to get Gadji back as well. According to Awi Bubu, they valued the tablet most highly. They

would have done a lot"—like forgive someone, I thought—
"to have it in their possession once again."

"So what is it, *exactly?*" he asked. "And why is Chaos so
intent on having it?"

I waged a small war with myself. I was not supposed to
tell anyone of the tablet's true purpose, but Gadji's life was
at stake, a life that, by all accounts, Awi Bubu should value
more than anyone. Not only that, Gadji was my friend.
Hopefully, Awi Bubu would understand. "It is an encoded
map, sir. A map that leads to the hidden cache of the artifacts of the gods, the ones that were hidden by the ancient
priests of Egypt thousands and thousands of years ago.
Artifacts with such power that they make the Orb of Ra look
like a child's toy."

Major Grindle grew still. "Are you serious, Miss Throckmorton?"

"Most serious, sir. And now Chaos has taken Gadji in the
hopes that we'll be so desperate to have him back, we'll be
willing to give up the tablet. Which I no longer have."

"Well, we'd better hope those men from the temple don't
get wind of this or they'll have our guts for garters," he said
dryly.

"Don't we need to tell them so we can get the tablet from
them?"

"I have no intention of putting that tablet in the hands of

Chaos. The havoc they could wreak doesn't bear thinking about." His tone left no room for argument.

"But what about Gadji, sir? We have to get him back. And not just because they think he might be their pharaoh. He's my friend and has saved me more than a time or two." My voice wobbled at the end, and I had to clear my throat.

Major Grindle gave a crisp nod. "And that is the best reason of all. We'll work something out." He turned his attention from me to the monkey on his desk. "Is this creature going to sit here all evening?"

"I have no idea, sir." Isis, on the other hand, appeared to have fallen in love with the major's leopard skin rug. She sat face-to-face with it, staring into its glass eyes, purring loudly.

Major Grindle muttered something about a zoo, then got up and went to his shelves. Sefu followed, leaping to a shelf just above the major's head.

Ignoring the monkey, the major began searching among the things on one shelf. "Have any of the Serpents of Chaos seen the tablet up close before?"

"No, sir."

"Perfect." He removed an old, unremarkable stele, a brass chafing dish, a large brick of beeswax, and a chisel that looked to be from the Old Kingdom. "I think that ought to do it." He saw me staring at the chisel and leaned in close. "It belonged to Ptah, Miss Throckmorton."

I gasped. "How do you come to have it? Shouldn't it be in the Brotherhood's vault?"

"It was a personal gift and bears no curse or dark magic, only a small power of making."

Of course, because Ptah was the maker god.

"Miss Throckmorton, may I suggest you take that turban away from your monkey? If he puts it on his head, he will either go up like a cinder or become possessed of an evil sorcerous spirit. Neither one is what we need this evening."

"Yes, sir!" I jumped forward and gingerly removed the battered yellow turban from the monkey's tiny hands. As I replaced it on the shelf, Sefu turned and grabbed a small bronze bell with an ebony handle.

"Careful—he'll wake the dead, Miss Throckmorton."

For some reason, I was certain he'd meant that literally. I quickly took the bell away and picked up the monkey. He wasn't thrilled to have me holding him, but he didn't attack me or try to escape, either. In truth, he clung to me a bit, like a baby might have.

Major Grindle returned to his desk and rummaged around for a piece of paper and a pencil. "Could you sketch me a copy of what the tablet looked like?" he asked.

"Certainly." Juggling Sefu in my left arm, I sat down at the major's desk and began drawing.

As I sketched, Major Grindle began working at a long table against the wall. I watched out of the corner of my eye as he laid the stele down on the table. Then he pulled the brass chafing dish close, lit a candle under it, and put the beeswax in the dish.

"How's that sketch coming, Miss Throckmorton?"

I quickly turned back to the paper. "Almost done," I chirped, blushing furiously at being caught not minding my own business.

"Excellent."

I put the finishing touches on the drawing, then hopped to my feet and carried it over to him. "Here you are, sir."

He took the drawing from me, glanced at it, then narrowed his eyes. "Thoth, eh?"

"Yes, sir. And Horus. It looks as if Thoth is giving Horus something, although I can't make out what, exactly. The glyphs are Chaldean," I pointed out helpfully.

He cocked an eyeball at me. "I know Chaldean when I see it, Miss Throckmorton."

"Sorry, sir."

However, I quickly forgot my embarrassment and became absorbed in what the major was doing. When the beeswax had fully melted, he took a pair of tongs, grabbed hold of the stone tablet, and dipped it into the wax. When he pulled it back out, a thin layer of the white wax clung to its surface. He repeated the process three times until the tablet was thickly coated.

Once it had cooled, he laid it on the table, picked up the chisel, and very carefully began to re-create the images and glyphs from the original Emerald Tablet.

I craned my neck to see better. He'd managed a very good likeness, but I didn't think the wax was going to fool anybody.

"I'm not done yet," he said, a faint tinge of annoyance in his voice.

Was he reading my mind? "I know you're not, sir."

Next, he unstoppered a small jar and shook out a few grains of something into a shallow dish. I was dying to ask what the granules were, but I was afraid he would shoo me away if I reminded him I was there.

"Grains of sandstone from the inside of a pharaoh's tomb," he said, as if hearing my unspoken question.

"Thank you, sir. I *was* wondering."

"I know," he said dryly. "I could practically hear you."

Well, he didn't expect me to be incurious, did he? Not with such fascinating procedures going on right in front of my nose.

He took a feather—an ibis feather, I thought—and dipped the nib end into the sandstone granules, then began to write on the wax. He wasn't pressing very hard—in fact, only the barest marks showed. They looked like hieroglyphs, but no matter how closely I watched, I wasn't able to recognize any of them.

At last he was done and set the feather down. "One last step," he said, then lifted the top off a small box and took a pinch from it. "Powdered silver," he told me, "to call upon the power of the moon." He sprinkled it over the coating of the inscribed wax. He took another pinch of something— "powdered copper, for the green color"—and sprinkled that over the wax as well.

The effect was shocking and immediate. The symbols Major Grindle had drawn on the surface began swarming and writhing, moving in rippling waves. Sensing the magical activity, Isis lifted her nose from the leopard rug and watched.

As the glyphs moved, the wax began to discolor slightly and take on a different texture altogether. It also began to turn dull green, just like the original tablet. Within minutes, the mysterious symbols had disappeared, transforming the once-ordinary stone into a near-exact replica of the Emerald Tablet.

"Brilliant, sir!" No wonder he hadn't thought we'd need to bother the wedjadeen for the original.

"Thank you. However, the silver will only cleave the magic

to the wax until the setting of the moon. After that, the deception will be revealed."

"We'd best hope the moon doesn't set before midnight, then," I said.

"It doesn't." He fished around under the table for some old scraps of leather and began wrapping the tablet in them.

"However did you learn that particular piece of magic? I've never seen anything like it in the papyruses I've read."

He quirked an eyebrow at me. "Read many, have you?"

"Yes, actually."

His lips twisted in a brief grin. "Chip off the old block," he muttered, and I swelled with unexpected pride.

"One of our brightest and bravest Keepers spent some time with a mysterious tribe in the desert—I'm guessing the very same tribe those men you know belong to—and learned a great deal of arcane magic at their hands. He recorded a few of the rubrics in his journals. Reginald Mayhew was his name."

"Mayhew?" I asked sharply.

For the first time, Major Grindle took his eyes from the faux tablet and stared at me intently. "Yes, why? Have you heard of him?"

"Yes," I admitted. According to Wigmere, it was Mayhew who had snatched the cache of artifacts out of the hands of the French and had them shipped to England, where they'd eventually been purchased by Augustus Munk and ended up in our basement. "But Wigmere hadn't said he was a Chosen Keeper." Oops. Had I said that last part out loud?

Major Grindle turned his attention back to the tablet. "Neither did I."

"But you did, sir! You just now said he was one of your brightest and bravest—"

"Must have misheard me, Miss Throckmorton."

"I must have," I said, catching on at last.

"Now, let's see about getting Gadji back, shall we?"

At the sound of his master's name, Sefu woke from his nap, scrambled up onto my shoulder, and looked around the room expectantly. "No, not yet," I told him. "But soon."

Major Grindle slipped the leather-wrapped tablet into a satchel. When he handed it to me, Sefu leaped from my shoulder and scampered over to the door, waiting.

As I was settling the load around my shoulder, the major crossed the room to his cabinet and quickly took a few things from a shelf: a large bronze arrowhead ("one of the Seven Arrows of Sekhmet," he explained), a small clay jar ("Rain of Fire"), two knives, and a sword.

"Don't you have a pistol, sir? Surely that would be more reliable. Von Braggenschnott seems very fond of his."

"Wouldn't be sporting, Miss Throckmorton, using modern-day weapons in an ancient temple."

Sporting? *Sporting!* This wasn't a game of cricket we were playing.

He looked up from hiding the weapons on his person. "Ready, then?"

"As much as I'll ever be," I said.

"This way." He led me to a back door that opened off his study into a side yard. I followed him around to a small stable and waited in silence as he saddled up his horse. When he was done, he gave me a leg up. As I settled myself into the saddle, I couldn't help but ask, "I wonder why they chose the temple at Karnak rather than Luxor?"

"Probably because the Luxor Temple has too bloody much traffic the past couple of days," he said as he vaulted gracefully into the saddle behind me. He took the reins, slapped them against the horse's neck, and steered us out of the courtyard, then set the horse on the road toward Karnak.

The short journey through the city of Luxor to the village of Karnak passed in a blur. My mind was utterly absorbed with worries for Gadji, if we'd get there in time, and if we'd be able to set up our operation before the Serpents of Chaos arrived. I was one big puddle of nerves.

I hoped that both Isis and Sefu were following. I kept peering over my shoulder, straining to see my cat's sleek form among the shadows or the scampering movements that would indicate the monkey was there. Finally, Major Grindle got exasperated with me. "It's hard enough on this poor horse carting around two riders. It would make it much easier on him if you would at least sit still."

"Sorry," I muttered.

The shadows of night had robbed the countryside of all color. Under the light of the gibbous moon, everything looked to be a shade of gray. But what gray! From deepest graphite to the pale silver of moonlight, and every shade in between. In the distance, huge boulders and blocks taller than a man littered the landscape, looking as if immense giants had once played here as children and left their toys behind. It turned out to be the ruins of Karnak itself, glinting under the light of the moon, casting long shadows.

"Almost there," Major Grindle whispered. He steered the horse down toward the bank of the Nile until he reached a faint road. It wasn't a proper road, really. It was the remains of an ancient canal that had once run from the temple to the quay. A lone obelisk stood on the southern corner, a silent sentinel guarding over a lost era.

The major reined up near the obelisk. "Here is where I will leave you." He slipped off the horse. Suddenly, my back was very, very cold and unguarded. I suppressed a shiver.

"I'll get in position in the temple so that I can guard you

and Gadji. Remember, do not tell them where you've hidden the tablet until they show you the boy. I fully expect them to try to take you, so do your best to keep some distance from them to give me some working room."

"Yes, sir."

"Keep heart, Miss Throckmorton," the major said. He stood up straight and gave a stiff salute before disappearing in the shadows to my left.

CHAPTER TWENTY-THREE
SHOWDOWN AT KARNAK

AHEAD OF ME LOOMED TWO LONG ROWS of criosphinxes guarding the entrance to the temple. I glanced one last time into the darkness behind me, heartened to at last see Isis. Surely Sefu could not be far behind. Feeling somewhat braver with the animals at my back, I squared my shoulders and directed the horse toward the first pylon.

Many of the sphinxes were missing their ram-shaped heads, but the ones who still had them seemed to watch me as I passed. Faint, shadowy symbols of power and magic drifted lazily across their surface. The glyphs were corroded with age and decay but still faintly discernible. I would have loved to have stopped to record them, to see what sort of magic held them in place or what they had been charged with, but now was not the time. Perhaps once this was all behind me, I could come back with Mother and explore the temple properly. Although probably not in the moonlight.

The pylon loomed in front of me, a huge, massive wall of cut stone nearly a hundred feet high. I shivered. The Pylon of Nectanebo I. How fitting that I should pass through it in order to rescue the last true pharaoh.

The walls of the pylon were thick, and it seemed to take forever to pass through the gate. I could feel no magic emanating from the structure, only the enduring strength of thousands of years. Immediately inside the courtyard, an enormous mound of dirt was piled up high along one of the pylon walls, as if the workers had abandoned the temple while they were still working on it. It was hard to imagine what sort of threat or power would have caused them to abandon their important work for the gods. Perhaps it was the gods themselves.

Now, *that* was a disturbing thought. Pushing it to the back of my mind, I focused instead on the large courtyard in front of me. Porticoes of columns ran along both sides. In the back, toward the second pylon, a lone column stood. Just behind it, guarding the entrance to the second pylon, were two enormous statues, their sightless eyes staring straight ahead.

The agents of Chaos could be hiding anywhere. I paused,

wanting to see if I could sense another human presence. I didn't *think* I could, but I was too nervous to risk closing my eyes and really focusing.

I considered searching among the columns to see if anyone was hiding there, then thought better of it. I had already played a game or two of cat and mouse among ancient ruins with the Serpents of Chaos. I was not eager to repeat the experience.

I glanced at my watch. Just past eleven o'clock. I was nearly an hour early. Feeling slightly more confident with this realization, I turned to my left, where Major Grindle had said the Seti Chapel would be.

A squat, square building of stone blocks lurked there, with three dark doorways gaping like giant mouths. That's where I was to leave the tablet—in the rightmost doorway, the altar of Khons.

Instead, I returned to the enormous mountain of dirt piled up against the pylon wall and used my foot to push aside some of the rubble. I carefully laid the satchel down, then covered it up.

At a small scritch of movement behind me, I whirled around. But it was only Sefu, climbing atop the Seti Chapel. "So nice of you to join us," I whispered.

He made a rude gesture, then scampered up to squat on the carved lintel above one of the doorways.

Ignoring him, I went over to find a place to sit and wait. Liking the idea of having a forty-foot-thick wall at my back, I chose a spot up against the pylon. Once I was settled, I searched among the shadows pooling on the temple floor, trying to spot Isis, wishing she would come over and wait with me. Alas, she had disappeared on some unknowable cat business of her own and was nowhere in sight.

Sometimes I thought waiting was the hardest part of all this. The constant rush, rush, rush to get these wretched men what they wanted, then the interminable waiting for them to come get it. Just as I was contemplating the unfairness of it all, I heard a faint sound somewhere beyond the second pylon.

"Isis?" I whispered, getting slowly to my feet. But truly, Isis never made any noise by accident. I saw a shadow move against the other shadows, and then it separated itself, drawing closer until I could make out the shape of a man. Another man followed him, and another. Six in all.

Once the lead figure had passed through the second pylon into the courtyard, he spoke. "You're early."

I recognized the voice. Von Braggenschnott. "So are you," I answered.

He jerked his head toward Seti Chapel, and one of his men trotted over and disappeared into the right-hand doorway. He reappeared a moment later and shook his head. Von

Braggenschnott turned to me. "You are playing games, fräulein?" he asked, looking around the courtyard. "Perhaps you do not think we are serious?"

"No games. Just being cautious. You don't think I'd hand over the tablet before seeing that Gadji is safe, do you?"

After studying me a long moment, von Braggenschnott finally said, "Reasonable enough. Bring him!" he called out over his shoulder.

Within seconds, two men appeared, each one hanging fast to one of Gadji's arms and nearly dragging him between them. They had put a black hood over his head, probably so he wouldn't be able to lead his rescuers back to the Serpents of Chaos stronghold, wherever that was.

"Gadji?" I asked. He was the right size and shape and wearing the same clothes, but that would be easy enough to manage.

The hood nodded vigorously.

"Are you all right?" I asked, hoping to hear his voice.

There was a pause, and then the man holding Gadji's right arm reached out and thumped him on the head.

"Stop that!" I said, but it worked. Gadji began nodding enthusiastically. When he reached up to keep his hood from slipping, I spotted the scratch that Isis had given him a few days ago.

"Enough!" von Braggenschnott said. "You have seen him

with your own eyes, fräulein. He is safe. Now hand over the tablet if you wish him to remain so."

"Very well." I was dying to look for Major Grindle but knew that would risk exposing him. Instead, I turned my back on von Braggenschnott and his men and walked calmly to the dirt pile. Every muscle was taut with the fear, but I assured myself they wouldn't do anything until I'd fetched the tablet.

When I reached the mound, I bent over and shoved my hand into the dirt, hard gazes boring into me as I felt around for the satchel. When I pulled it from its hiding place, I carried it back to where von Braggenschnott waited, stopping a few feet away. "You release Gadji first," I told him.

Von Braggenschnott waved the fingers on his remaining hand, and the two men let go of Gadji, who stumbled forward.

My eyes still on Gadji, I thrust the satchel at von Braggenschnott. "Here."

He jerked his head again, and a man came forward and took the satchel from me. I took a step toward Gadji, but von Braggenschnott stopped me.

"Ah, ah, ah!" he said, wagging his finger. "Not until I see what you have brought me."

I had no choice but to wait while they unwrapped the

tablet, my skin twitching with a nearly overwhelming desire to get out of there.

As his man worked to reveal it, von Braggenschnott narrowed his eyes at me. "I do hope you haven't tried to trick us."

"Not with Gadji's life at stake," I said. Which was true. I would never have dreamed of tricking them. That had been Major Grindle's brainstorm.

The man finally removed the tablet from its wrappings and I held my breath. I could only hope that Major Grindle's magic would hold up under Chaos's scrutiny.

Von Braggenschnott drew closer to the tablet and inspected it closely. Then he smiled, a truly sickening sight. "You have done well," he said.

I let my breath out in a whoosh. "Excellent. I think we'll be going, then." I jumped forward and grabbed Gadji's arm.

"Seize them!" von Braggenschnott shouted.

Two men leaped forward and pulled me away from Gadji. "Wh-what is this? You said we would make a fair trade!" Two others closed in on Gadji, whose head whipped back and forth blindly within his hood as he wondered what was going on.

"I lied," von Braggenschnott said. "Surely that does not surprise you. Besides, you and I have old business to settle between us." He lifted up the empty glove of his left hand.

"I'm afraid it will have to wait." Major Grindle's voice rang out through the courtyard. At his disembodied voice, the Serpents of Chaos looked up, trying to locate him. I looked over at Gadji. "Be ready," I whispered.

"The curse-repelling device, Miss Throckmorton," Major Grindle reminded me. I reached down and adjusted the knob as he called out, "Then the fountain pen, when you're able."

No sooner had he stopped speaking than there was a whooshing noise as hundreds of small sparks rained down on the men on either side of me. They screamed and let go of my arms, slapping at the Rain of Fire's sparks. With both my hands free, I shouted, "Duck, Gadji!" then gave the fountain pen a violent twist.

The effect was instantaneous. A buzzing sound shot from the pen, followed by the screams and cries of the Serpents of Chaos. Something deadly and sharp came slicing through the dark. Von Braggenschnott gave a shout of pain as it embedded itself in his arm, the one that had been reaching into his jacket for a pistol.

"Run!" Grindle shouted as he leaped down from high above. But we were already halfway to the pylon. A man stepped out from behind the chapel—where had he come from?—and grabbed for me. Before he got a firm grip, however, a small, spitting shape hurled itself at his face.

Isis! As her sharp claws made contact with his face, he let go of me to protect himself.

That was all we needed. I dragged poor Gadji toward freedom, not even stopping long enough to remove his hood. I had a firm grip on him so he wouldn't fall.

There was a thud behind us and a ring of steel as a sword was drawn. When we reached the first pylon, I risked a quick look over my shoulder.

"Do not dawdle, Miss Throckmorton! Get to the horse!"

I turned back around, grabbed Gadji's hand, and ran pell-mell toward where the horse was waiting.

CHAPTER TWENTY-FOUR
AN UNEXPECTED DETOUR

WHEN WE fiNALLY REACHED THE HORSE, I stopped long enough to grab Gadji's hood and yank it off his head.

But it *wasn't* Gadji! "Who are you?" I asked.

The terrified boy said something in Arabic. My best guess was he was some peasant child the Serpents of Chaos had snatched off the streets to fool us. I glanced at his scratched hand, appalled that they would injure him in order to maintain the deception.

Before I could decide what to do, two cloaked figures glided from the shadows at the base of the pylon to one of the criosphinxes on either side. "Come on," I told the boy, not caring who he was. We both needed to get to safety before those men saw us.

I grabbed hold of the saddle, got my foot into the stirrup, then hauled myself up. I took the reins from the boy and held my arm down to him. He grabbed hold and scampered up onto the saddle behind me.

Afraid the two men were closing in on us, I glanced up, surprised to see that they weren't paying us any attention. Instead, they had drawn instruments and were doing something to the criosphinxes. They each tapped a ram-headed sphinx on the forehead, the chest, its elbows and hands, then its ears.

The moment they touched the sphinxes' mouths, I *knew*. It was the Opening of the Mouth ceremony—very similar to the one I had performed on Tetley's mummy just a few months ago! Done in about three and a half seconds, I might add. But the ceremony was designed to reanimate the deceased. I couldn't imagine what possible use it might have on a statue.

No sooner had I formed that thought than the night air shifted and there was a mighty cracking sound, as if one of the temple pillars had fallen. But no. My eyes nearly popped out of my head as one of the ram-headed sphinxes pulled one of its great lion paws from the plinth on which he rested.

My heart began to race. Surely the men hadn't—

Behind me the boy squealed, the terror in his voice perfectly mirroring my own as the sphinx shook its mighty head. It looked directly at the man in front of it, who said something I couldn't hear and then pointed into the temple.

There was another mighty crack, one that shook the very ground, as the second sphinx leaped off the plinth, twitched its long lion tail, lowered its horns, then charged into the Court of Nectanebo.

The boy tugged on my sleeve and I felt his raw panic, but I was loath to leave such a spectacular bit of magic. However, I suspected that even at this distance, we weren't truly safe. Besides, who knew how much control over those creatures the magicians actually had? After all the major had done to save us, it would be wrong to repay him with stupidity.

As I wheeled the horse around, I peered frantically into the shadows, trying to locate Isis and Sefu, but they were nowhere to be seen. They were small, I reminded myself over the thudding of my heart. They could easily get away and hide in small places where those sphinxes couldn't reach them. The boy began slapping at me, wanting me to *move*. Knowing he was right, I put my heels to the horse.

It bolted forward and I felt the boy tighten his arms around my waist. I bent my head down low over the horse's neck and held on for dear life. The sounds of chaos and fighting receded into the distance. Even so, I kept riding, not slowing down until we reached the Temple of Mut.

As we passed the sacred lake, the horse shied at a shadow in front of us. It checked itself and changed directions, veering left toward the temple.

Two more shadows stepped out in front of us, this time causing the horse to rear up and nearly pitch us out of our seat. "Hang on!" I shouted, praying we wouldn't fall and break our necks. Or be trampled by flailing hooves.

But one of the shadowed figures darted forward and grabbed the horse's bridle. As he quieted the horse, the others closed in on us. With a sinking feeling, I recognized the black robes of the wedjadeen.

A dozen more men mounted on horseback poured out of the darkness, encircling us. With a wedjadeen on either side of my horse, they began leading us toward the Temple of Mut.

My mind was a jumble of panic and potential explanations.

As soon as we reached the temple, they pulled the horse behind one of the remaining walls so it wouldn't be seen from the road. Bother. There went my hope of Major Grindle's spotting us on his way back to Luxor.

But wait—he had the detecting device from Dr. Quillings! He *would* be able to find me.

Comforted by that thought, I looked down at my wrist and switched the knob to the correct position.

After that realization, my spirits rallied and I slipped my hand into my pocket for the Babel stone. I would learn all I could from the wedjadeen before Major Grindle arrived.

One of the men reached up, gently lifted me from the saddle, and placed me on the ground. I recognized Khalfani from our meeting at the Luxor Temple.

"What are you doing here?" I asked him.

"There is great magic afoot tonight."

"And you thought of me?" I was flattered in spite of the events of the evening.

"We thought of our pharaoh," he corrected. "Of his safety."

I should have thought more, weighed the true implications of my next words, but I was overset. "He's been taken," I blurted out.

Khalfani stared back up at the boy on the horse. "Who is this?" he asked.

"Their decoy," I said. "They used him to trick us."

"And who is this *they*?"

"The Serpents of Chaos."

He frowned at the name, then turned and spoke to the other men in Arabic, before looking back at me. "Who are these serpents?"

"Honestly, what do you do all day? You've never heard of them?"

He glared at me. "I would watch my tongue if I were you."

"Sorry. They are followers of Seth, very interested in getting all the powerful artifacts they can lay their hands on in order to bring chaos fully into the world, then seize power."

He nodded. "The followers of Set, I know." He turned to the boy. "You are tired," he said. "Very sleepy. All that you have experienced, all that you have heard and seen tonight, is but a very bad dream." Then he made a snatching sign at the boy's forehead and snapped his fingers. The boy blinked, then turned and ran.

"See that he gets home safely," Khalfani told one of the others. "You!" he said to the wedjadeen still mounted. "Go back to the temple. Pick up the trail of Set and collect our pharaoh!"

As one, the men wheeled their horses around and galloped back the way we'd come.

Khalfani turned back to me. "And how did they learn of our pharaoh?" His voice was low, almost a purr, but the purr of a panther rather than a cat.

"I don't know," I whispered. "I certainly didn't tell them. They are my sworn enemy."

He studied me a moment longer. "And my enemy's enemy is my friend, yes? You are in luck, young miss. Our high priest wishes to see you. We will save the harder questioning for him."

"Just so you know, I have to be back before morning. My mother has no idea I'm gone."

Khalfani gave me an unreadable look.

"I won't be back before morning, will I?" I asked in a small voice.

"No, young miss. I do not know when you will come back here." He motioned with his arm, and a phalanx of wedjadeen drew in around me and my horse, boxing me in on all sides.

"My mother is not going to be happy about this," I said. "You've no idea how big a fuss she can raise."

Khalfani ignored my threats and offered a few of his own. "If you try to scream or attempt to escape in any way, we will have to tie you up and silence you. We would prefer not to do this, but we will need your word that you will not hinder our progress."

The stark image of Awi Bubu's assistant and his missing tongue filled my head. "I give my word," I said.

A surge of power bumped up against me, probing to see if I was telling the truth. "I gave my word," I said, annoyed.

Khalfani shrugged. "You cannot blame me for needing to test the strength of that word, young miss. Now come. Hashim will control your horse for you."

"Major Grindle will come for me, you know." I said it as much to reassure myself as to warn them.

Hashim exchanged a weighted glance with Khalfani. "The man with you back at the temple?"

"Yes."

Khalfani shook his head, and a sense of deep foreboding filled me. "No, young miss, your major will not be coming for you. By the time the criosphinxes we have awakened are done, there will be nothing left in the temple."

CHAPTER TWENTY-FIVE
QERERT IHY

WE PLODDED ON THROUGH THE NIGHT, the taste of failure bitter on my tongue. I was tired and heart weary and wondered if I would ever see Gadji or Mother or Isis again.

Just when I was certain I would tumble off my horse with fatigue, the wedjadeen turned off the road and headed to a small Roman ruin, just barely visible in the faint light from the setting moon. Khalfani helped me dismount and steered me to a clear spot on the floor. "Wait here," he said.

That was the last thing I remembered before tumbling headlong into an exhausted sleep.

It seemed like only seconds later that voices were calling at me to wake up. I yawned and stretched, wincing at the soreness in my legs. I noticed that someone had put something soft underneath my head and covered me with a blanket of some sort. Touched by this kindness, I blinked the sleep from my eyes and sat up.

"Good morning."

The surprise of hearing Major Grindle's deep voice brought me full awake. "You're not dead!"

"No," he said dryly. "I'm not."

I glanced quickly around, wondering if the others had seen him. "Are you here to save me?" I whispered.

"I'm afraid not." His tone was even drier, and he jerked his arms, which I saw were tied behind him. "Although that *was* my original plan. But these men are devilishly hard to sneak up on."

"Oh." My heart sank as dreams of being rescued quickly evaporated. "Well, I'm sorry they captured you, but I'm awfully glad you're not dead."

"And I you," he said. He turned his gaze to where the wedjadeen were breaking camp, his eyes hard. "Have they harmed you?"

"No, not really. Aside from a saddle sore or two."

He looked almost disappointed, as if he had been hoping for a bone to pick with them. Although I supposed being kidnapped was bone enough. I scooted closer. "How did you survive the criosphinxes?" I asked.

His head whipped back around to me, his eyes alight with a strange fire. "Saw that, did you?"

"I did! As best I could tell, they used an Opening of the Mouth ceremony, sir, to bring the statue to life. What happened once they got into the temple?"

The major shook his head in amazement. "They acted just like a couple of mousers cleaning out a nest in a barn. They plowed through the Serpents of Chaos in minutes, wreaking havoc and destruction. Only three of those men escaped with their lives, and they were badly mauled."

"Did you see any sign of Gadji, sir?"

"So that wasn't him?" He sighed. "I was afraid it wouldn't be when I saw that hood. Ah, look sharp, Miss Throckmorton. Here come our captors now." He lowered his voice. "Don't let them know I can speak Arabic."

Before I could ask him to explain, Hashim was upon us. He gave us each a stale piece of flatbread to munch on for breakfast, and then five minutes later they had us up in our saddles, ready to move on.

They bound and gagged the major, but he didn't seem to mind. In fact, except for the faint bit of whiskery stubble on his cheeks, he looked to be in high spirits.

We continued southward. The sun was merciless and the wedjadeen impervious to it. I felt like a wilted piece of lettuce. Where were they taking us? And would I be cooked to a delicate crunch before we arrived there? Thoughts of Mother filled my head. She would be frantic with worry. Had she sent word to Father that I was missing? Did Wigmere know? And what had happened to Gadji? Surely the Serpents of Chaos would do nothing to such a valuable hostage.

On the evening of the second day, the wedjadeen struck out toward the west, heading into the rocky desert. I soon lost all sense of direction. The sand and cliffs of the desert all looked alike to me. I tried to force myself to think of it as an adventure but failed miserably.

Just as dawn began to peek over the horizon, our horses stumbled into a Bedouin camp. Even as exhausted as I was, I recognized what a brilliant cover this was. The wedjadeen could move around at will, come and go as they pleased, and no one would question them.

Men came forward to take our horses and I tumbled from the saddle. Khalfani was there to steady me, which I thought very kind of him since I was more or less his prisoner. Major Grindle, I noticed, was not treated as gently, although he needed it far less, seeming almost to thrive on the hard ride and rustic provisioning. Never had I been more aware of what a true soldier he was, down to his core.

We were herded to a small black tent and bundled inside. "Sleep," was all Khalfani would say, which was just what I wanted to do anyway, so it worked out perfectly. I flopped onto one of the blankets on the ground and felt every portion of my body aching with fatigue. Never had I missed the soft, furry comfort of Isis more. Which is why I was so surprised that I fell asleep the second I closed my eyes.

I was awoken sometime later when the tent flap opened, letting in the blinding glare of the sun. I blinked awake and squinted at the figure outlined against the bright light.

"Greetings," she said softly, then came fully inside and let the flap close behind her. Once I stopped squinting, I could see she was a girl, slightly older than I was. She wore the less-restrictive dress of the Bedouin, which did not include a veil or burqa, so I could see her face plainly. When she glanced shyly at Major Grindle, there was something familiar in her gaze but I couldn't think what. Then she returned her gaze to me. "I bring you food for your stomachs and water to wash the dust from your faces."

"Thank you," I said. "I'm famished."

Major Grindle's response was much more formal. "We appreciate your hospitality."

The girl ducked her head and began setting out our meal. She lingered as we ate, studying us curiously. Or me, more precisely. Finally, she seemed to get up her courage. "They say that you are the one who found our lost pharaoh and brought him to Luxor. Is this true?"

"Ye-es," I said warily. Was this a good sign, that they were telling people I was responsible for getting him as far as Luxor? "I found him working as a donkey boy in the streets of Cairo. He was quite brave and helped me out of an awkward situation. In return, I offered him a place to stay."

She glanced down at her hands. "And how did you find him? He was well?"

And then it hit me, why she looked familiar. "Are you Safiya?" I asked.

Her head jerked up, her eyes wide with wonder. "How do you know my name?"

"Gadji spoke of you," I told her.

Her eyes misted over. "He did? He has not forgotten me?"

"No," I said. "He spent days and days trying to find you when he got to Luxor, hoping to be reunited with you. Unfortunately, there was no hint of where you had gone."

"That is good and that is bad. Bad that he could not find me, but good that no one recalls what has happened to me."

Then she returned to her original question. "He is well?"

"Yes, he is. A bit on the thin side, but he is in good spirits. Very kind, very brave, and most loyal."

She clasped her hands together. "Thank you, my lady, for having brought my brother closer."

"He's not home yet," I pointed out.

"No, but he will be. The warriors of Horus will find him."

Major Grindle cleared his throat. "Speaking of that, what are the men doing out there? Have they organized any search parties? Sent out any scouts?"

Safiya was too shy to look at him, instead addressing her answers to her feet. "They are meeting now with the *mudir,* telling him of what has transpired. That is why I have been sent. You are to eat, then wash, and then I am to take you to them so they may question you."

"Excellent," the major said.

Excellent was not the word I would have chosen. Even so, we quickly finished our small meal, and then Safiya stepped outside while we washed in the water provided. Major Grindle turned his back while I washed my face and arms, and then I did the same for him. It was surprisingly intimate washing oneself—even just one's face and hands—with someone else nearby.

Not to mention, the results were most unsatisfactory. My

face might have been clean, but my clothes were still filthy and coated with dust.

As Safiya escorted us across the campsite, I saw then what I'd been too distracted to see earlier. The camp was pitched in the shadow of a great temple. Although it was smaller than the Luxor Temple, it was in excellent condition.

We arrived at a large, central tent, and Safiya held the flap for us as we went inside. My first impression was that I hadn't realized tents could be so very big, nor hold so many people. A dozen men were seated on thick rugs on the ground. I recognized Khalfani, Hashim, and the old grumpy wedjadeen who had wanted to kill me and be done with it. Fenuku, I think they had called him. He now wore the leopard skin of a *sem* priest. Bother. I knew that ancient Egyptian priests had often served for only a few months out of the year, but it seemed rather unfair to have them traveling about incognito. Priests ought to have warning signs on them.

Khalfani nodded at us, then turned to the man on his left. "This is the girl, *mudir,* and this man is the *Inglaize* we told you about."

"The one that put a knife to our pharaoh's throat," Fenuku spat out. Clearly he had not forgiven Major Grindle for that yet.

The *mudir*'s unblinking gaze passed over the major and landed on me. "Tell us what transpired."

I stood very straight and cleared my throat, determined that my voice not quiver. "When I returned home from my mother's excavation, there was a note on my pillow, demanding that I bring the Emerald Tablet to exchange for Gadji."

The *mudir* shook his head. "No, no. I mean, start at the very beginning. How did you come to have Gadji in your household?"

"Oh, *that* beginning! Well, we were leaving the Cairo museum for our hotel, and we needed to hire some donkeys . . ." I told him of hiring Gadji as a donkey boy (although not about Sefu's masquerading as his hump and eliciting sympathy from me) and his following us to Luxor and my subsequent hiring of him. When I had finished, they all looked faintly shocked that I had hired their pharaoh to muck out our stable.

"Sir, I'm very sorry," I rushed to add. "But at no time did Gadji mention anything about being a pharaoh. He didn't even know himself, until your men told us. He never balked at performing his duties nor suggested they were beneath him. The first I—we—learned of this was at the Luxor Temple when one of your men called him a pharaoh. I meant no disrespect. I was only trying to help out someone who needed food and shelter."

The *mudir* said nothing, and his gaze hardened as he turned to Major Grindle. "And you, where do you come into all this?"

Standing at full attention as if being inspected by the king, Major Grindle explained how he had first learned of Gadji's existence when the boy had shown up on his doorstep, begging the major to come help the effendi miss because Gadji was afraid she would get herself in trouble. He finished with me showing up on his doorstep, asking for help in getting Gadji back from the Serpents of Chaos.

"And why did you not come to us?" asked one of the seated men.

Major Grindle looked at him blandly. "I did not know of your existence until four days ago, let alone how to get hold of you in the four hours we had to respond to the demands. It seemed best for the boy that we move as quickly as possible to secure his release."

Fenuku leaned forward. "And how do you come to know such powerful magic, to create a tablet such as the one that fooled those men?"

"Years of study," was his clipped response.

Fenuku opened his mouth to say something else—

something unpleasant, by the look on his face—so I cleared my throat.

The *mudir* turned his attention from Grindle to me. "You may speak," he said.

"Sir, if you don't mind my asking, even if Gadji didn't go with your men that night, why didn't they put a guard on him as soon as they recognized him? I mean, with him being so valuable and all."

Fenuku looked as if he wanted to cut out my tongue for my impudence.

The *mudir* turned narrowed eyes to Khalfani. Oh dear. I hadn't meant to get anyone else in trouble, merely sought to shift the blame from us. But honestly, what had they been thinking? I'm just a child and I knew he should have been watched from the moment they first caught sight of him again. If they had, then the Serpents of Chaos would not have been able to nab him in the first place.

Khalfani shifted slightly in his chair. "We did, indeed, post guards, *mudir*, but they were attacked. We found them later, bound and gagged."

"I understand, sir," I said sympathetically. "The Serpents of Chaos have caught me off-guard a number of times."

"Yes, but how did you come to lose the boy in the first place?" Major Grindle asked. "If he was important to you, there should have been more than one old tutor to watch over him."

Fenuku's face flushed a dark, ugly red. "You know nothing about which you speak."

"But if you are going to judge us for not watching him more closely," I said, "it is only fair that we understand how you came to lose him in the first place."

The *sem* priest looked apoplectic, but the *mudir* inclined his head. "It is a fair question. And their knowing will not harm the Son of Re in any way.

"When our last native pharaoh, Nectanebo II, was driven from his rightful throne," the *mudir* began, "he took up refuge in the land of Macedonia. In hiding there, he realized his chances for reclaiming his birthright were meager. His only hope to reclaim the throne lay in any future heirs he might have. He could not risk having the blood of the pharaohs die with him, so he went forth and sired as many children as he could."

"Including Alexander the Great?" I asked. I had not quite believed Awi Bubu when he had first made that claim.

The *mudir*'s eyes sharpened. "Yes, even so. But he was only one of many sons fathered by Nectanebo. The responsibility was given to us, the Eyes of Horus, to watch over these sons, these children in whom the last drops of pharaonic blood flowed. We were to keep them safe, help raise them in the old ways, teach them of their heritage.

"But there were many of these children, in seven different bloodlines, and then these children had children, and so on. At one time there were nearly two score separate descendants of Nectanebo and we looked after them all.

"But one can have only one pharaoh at a time. What to do with all these extras that would not incite feuds and infighting? And when one's country grows poor and weak, overrun by foreign overlords who would use it for their own purposes, of what good is it to be a pharaoh?

"So most of these children lived in obscurity, closely guarded, taught by learned men who ensured they had the knowledge necessary to be pharaoh should the need arise, but never knowing their own true identity until the line of succession indicated they would be needed. This system worked well for us for hundreds and hundreds of years."

"Like a ruddy bank account," I heard Major Grindle mumble under his breath. "Then you could collect them at your whim."

"We lost many during the Turkish occupation of our land, for they were harsh masters. We lost more when Napoleon came to our shores. At the turn of this century, we had eleven descendants of Nectanebo. But the past few years have been hard on our people. When Gadji was born, he was one of only five left, and last in the line of succession.

"Soon there were two in line before him, but when they died of a wasting sickness, he was the only one left. But before we could summon him here to take his place at Qerert Ihy, disaster struck and the boy's tutor came to us, shame-faced with the tale of having lost the boy."

I was incensed that Gadji had been valued so poorly until the others were dead. "So you didn't appreciate him while you had him," I said.

"It is more that his value increased while we were focused elsewhere."

"And what of his sister, Safiya?" I asked. "Doesn't she have the same royal blood?"

"Women cannot serve as pharaoh," Fenuku said curtly.

The *mudir* held up his hand, and we all fell silent.

"Have you launched a rescue party yet?" Major Grindle asked, drawing all eyes back to him.

The *mudir* and Khalfani exchanged glances, and then Khalfani spoke. "We left half our men behind to see if they could find traces of the boy. When we first arrived here at Qerert Ihy, we sent a second wave of scouts to see if they could find where those men had gone. As soon as they report back, we will launch a full assault and rescue our pharaoh." When he stopped speaking, he brusquely clapped his hands. We were dismissed.

Safiya appeared and escorted us back to our tent. Neither Grindle nor I spoke until Gadji's sister left us. "I can't believe they are trying to hold us responsible for Gadji's kidnapping!" I exploded.

"It is always easier to blame others rather than oneself," Major Grindle said. "Especially when they have made so many mistakes along the way." He began pacing, and at first I thought he was agitated, as I was. But after a moment, I realized he was practically quivering with excitement.

"What is it?" I asked. "Why are you so wound up?"

His face brightened, as if by mentioning it I had given him permission to speak. "Did you see those men?" he asked, his face glowing.

"I saw twelve men," I said dryly. "Which ones do you mean?"

He glanced around the tent, as if checking to be certain no one had slipped in while he hadn't been watching. "At least six of those men in that tent were Weret Hekau."

"Weret Hekau? You mean the goddess of magic?" Truth be told, I was feeling a little dim. I'd had only a few hours' sleep and a handful of dates and some rather foul cheese to eat, and I had been called before a rather hostile group of judges; I was not able to equate six men with the goddess of magic.

The major snorted. "Of course they weren't the goddess of magic." He'd returned to his pacing.

"Oh, good. I'm glad we got that sorted out, because I was feeling a bit confused . . ."

"Weret Hekau was also a title given to ancient Egypt's most accomplished magicians. Those that had reached the highest degree of magical mastery. And six of them were sitting in that tent."

"How could you tell?"

"They were the ones with the snake tattoo running up their wrists."

Ah. I had noticed *that* and had meant to ask Major Grindle about it, but he had beaten me to it.

He stopped his pacing. "Don't you see? This means that not all the secrets died with the library at Alexandria. The knowledge needed to attain mastery hasn't all been lost!"

"Oh. Do you plan to ask them to write it down for you? So you can put it in your vault?"

Before he could answer, Safiya came bustling back into the tent carrying an armful of clothes. Two other women trailed behind her. "The *mudir* has spoken. You are to appear before the high priest tomorrow to plead your cases. I have brought clean robes for you to wear so that we may wash your clothes for you. And more water for washing," she said, wrinkling her nose.

CHAPTER TWENTY-SIX

THE RITES OF MAAT

I DID NOT SLEEP WELL THAT NIGHT, knowing that I was to face an official trial in the morning. And Fenuku would no doubt be sitting in judgment. He'd made it clear that he held no love for me or Grindle or even—perhaps especially—Awi Bubu. Safiya awakened us when she came in with our freshly washed laundry and a hearty breakfast. After eating and donning my own clothes, I felt more like myself and ready to face our judge and jury.

We were led from the camp to the giant temple ruins nearby, although truly, they were the best preserved ruins I had ever seen. As we drew closer, I realized that this was no mere ruin whose shadow they camped in. It was a working temple, still used in the worship of their gods. Bald priests wearing pleated linen kilts bustled about the courtyard. Some carried vessels of purifying water, and others carried baskets of fruit or grain. A goat bleated nearby, and a scribe hurried into one of the side chambers.

We were led past the first pylon, then the second. As we entered the temple chambers, I saw that our trial was to be held in front of three *sem* priests. They sat in front of a wall that held a huge painting depicting Horus presiding over a Weighing of the Heart ceremony. Would our hearts be determined to weigh less than a feather? Did they have a Devourer nearby who would eat us if we failed the test?

Furthering the bad news was the fact that their ranks included Fenuku, just as I had suspected. The good news, though, was that Baruti, the kind priest who had sent the falcon to summon the wedjadeen that very first time, was also a *sem* priest, and he had proved himself quite friendly to us. The third appeared to be the high priest.

We were made to kneel on the hard stone floor. Once we had, the high priest began to speak. "You are brought before the judgment of Maat, to be held accountable for your actions in regards to the abduction of our pharaoh. Furthermore, you are to be examined so that we may understand how you came to be in possession of your knowledge of our existence as well as some of our most closely guarded secrets. Lastly, you are here to tell us what you know of the traitor, Awi Bubu, so we may determine if your actions in losing our pharaoh were carried out on his behalf."

"No!" I said, shocked. "Awi Bubu never mentioned the pharaoh to me—"

"Silence!" Fenuku boomed. "You will be given a chance to speak and will remain silent until then."

The unknown priest leaned forward. "The charges made against you are serious, child. To even know of our existence can bring a swift and terrible death. To have meddled in our affairs, to have lost what is most precious to us—those things have even more dire consequences."

"Although," Baruti interrupted, "those laws and punishments have been devised for adult transgressors. Trials such as these have never involved a child before."

"Then let her go." Major Grindle was quick to step into the opening Baruti gave him. "As you say, she is but a child, and a girl child at that. She has little value and should not be held responsible for what has transpired."

I appreciated what he was doing, trying to get them to free me, but I did not like being accused of having little value; it cut too close to the bone.

"That, too, will be decided over the course of this trial," the high priest said. Then he turned to me. "How did you come to know Awi Bubu?"

Before I could answer, Fenuku leaned over and whispered in the high priest's ear. After long moments of whispered debate, the high priest spoke again. "The point has been made that we have no way to be certain you speak the truth. We would ask that you willingly subject yourself to the Rites of Maat so we may determine the veracity of your words."

"Um, what is that, exactly?" I asked.

"With the goddess of truth guiding your tongue, false words cannot pass your lips. Are you afraid?" Fenuku smirked.

"No," I lied. "Just curious." And wondering if it would hurt.

"I will endure the Rites of Maat." Major Grindle's loud voice rang out through the chamber.

Fenuku looked surprised, while Baruti did not. The high priest merely clapped his hands. "Let the Rites of Maat begin!"

Three lesser priests hurried into the room. I could not help but assume they'd been listening at the door, so quick was their response.

They approached Major Grindle bearing vessels, bowls, reed brushes—all manner of strange equipment. They bowed before him, then got to work. One of them poured oil from an ornate vessel into a shallow bowl. Another one unstoppered a clay jar and transferred some dark, sticky paste from it to the bowl, then stirred. When it was the right consistency, they had Major Grindle open his mouth. While he said, "Ahhh," one of the men dipped a brush into the special ink and began to paint on Major Grindle's tongue. Burning with curiosity, I inched forward to see better.

The man was painting a figure on the major's tongue. A woman—a goddess, to be exact. But of course! The goddess Maat.

When he had finished, he dipped the reed brush back into the special ink and drew three more hieroglyphs next to the figure of the goddess. When he was done, he withdrew a respectful distance.

The major looked at me, and we waited a long, breathless moment. When it became clear he wasn't going to keel over dead from poisoning, he gave a brisk nod. "Nothing to it, Miss Throckmorton."

"What did it taste like?" I asked.

He tasted his tongue. "Honey and ashes, I think."

"And what of you, young miss?" Fenuku was leaning forward again, his dark eyes shining. "Will you, too, undergo the Rites of Maat to assure us that you speak nothing but the truth before us?"

"Yes," I said. "I have nothing to hide." But of course, that wasn't exactly true. I had many things I needed to hide from lots of people; the wedjadeen just weren't among them.

The lesser priest stepped forward with his mixing palette—I was glad to see that he'd picked up a new brush—and motioned for me to open my mouth. When the ink touched my tongue, it tingled, a faint burning on my taste buds. When he had finished his artwork, he motioned to the *sem* priests that they could begin the questioning.

"How did you come to meet Awi Bubu?" Fenuku asked.

My tongue buzzed and hummed and began moving of its own accord. "I met him when he was performing a magic show at the Alcazar Theater in London." I tried to look down at my tongue, but my nose got in my way. "We went backstage to meet him and grew, er, friendly."

I saw no need to mention that I had sensed he was working true magic rather than tricks. I waited to see if my tongue would volunteer that information, but it did not. The magic seemed to be very literal—it only forced me to answer the questions asked, not volunteer anything extra. "He then came to visit my parents' museum, and while he was there he sensed an artifact of great power."

"Which was?"

"The Emerald Tablet that I returned to your men."

The high priest nodded. "Go on."

"It took him a while to convince me of what it was and its importance. There were a number of other men after it, and I didn't know whom to trust. Some of these men are the very ones that have Gadji now. Anyway, in the end, I guessed some of it—"

"What did you guess?" Baruti asked, eyeing me with a keen gaze.

"Well, he'd told me he was exiled from his own country. And I quickly became aware of his powers—"

"How did you learn of these powers?" Fenuku asked.

Honestly, would they just let me answer one question at a time? "I-I felt them. When he tried to use them against me or to bend me to his will, I was able to sense it. Anyway, I began to do some research, wanting to get to the bottom of the whole affair. In my research I came across the name *wedja*—" I hesitated.

Baruti nodded. "You may speak that name in this place."

I nodded. "I came across the name *wedjadeen* scribbled in a few books."

The high priest grew visibly disturbed. "What mention was made of us in these books?"

"Well, the book talked about the Emerald Tablet and claimed that it had been lost in the fire that destroyed the Alexandrian library."

Beside me, I felt Major Grindle stiffen.

"But in the margin was a handwritten note, and it said that there was a rumor that some of the books from the library had been rescued and were hidden in the desert by the wedjadeen."

The three priests grew upset and began talking in low, urgent undertones. After a moment, they turned back to me. "Is that all?"

I swallowed. "No. There was another mention of you made in a diary written by one of Napoleon's men during his occupation of Egypt."

There was more hushed whispering, and then Baruti turned back to me. "But how did these small pieces of knowledge lead you to us, child?"

Fenuku leaned forward. "Did Awi Bubu reveal our secrets to you?" He spoke kindly for the first time, clearly hoping to lull me into trusting him.

He needn't have bothered. I would have sooner trusted a cobra. But I had no intention of finding out what the goddess of truth and justice would do to me if I spoke falsehoods with her symbol painted on my tongue. "He did tell me some of them, sir, after I had guessed quite a lot. Once I read of the wedjadeen's existence, I pieced together that it was they who had once held possession of the artifacts of the gods—"

The high priest gave a bark of frustration. "You know of those? Which of our secrets do you not know?"

I ignored his outburst and waited to see if my tongue would answer on its own. It didn't. Interesting that the Rites of Maat allowed for rhetorical questions. "I had to discover whom to trust, you see. Whom to believe about the Emerald Tablet. When I presented Awi Bubu with what I had learned and told him I would not give him back the tablet without the full story, he finally filled in some of the blanks in my knowledge."

"Traitor," Fenuku spat out. "The man is still a traitor to his people."

"No, sir. It wasn't like that. He—he had another reason for telling me. Only me."

That got their attention. They all looked at me expectantly. "He said he thought I had a role to play in all this." I was finding it surprisingly difficult to stand in front of a group of strangers intent on judging me and try to convince them I was unique. "He said there was something special about me that he could see," I rushed to get out.

I felt rather than saw Major Grindle turn to stare.

The priests put their heads together again and talked among themselves. Finally, they calmed down somewhat and turned back to me. "And as for your role in the disappearance of our young pharaoh . . . ?" the high priest asked.

I quickly told him all that I had explained to the *mudir* about meeting Gadji and his subsequent disappearance. At last they were satisfied and waved to the priest to let me rinse my mouth. I felt as limp and wrung out as an old rag.

Now it was Major Grindle's turn. Like me, he repeated the exact same story he had told the *mudir*, which corroborated my own. When he had finished, Baruti leaned forward. "And have you met or do you know of Awi Bubu?"

"No, sir, I'd never heard of the man before five days ago, when Miss Throckmorton and Gadji told me some of their stories."

"So she did not share his confidences with you?"

"No, she did not. Not until I had come face-to-face with your people myself at the request of your young pharaoh. When I demanded an explanation, she gave me one, although"—he tossed a recriminating glance my way—"not the full one."

"And now you know why," I murmured.

"Silence!" Fenuku barked. I must confess, that *sem* priest was getting on my last nerve. "The most serious charge against this *Inglaize* is that he put a knife to our pharaoh's throat and threatened his life."

"Nonsense!" Major Grindle said. "I was merely bluffing, and if you were ever to find your precious pharaoh, you could ask him and he would tell you. As soon as I knew he had value to your men, I pretended to be willing to harm him in return for her safety. And he knew I was bluffing. But I will remind you, you were the one that began using children as pawns," he pointed out.

They put their heads together for one more of those beastly, whispered conferences. "Very well," the high priest said at last. "We have heard your testimony and will render judgment on the morrow. You are dismissed until then, but you may not leave the camp."

CHAPTER TWENTY-SEVEN
AN UNEXPECTED REUNION

I AWOKE EARLY THE NEXT MORNING to the sounds of a commotion outside our tent. I scrambled out of my bedroll onto my feet and fumbled over to the tent flap.

Major Grindle beat me there.

"What is it?" I asked, pushing my hair out of my eyes.

"The scouts have returned," he said. "Shall we see what they have to say?"

"Yes, please!"

Together we stepped out into the soft light of dawn. The sun had not even risen over the eastern peaks yet, so it was surprisingly cool out. People had begun to gather where the scouts were dismounting. We hurried to join them.

Safiya stepped next to me just as Khalfani came out of his tent. He spoke to the scouts in Arabic, and I slipped my hand into my pocket for my Babel stone.

"Any sign of the boy?"

The taller scout shook his head. "No. Nothing. When we returned to Karnak, there was nothing, no sign of anyone."

"We separated into three different directions, all trails turning cold," the other scout said. "They have gone to ground, I am afraid."

I wondered that they hadn't asked the god of air to tell them where the men had gone, he being such a big friend of theirs and all.

"Did you question those who lived near the area? Go door to door in the village of Karnak?"

The scout bowed. "But of course. No one knew anything."

"Which is in itself unusual," Khalfani muttered.

The shorter scout stepped forward and pulled something from his robes. "The only sign of their passing was this." He unwrapped the small bundle, and my heart shot to my throat. It was Gadji's monkey, lying limp and lifeless in the man's hands.

Unaware of what I was doing, I pushed to the front of the crowd. "Sefu!" The scout looked at me in surprise. "Is he dead?" I asked.

"Yes, the worthless creature is dead."

The other scout spat onto the ground. "He was to watch over our pharaoh for us. Twice now, he has failed in his duties. Let the jackals have him," he ordered.

The scout holding the dead monkey hurled it off to the side, onto the midden heap on the outskirts of camp.

"No!" I whispered, staring frantically at poor dead Sefu. He and Gadji had been so close, such friends. If Sefu had failed his master, it was through no fault of his. A small monkey is no match for the Serpents of Chaos.

While the others continued to talk, I inched over to the side of the crowd. A quick glance told me everyone else's attention was still on the scouts and their report, so I hurried over to the lifeless monkey. Bending over, I picked Sefu up and cradled him in my arms. I placed a finger on his chest where I guessed his heart to be. Nothing.

"What are you doing, Miss Throckmorton?"

I looked up to find Major Grindle watching me. "He and Gadji were such good friends and he served the boy faithfully. Surely he deserves a proper burial." I did not tell him that I could not bear the idea of such a thing happening to my cat.

The major glanced over to the others. "I'm not sure that's the most important of our worries today."

"It's wrong," I said stubbornly. "What did they expect the poor monkey to do?" I was surprised to feel that my cheeks were wet. I transferred Sefu to one arm and used my other hand to wipe the tears from my face. Embarrassed, I turned and blindly made my way back to the privacy of our tent.

Inside the tent, I found a small pillow and laid the monkey on top of it. He sprawled awkwardly and I leaned over to arrange his limbs.

Wait a moment. If he was dead, wouldn't he begin to stiffen? And cold—shouldn't he be cold? I reached back down to touch him and found that he was cool to the touch, but by no means dead cold. Could he possibly still be alive?

There was a whisper at the tent door as Safiya entered. "What are you doing?" she asked.

"I'm tending to Gadji's monkey," I said. "Do you still have that mirror you lent us when we were preparing for our trial?"

"But of course." She slipped back out of the tent and I turned back to Sefu, the hope inside me rising.

When Safiya returned, she held the brass mirror out to me. "I remember when Gadji got that monkey," she said. "It was given to him by Master Bubu, who told Gadji to keep the creature with him always." Her voice broke.

I looked up at her. "He did, Safiya. Gadji and the monkey were inseparable. Both of them kept their word to Master Bubu." I lowered the mirror down in front of the monkey's face.

"Whatever are you doing?" she asked.

"Trying to see if he's really and truly dead." As I watched, the faintest bit of fog appeared on the mirror's surface and hope surged through me. "He's breathing!"

"He is?" Safiya leaned forward to see. I showed her the mirror, and she nodded. "It is so."

I felt gently along Sefu's arms and legs to see if anything was broken. Nothing, as far as I could tell. I had no idea how to check the creature's internal organs. "We need to keep him warm," I told Safiya. "And we should probably try to get some water down his throat."

"I will be right back." She got up and hurried out of the tent. I grabbed one of the extra blankets and gently covered the monkey, tucking the ends in close to preserve as much of his little body's warmth as possible. To say I surprised myself was an understatement. Sefu and I had not cared for each other particularly, but even so, I recognized that his relationship with Gadji was much like mine with Isis. It was almost as if by taking care of Sefu, I was also taking care of those I missed even worse.

Safiya returned with a shallow bowl of water and a rag. "Here," she said. "This is how we feed baby goats when their mother has been taken by the jackals." She twisted the rag tightly, then dipped an end into the water. She held the saturated tip over the monkey's mouth, which I had gently pried open. One drop, two, three, slipped down Sefu's throat. His eyelids fluttered, and I nearly cheered.

Major Grindle stuck his head into the tent just then. "Miss Throckmorton? They are ready for us."

I looked at him blankly, all memory of our awaiting judgment having evaporated as I cared for Sefu. "Oh. Right. Coming." I looked at Safiya. "Will you watch him for me?"

"But of course. I will nurse him as I would my own brother."

"Thank you," I said, then got to my feet, straightened my skirts, and went out to meet my fate.

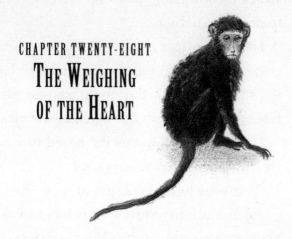

CHAPTER TWENTY-EIGHT
THE WEIGHING
OF THE HEART

OUTSIDE THE TENT, Khalfani and Hashim were waiting to escort us to the temple. Khalfani gave me an encouraging smile that didn't quite reach his eyes.

As we made our way through the tents to the temple, we picked up a bit of a following, much like a cat's tail picks up a collection of burs. By the time we'd reached the temple proper, we were a small crowd. As Major Grindle and I made our way across the courtyard, the throng followed, silent as a shadow. They stayed with us as we crossed the Hypostyle Hall and, much to my surprise, followed us into the first antechamber, crowding around us as best they could. We were to have an audience, then.

The three *sem* priests filed in and took their seats. I was struck by how many times I'd seen this exact tableau—on a tomb wall painting.

The high priest stood. "The accusations before you are grave. Yet you have also done much to commend your actions. We have looked to the stars, cast the bones, and scattered the entrails, yet the signs are not clear."

The rustling behind us increased to a muttering. Apparently the signs were *always* clear.

"You"—he looked straight at me—"have traveled far and endured much to return what belongs to us, and for that you have our gratitude. But you have also seen our secrets and been exposed to our mysteries, and this is forbidden."

The room grew so quiet, I could hear the faint wheezing of one of the priests.

"Because your actions were carried out in good faith, Maat will be served when you have drunk of the Wine of Forgetting. Then we will return you to your family."

"What exactly is the Wine of Forgetting?" I asked, not liking the sound of it one bit.

"It is a draft that will wipe us from your mind, child." Baruti looked sad. "But it will do you no lasting harm."

"But Awi Bubu said—"

"He lost his right to speak for us when he was cast from

our midst," Fenuku said, with far more relish than necessary, I thought.

"But if I forget, how can I help? Awi Bubu was certain I
had a role to play. Forgetting will not help me fulfill that."

"The wedjadeen have survived millennia without the help
of an *Inglaize* girl," the high priest said. "I feel certain we
shall be fine."

"You would be wrong!" a feeble voice called out from
somewhere behind me. I turned around in time to see the
crowd parting as someone worked his—or her—way forward. In the silence, I heard a . . . cowbell?

An old woman pushed her way out of the crowd. She wore
an ancient, tattered black gown lined with gold on the hem.
From the sash at her waist was a red cord. An ancient
bronze cowbell hung at the end. As she drew closer, she
lifted her head and I bit back a gasp. She did not wear the
traditional veil that so many of the women in Egypt did. Instead, she had a tattoo on her forehead, a large disk with a
horn rising up on either side.

Fenuku scowled at her, and I slipped my fingers around
my Babel stone just in time to hear him say, "What do you
want, old woman?"

The high priest poked him in the ribs—hard—and hissed
at him to be silent. "Be welcome, Mother."

She smiled, revealing a number of missing teeth. "That's better," she said. "I have come to speak on the girl's behalf."

A collective gasp went up from those behind her, and Fenuku's scowl deepened. Major Grindle looked as though he were watching a particularly close cricket match.

"What gives you the right to speak on her behalf?" Fenuku demanded.

The old woman glanced at me then, and her eyes softened. "Because I attended her on the seventh day after her birth," she said. "And foretold her fate that day. I would tell it again before all of you."

Pandemonium ensued. The *sem* priests began arguing among themselves and the assembled wedjadeen behind us exchanged excited whispers. Major Grindle stared at me with what looked remarkably like envy. "You were born in Egypt, Miss Throckmorton?"

I smiled sheepishly. "Yes, apparently."

"Did you know that you had been attended by one of the Seven Hathors?"

"Hardly. I don't even know what the Seven Hathors *are*," I pointed out. Even so, I was trembling with excitement. Here was someone who knew something about my birthplace, something about what made me *me*.

"Silence!" the high priest finally demanded. "We will let this Hathor speak."

"Nearly twelve years ago, my sisters and I were summoned by the goddess to attend a newborn."

"But she is an *Inglaize* girl!" Fenuku interrupted. "Surely the Seven Hathors only visit Egyptian babes."

The Hathor scowled. "But she was born in the Temple of Isis, on a fortuitous day, and the goddess summoned us nevertheless. It was clear we were to bestow such blessings as we could, in order to prepare the child for the great fate that awaited her."

The high priest leaned forward. "And what fate is that?" he asked.

"Are you too blind to see what is before your own eyes? The girl is *hekau*," the Hathor's voice rang out. "A possessor of great magic."

Honestly, Fenuku looked as if someone had put a dead scorpion in his honeyed wine.

"Not only that, she is Rekhet."

Voices erupted at that proclamation and even Major Grindle looked at me with new eyes. I just wished I knew what on earth it *meant*.

Baruti's eyes sparkled—with pleasure or mischief, I couldn't tell. "This changes everything," he pointed out.

The high priest sighed. "This girl is much trouble for one so small. But you are correct. We will have to consult with the Seer of Maat."

At that announcement, the old woman reached out and patted my hand. I smiled into her ancient eyes and, for the first time, felt that someone here was glad to see me.

Fenuku was wretchedly unhappy with this turn of events. "There is still the matter of the *Inglaize* major to be settled," he reminded us. From the evil smile he wore, I did not think we were going to like this one.

The high priest picked up a piece of papyrus. "Major Harriman Grindle, you have been charged with laying hands on the pharaoh, penetrating our secrets, and having knowledge of our whereabouts. You also display a disturbing grasp of magic, magic that no one but the wedjadeen should know. Maat will be served only when your life is forfeited."

"No!" I shouted, forgetting myself. "You can't be serious!"

"Silence!"

"He did everything in his power to save Gadji."

"Now, now, Miss Throckmorton. Enough of that." Major Grindle gave me a bracing pat on the back. "We've played our hand and it's run out."

I stared at him. "Are you off your nut? They're talking of killing you!"

"I am an old soldier, Miss Throckmorton. A threat of death is nothing new to me. Indeed, it may be the beginning of a whole new adventure."

I wanted to scream. Did he have to be so noble minded about it? Why didn't he fight, argue, make them see—

That was it. *See.* "Wait!" I said. Baruti looked at me with interest, while the other two *sem* priests seemed annoyed. "Wait. All these things he did—touching the pharaoh and knowing your magical secrets and where you live—those are only a crime because he isn't one of you, correct?"

"Yes," the high priest said.

"Well, what if he *was* one of you?" I asked.

"What do you mean, child?" Baruti asked.

I marched over to Major Grindle. "Forgive me, sir, but I would never ask this of you if your life wasn't at stake."

"Ask what, Miss Throckmorton?"

I cleared my throat, suddenly embarrassed. "Ask you to unbutton your jacket, if you please."

"What?" he blustered.

Under my breath, I whispered, "Trust me, please?"

He stared into my eyes, then slowly nodded. "If you insist." He lifted his callused hands to the brass buttons on his red coat and began to unbutton them.

"Now your shirt," I said softly. "I want them to see your tattoo."

Raising an eyebrow, he did as I asked and unbuttoned his shirt.

"Now open it wide so they can see," I said.

He grasped his shirt in his hands and pulled the collar apart. A brilliant wedjat eye stared back.

Slowly, like a fire catching at tinder, murmurs spread throughout the sanctuary. The high priest leaped to his feet while Fenuku sat blustering, as if he'd sprung a leak. Baruti, who I was beginning to suspect must be Awi Bubu's twin brother, merely stroked his chin thoughtfully.

"Would you care to explain why they're all agog, Miss Throckmorton?" Major Grindle asked out of the side of his mouth.

"Because that tattoo that you consider to be a mark of the Brotherhood? It is the very same mark they bear as members of the wedjadeen."

His eyebrows shot up to the top of his forehead, and Khalfani murmured, "It is so."

The high priest and Fenuku were engaged in a fierce debate, so Baruti rose to his feet to address the crowd. "This entire matter is more complicated than we first knew. Both matters will have to be brought before the Seer of Maat. That is all." With one last curious glance in my direction, he turned and disappeared through the door.

Baruti's announcement took the heat out of the two arguing *sem* priests, and they, too, rose to leave the chambers.

As I watched them exit, my knees grew wobbly with relief and I decided I needed to sit down in the worst possible way. Silently, I lowered myself to the floor and leaned up against one of the columns.

Major Grindle looked up from rebuttoning his jacket. "Are you all right, Miss Throckmorton?"

"Yes. Just having a little rest." But the truth was, my head felt as if it might explode. "What happens now?" I asked Khalfani.

"They will take the matter before the Seer of Maat, and he will most likely summon you so that he may discern the truth in your words."

Word of the trial's results—and surprises—traveled quickly and I felt everyone watching me as I made my way back to our tent. I couldn't tell if the looks were filled with judgment over my guilty sentence or awe and fear because I was a Rekhet. I kept my head down and refused to meet anyone's gaze.

When at last I reached the safety of our tent, I hurried inside, anxious to see how Sefu was doing. However, word of this morning's events had reached even here. As I greeted Safiya, she sank gracefully into a deep bow.

I couldn't bear it. "Oh, stop that, Safiya! Please! Get up."

She lifted her head and peeked up at me. "Effendi miss is not angry that I have treated her without the proper honor?"

"No! Not at all. I didn't even know until fifteen minutes ago, and I still don't really understand what it *means*." As I spoke, I crossed the small tent and knelt beside Sefu's still form. "Has he changed at all?"

Safiya got to her feet and shook her head. "Not really. But I did get some more honey water down his throat."

"Good." Still afraid of what I would see in her expression, I busied myself with straightening the monkey's bedding.

"What happened to your major?" Safiya asked.

"He lingered behind to speak with Khalfani. I think they might be comparing tattoos," I muttered.

"Tattoos?" she repeated.

Interesting that bit of news hadn't reached her yet. "Major Grindle—all the men in his organization—wear the same wedjat-eye tattoo that the warriors of Horus do."

"How is this possible?"

"Well, that is what everyone is dying to find out."

She frowned. "Does it mean that he, too, is a warrior of Horus?"

"I'm not certain." During the trial I had claimed that it did, but I didn't know that for a fact. It was a bit of a bluff, actually.

Between talking of Major Grindle and tending to Sefu,

things had grown easy between Safiya and me once more. "Safiya, what exactly does being a Rekhet mean? No one's told me anything."

She glanced up at me shyly. "It is a great honor the gods have bestowed upon you, miss. They have given you the power to see the *heka* that lurks in our world, *heka* both good and evil. This makes you very valuable in our fight against Set."

I sat back on my heels. So that was it. That was why I was able to detect curses and lingering *mut* so easily. "Are there many Rekhet among you?"

Safiya shook her head.

"Why me?" I wondered, then nearly jumped out of my skin when a voice behind me answered.

"Why not you, child?"

I whipped my head around and saw the Hathor standing just inside our tent. I heard a faint *thunk* as Safiya dropped her forehead onto the ground in a deep bow. I wondered if I was supposed to bow, too.

"The gods select what tools they may, child," the old woman continued. "It is not for us to question them. May I sit down, please? I have traveled far these past few days."

"Yes, yes. Of course." I jumped to my feet at the same time Safiya did and we bumped into each other in our eagerness to see to the old woman's comfort.

Once we'd gotten her settled, Safiya brought her some water, which she drank gratefully. When she was done, she turned her attention back to me. "When my sisters and I attended you on the seventh day after your birth, we sensed this great power in you, and because of that, a great destiny was foretold. We briefly considered taking you with us so we could train you in the full use of your gifts. In the end, we decided that the gods surely knew best in giving such power to a foreign babe, so we did not meddle."

"Did my mother know of your visit to me?" I tried—without success—to picture my mother letting seven women who looked as if they'd stepped right off a temple frieze into her house, let alone into her newborn's room.

The Hathor shook her head and snorted. "No. It was the housekeeper who let us in while your mother slept. She never knew we were there.

"If you had grown up with us, we would have begun your training at five years of age. We Hathors would have had a hand in such training, and the *sem* priests as well. Even so, you seem to have done quite well on your own. A thirsting mind seeks knowledge like a withered vine seeks water."

The old woman leaned forward then. "And Awi Bubu was right. You do have a role to play in our fight against Set. You are, I think, to lead us to wholeness. So, how does young Awi Bubu fare?"

I blinked rapidly, trying to keep up with the lightning-quick change in her manner from prophetess to village gossip. "He is well enough, but he could be better."

"Tell me how you came to know him?"

Honestly! I should just publish the story in the local paper and be done with it! I repeated the story, the entire story this time, leaving nothing out. When I was done, the Hathor cackled. "You see? Even his fall from grace has a role to play, for without him in your country, how would you have learned of us?" She fell silent as the import of her own words struck her. "Hmm. I must go point that out to the council. Surely they will see the gods' hands in this and revoke the order of exile they placed upon Awi Bubu's head."

At last! "Oh, thank you! That would be wonderful. He's wanted nothing more than to be forgiven by his people and allowed to come home. If," I said sadly, "he ever makes a full recovery and is well enough to travel."

The old Hathor took her leave and Safiya had other duties she had to attend to. I was actually grateful for the solitude and laid my spinning head down onto the pillow next to Sefu. I carefully placed my hand so that it touched his furry little body, wanting him to know he wasn't alone. Or perhaps I was the one who didn't want to be alone.

CHAPTER TWENTY-NINE
MONKEY BUSINESS

THE NEXT MORNING WHEN I WOKE UP, I checked on Sefu first thing. There wasn't any change and I wondered at the nature of his illness. Was he sick? Was he weakened by lack of food and water? Had he been struck with some powerful *heka* or horrible curse?

However, the good news was that sometime during the night, my mind had formed a plan all on its own. Even better, the plan held up when examined in the harsh light of day.

If I was a Rekhet, then it seemed time to use those skills to my own advantage. All my life, whatever abilities I possessed had given me mostly grief. And while it was true that they had allowed me to keep my friends and family (relatively) safe, those abilities had also made my life wretchedly difficult. They had forced me to lie to my family, created discord between me and my brother, and caused my grandmother to disapprove of me, not to mention all the untold terrifying moments and haunting nightmares.

But what if that was because of my inability to understand the true nature of my gift? So far, I had seen only the dangerous aspect of magic in the world. What if my abilities could also tap into the good *heka*? If I was stuck being peculiar, I'd prefer to be peculiar on my own terms, thank you very much.

I looked down at the unconscious little monkey. Who was more deserving than the pharaoh's loyal pet?

I got up out of my blankets and saw that Major Grindle had left the tent already. I wasn't particularly worried, as he and Khalfani had been talking almost nonstop ever since learning of their matching marks. Probably exchanging war stories or battle tips, I thought.

Using the last of the water in the pitcher, I washed, ate a cold piece of flatbread, then went to collect Sefu. I wrapped the monkey in a blanket, tucked him close to my chest, then went to the tent flap and peeked out.

There were a number of people about, all of them busy with their morning chores. Hopefully they wouldn't notice me. Or if they did, they'd be too in awe of a Rekhet to stop me.

As I headed for the temple, I kept my eyes down and ignored the occasional curious glance that came my way. I entered the vestibule and wound a path among the columns of Hypostyle Hall until I came to a small door on the right that led to the sanitarium—the ancient room of healing. I paused at the door. "Hello?" I called out, but there was no reply. There didn't seem to be any doctors about, nor *sem* priests, nor attendants of any kind. Still, the door had been opened and unlocked. Cautiously, I stepped over the threshold.

It felt as if I had passed through a shower of minuscule sparks, their burn cool and clean rather than fierce like the heat of fire.

The room held a small healing bath filled with water, which sat in the middle of the room. On either side of that was a row of three beds, all empty. On the far wall was a long table, above which stood shelves and cupboards. The wall closest to me had an alcove with three statues. The first was Sekhmet, the goddess of fire and destruction. It had always seemed odd to me that she was the goddess who had brought the plague and general destruction but was also in charge of healing. The next two statues were of Thoth and Horus. Thoth had taught the healing arts to mankind and Horus was the god Thoth had so spectacularly healed that it had inspired one of the most powerful amulets ever—the wedjat eye. Along the foot of the statues ran rows of hieroglyphs.

I gently laid Sefu down on the bed closest to the shelves, then went back to the statues to read the inscriptions at their bases. I was in luck! These were just like the statues back at our museum, the ones that had come from the sanitarium at Dendera. Those statues had been inscribed with healing rituals and spells. I chose the spell on the Horus statue, thinking his sort of miraculous healing would best correspond with Sefu's problem.

Prepare an ink made of honey, the juice from a flaming red poppy, and sour wine. Mix thoroughly.

I stopped there and got up to examine the shelves. I had seen two mortars and pestles sitting on the table. Since this was a working temple, perhaps the sanitarium cupboards contained some of the ingredients I would need.

The cupboards turned out to be a veritable treasure trove of ancient Egyptian healing ingredients! There were jars and vessels, small bowls and tiny boxes, filled with all manner of strange things. Small hieroglyphic labels were affixed to each of them. Bat dung, crocodile urine, lettuce milk, honey, fly dung, ostrich dung, scorpion venom, lotus seeds, hippopotamus dung, ibis dung. (Who knew so many different types of dung had healing properties? Although I must confess to being grateful that the spell I was working with did not require any.)

I removed the three ingredients I needed and carefully poured them into one of the mortars, then began stirring it with the pestle. When it was well mixed, I went back to the statue to read the rest of the instructions. (Honestly, they should have placed the statues closer to the workspace, for efficiency's sake.) I knelt at Horus's feet to read what came next.

Using a new reed, dip it into the prepared ink, then write the following spell on the inside of a clay bowl. When the spell has dried, pour water from the healing bath into the bowl. Swirl nine times, then have the patient drink it.

I glanced over at the poor unconscious form of Sefu. I wasn't sure how I was going to get him to drink it, but I'd cross that bridge when I came to it. I got back to my feet and returned to the worktable. There was an entire stack of unused clay bowls on one shelf, so I helped myself to one of those. Next I searched in a drawer for an unused reed. The hardest part was remembering the beastly spell. I'd write three words, then forget it and have to return to the statue to refresh my memory. I finally got so vexed that I carried the whole thing over and worked at the foot of the statue, just to save time.

At last it was finished. But how long did it need to dry, I wondered?

A shuffling step outside in the hall drew my attention. I looked at the door, holding my breath to see if whoever it was would come in here. I was not doing anything wrong, I reminded myself. Besides, I was Rekhet. Surely that stood for *something*.

An old man came to a stop just inside the doorway. He was dressed in a traditional peasant robe and held a staff in his right hand. That's when I noticed that his eyes were cloudy and he held his head at an alert angle.

"Hullo," I said, not wanting to startle him.

He turned his head in the direction of my voice, confirming my suspicion that he was blind.

"Greetings," he said, coming more fully into the room. "Are you the new *senau* priestess, then?"

"Oh no! Not at all. In fact, I'm hoping no one minds that I'm in here."

"Are you ill, then?"

"No, my, er, friend is." I looked over my shoulder at Sefu, then back at the old man. "Actually, he's a pet, not a person, but he belonged to Gadji—I mean, the young pharaoh—so I don't think the gods will mind, do you? I mean, they used to

317

mummify monkeys, once upon a time, so surely they won't think it wrong if I'm trying to heal one?"

"I should not think so," he said, shuffling farther into the room.

"Oh, here, let me help you." I hurried forward, gently took his elbow, and steered him to the bed next to Sefu's. "Is there something I can get for you? Or help you prepare?" I asked.

His face creased in puzzlement. "Prepare?"

"You know." I gestured toward my face, then realized he couldn't see me. "For your eyes," I whispered.

"Ah." His face cleared. "These old eyes can wait. Tell me what you have tried so far on your small friend."

I told him of the ink and the spell I'd written on the inside of the bowl. "Only—only he's unconscious and I can't figure out how to get the potion into him."

"Perhaps I could be of some help with that." He put his staff down on the bed. "If you were to place him in my arms and show me where his mouth is, I could hold it open for you, and then we might get some down his throat?"

"Oh yes, that would be perfect," I said. "Thank you so much!" I hurried over to Sefu's bedside, gathered him up in my arms, then carried him over to the old man. "Here you go," I said. "Hold your arms closer together—he's very small," I explained.

The old man took the monkey gently in his arms, cradling

the head in the crook of his elbow. "Show me where his mouth is."

"Here." I placed my hand on his, then carefully guided it to Sefu's cheeks.

"So if I squeeze like this, does his mouth open?"

"Yes! That's perfect. Hold it just like that." I hurried to fetch the bowl. I poured water from the healing bath into the bowl and swirled it carefully nine times. Then I returned to the old man and tentatively began dribbling the potion down Sefu's throat. It was painfully slow going. The monkey's mouth was small and the bowl quite large. It took forever to get all of it down his gullet, but at last we were finished. "That's the last drop," I said, then put the bowl down.

"That is good, for I fear his stomach might pop if we were to give him any more." The man reached down and very gently patted Sefu's stomach, then held the monkey out to me.

"Thank you ever so much," I said, taking Sefu from him. I stared down at the monkey. "I have no idea how long it will take to work, do you?"

The old man shook his head.

"Would you like me to help you now? I could, you know. All you have to do is tell me what you need and I can mix it up for you. Or I can see if there is a seeing spell on the Thoth statue. Or perhaps it would be the Horus statue," I mused.

"No, child, I am fine, but thank you for your offer."

An uncomfortable feeling came over me. "You didn't come here to be healed, did you?"

He smiled and shook his head, and as I looked at his cloudy eyes, I knew. He was the Seer of Maat. It made sense in a perfectly ancient Egyptian sort of way—in order to see the truth, you had to be blind to the distractions of the physical world.

Before I could confirm my suspicion, there was a strange rumbling sound. I looked down in time to see Sefu struggle to sit up, and then a veritable gusher of water erupted from his mouth.

"It sounds as if it's working," the old man said dryly.

"It is!" I said. I was so happy, I didn't even mind having to clean up what Sefu had just spewed forth. However, by the time I was done, the old man had disappeared.

I felt bad about that and hoped I hadn't offended him. However, I was thrilled with my success. Before long, Sefu began to chatter quietly to himself, and I knew he would make it. I lifted him in my arms and carried him off to show Safiya. It wasn't exactly her brother, but it was a hopeful sign.

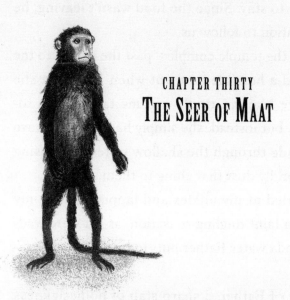

CHAPTER THIRTY
THE SEER OF MAAT

THE NEXT MORNING the word came down that the Seer of
Maat was ready to address the wedjadeen. We ate a hurried
breakfast (me feeding most of mine to Sefu, who was raven-
ous). When we were done, Safiya arrived and announced
that we'd need to undergo rites of purification before being
allowed into the presence of the Seer of Maat. She headed
for the door and motioned for us to follow.

"But what about Sefu?" I asked. "Can he come, too?"

Safiya shook her head. "I am sorry, but no. Nothing made
from animals may pass into the birthing room."

Birthing room! That part sounded promising. I didn't
think they'd execute us in something called the birthing

room. I told Sefu to stay. Since the food wasn't leaving, he showed no inclination to follow us.

Safiya led us to the temple complex, past the pylons to the sacred lake. I had a horrible moment when I thought she was going to have Major Grindle and me take a bath together in the lake, but instead, she simply bade us to remove our shoes and wade through the shallow waters, cleansing our feet of the worldly dust that clung to them.

The water swirled at my ankles and lapped against my shins. There was a faint tingling sensation, as if I were wading through the soda water Father puts in his whiskey sometimes.

At the thought of Father, a sharp stab of homesickness sliced through me, and I realized I would have given just about anything to be back in London, in our museum, with Mother and Father and even Henry all around me. I refused to entertain the idea that I would never see them again.

I stepped out of the sacred lake onto a square of pure white linen, then into a pair of sandals made from reeds. Two lector priests showed Major Grindle to his changing room, while Safiya and another girl escorted me to mine.

Inside the small changing room, I saw that they had a large basin of water, presumably from the sacred lake. I stepped out of my gown, then stood shivering in my petticoat—not from cold, mind you, but from sheer nerves. They dipped linen cloths in the water and made as if to wash me with them. I leaped aside. "I can do it myself!" I said. Honestly, I hadn't had anyone wash me since I was two years old! I snatched the wet cloth from Safiya's hand and began scrubbing at my face and neck. When they were clean, I dipped my arms into the basin up to the elbows and scrubbed some more. I insisted that both girls turn around before I would wash anything else.

When they had, I did a quick, thorough job of it, then hastily slipped into the pure linen shift they had laid out for me. I hesitated for a moment, then searched for a pocket of some sort. I daren't be without my Babel stone. Not when so much could be at stake. Surely I needed to understand every word spoken.

But the wretched shift had no pockets. In the end, I decided to stick the stone between my foot and the sandal, and I'd just be sure to shuffle my feet. Before I could tell the girls to turn around, a strange sound came from far off, as if someone had dropped hundreds of dried peas onto the floor.

"That is the summons. It is time." Safiya straightened my shift and fussed with my hair one last time. She dismissed the other girl, then came and put her hands on my shoulders. "No matter what happens, I know that you did all in your power to help my brother. I, as well as the gods, will always be grateful for that." Then she kissed me on both cheeks, took me by the hand, and led me out into the hall to the doorway of the birthing room. Major Grindle was already there and waiting for me, a lector priest on either side of him. He looked quite different in his white vestal robes, but no less commanding a presence. His wedjat eye showed quite plainly. All for the better, I thought.

"I am not allowed to enter," Safiya said. "Nor are they." She indicated the other servants. "You are to go on from here alone."

My heart was beating so rapidly, it made my voice thin and a bit wobbly. "Thank you for everything. Take care of Sefu, will you?"

Safiya bowed low, and Major Grindle offered me his arm. "Shall we, Miss Throckmorton?"

How could he be so calm? "I suppose so," I said, taking his arm. Then together, we stepped into the birthing room.

The entire place was thick with incense, and I began coughing at once. "What do we do now?" I asked, waving my hand frantically in front of my face, trying to clear the air.

"I believe we proceed to the door on the far side, where the others await."

We made our way to the far door. When we reached it,

Major Grindle paused just long enough to give my hand a reassuring pat, and then we stepped into the inner sanctum.

The room was dark as night, or so I thought. As I blinked rapidly, my eyes adjusted and I saw that there were actually small braziers burning throughout the chamber. The room felt crowded. Nine black-robed wedjadeen with bare heads stood in a semicircle facing a stone statue of Maat. In front of them were the three *sem* priests. As Major Grindle and I entered, they silently parted to make a path for us. Clearly we were meant to stand before the statue.

The high priest bowed formally, then turned to the statue and began reading from the scroll in his hand. "These two are brought before you on grave charges, O Seer of Truth and Wisdom. We bring them before you so you may see justice served.

"The girl is charged with knowing that which she should not know, and for that we have sentenced her to drink the Wine of Forgetting. However, it is claimed by one of the Hathors that she is Rekhet and therefore one of us, and knowing is no crime for her."

He waited a long moment, as if expecting the statue to say something. When it didn't he cleared his throat and continued. "The man has greater charges against him. In addition to knowing what he should not know, he has also laid hands upon the pharaoh and used magic that is forbidden to any but a Weret Hekau. For this we have determined he should die. However"—the priest's face contorted, as if the next words pained him greatly—"it appears that he is marked with the sign of Horus, and the girl claims this makes him wedjadeen, and so that which he knows and has done is not forbidden to him; therefore his life should not be forfeited. We await your justice."

"Um, excuse me," I said in a tiny voice.

The high priest looked at me, incredulous that I'd been so brazen as to speak.

I ignored him. Justice was, after all, at stake. "Don't forget to tell him that I returned the Emerald Tablet. I should get points for that. And that Major Grindle almost got himself killed trying to rescue the pharaoh from the Serpents of Chaos. Also, we need to ask him if having me return the tablet was enough to get Awi Bubu forgiven and his exile lifted."

The priest stared at me with his mouth hanging open, jumping when the statue spoke. "Is that all?" it asked. I recognized the old man's voice, the one who had helped me with Sefu.

"Yes. Sir."

"Be quiet!" the high priest hissed, and I stopped talking, mostly because I had said everything I needed to say.

The room fell silent then, and a heaviness descended over all of us, like a thick, invisible blanket.

At last, the statue began to speak again. I looked briefly around, trying to see how the old man was doing that. "This girl has been sent to us by our gods, to help us heal the great breach that tore us asunder when our world fell apart. She and the man are a reminder to us that it is not we alone who must bear the burden of protecting our world. That we have brothers in this fight against Chaos."

To say that a shocked silence filled the holy of holies would be a gross understatement. Major Grindle and I exchanged a look, his entire face alight with good humor.

"When the heretic Akhenaten tried to replace our gods with his own, and the covenant was entered into between the priests of Egypt and the gods they served, we were all as one. We dedicated our lives to serving them, and when the gods left our lands for the West, we guarded those gifts they left behind until a time when we could restore the One True Pharaoh to his rightful throne.

"Wave after wave of foreigners have ruled our lands since then, from the Persians to Alexander, the Ptolemies, the

Greeks, and the Romans, and through each of them the wedjadeen have endured. However, a great schism occured, and we have been weakened ever since."

The high priest—indeed, all the *sem* priests—looked sorely confused. "What schism, O Seer of Truth?"

"When the pharaoh Ptolemy put forth the call to bring all the sacred items from our temples and house them in the Alexandrian library, it was his intention to centralize the power of our land. However, he, like Alexander and others before him, wished to bring his foreign gods and marry them with our own. This, as we all know, was an abomination. We did what we could, spiriting our most powerful and sacred relics of the gods into places of hiding. We got many, but not all. In spite of our efforts, some made their way to the great library."

Awi Bubu had explained to me that the wedjadeen had sent a few of their lesser, least powerful artifacts to the collection at the Alexandrian library but that they had kept the most powerful artifacts of the gods and hidden them away in the desert.

"But it would be a poor commander who tried to win a war with only a single tactic. When it became clear that some of our holy treasures had slipped through our fingers, we vowed to see our own wedjadeen installed in the library. We were not willing to let even the lesser artifacts fall into the hands of unlearned or unscrupulous men. A small band of wedjadeen was chosen to accompany these lesser artifacts and become librarians at this new place. These men were charged with watching over the artifacts in the library and keeping them safe. Their sole charge was the artifacts and texts contained within the library. In that way, we could keep our covenant with our gods and watch over all that was in our keeping."

I couldn't help but glance over at Major Grindle to see how he was taking this. I needn't have worried. His face was aglow with hope and longing and a shocking hunger.

"These sacred librarians would guard the artifacts housed there, be certain that no one else used their power, and spirit them away when the opportunity arose. And that worked for a time. We were able to keep watch over the artifacts and occasionally slip one to our brothers outside the library, who would take it to protect with the others.

"And then Caesar came. He burned the city, and the fire reached the walls of the library. There was much damage, though the library itself still stood. But it was a warning to us. A warning that the chaotic forces of the outside world were once again beating upon our shore. We redoubled our forces at the museum, but it was not enough.

"When the library fell for the last time, at the proclamation of Emperor Theodosius, it was these librarians who tried to save the last remaining artifacts in the library. Many lost their lives to the rioting mob and had the very artifacts they were trying to save wrenched from their dying hands.

"This man is one of us, descended from our brothers who had become lost to us when the library was destroyed and the librarians overrun by those sent to destroy it."

Even the strict discipline of the wedjadeen couldn't hold back the wave of surprise that rippled through the room.

"That is the Rekhet's destiny that the Hathor spoke of, to rejoin that which had been torn asunder, to allow the two halves to be made whole once again. For only when we are whole will we be able to face Chaos in the fullness of our power. That is the role this young miss has played. And that is the role Awi Bubu has played."

"The contending of Horus and Set is never-ending, and even now the forces of Set are gathering, growing in power and strength. Do you truly believe the struggle was fought in Egypt alone? That chaos and evil have been contained within our borders?"

"B-but, O Seer of Truth, what of our young pharaoh?" Fenuku asked.

"Do not fear. You will find him. Even now, more warriors of Horus arrive. You will need them to retrieve the Son of Re."

More warriors of Horus? Whom could he mean? But the

statue fell silent then, and after a long moment, it became clear that it would not speak anymore that day. I glanced over at Major Grindle, whose stiff upper lip was curled into a gleeful grin. "An interesting turn of events, wouldn't you say, Miss Throckmorton?"

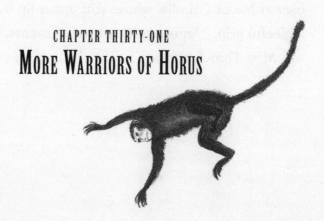

As we filed out of the inner recesses of the temple, a great commotion reached our ears. "The additional warriors of Horus must have arrived," Khalfani said.

"Who are they?" I asked, trying to keep up with his and the major's longer strides.

"I have no idea." He sounded faintly aggrieved.

We stepped out of the temple courtyard into the camp, a handful of riders heading our way. Three were garbed in the traditional robes of the wedjadeen, but two were distinctly European.

"Kazimerz! Gunter!" Major Grindle yelled, waving his arm. He gave a short bark of laughter. "But of course."

Unable to help myself, I reached up and rubbed my eyes, but my vision didn't waver. There, indeed, rode Jadwiga and Rumpf into camp, accompanied by three wedjadeen scouts.

The sight of them produced a giant lump of homesickness in the middle of my throat. I'd been trying so hard not to think of Mother or Father or Isis. A small hiccup of a sob escaped before I clamped my mouth shut. Wait a moment. "What do you mean 'of course,' Major?"

"What?" he said distractedly.

"When you saw Mother's assistants, you said, 'of course,' as if it made perfect sense that they were here."

Khalfani sent the major a sidelong glance. "They are two of yours, are they not, Major?"

"In a manner of speaking," he said. With a sheepish look, Major Grindle turned to me. "They belong to the Brotherhood," he said.

I gaped at him. I couldn't help it. Then I turned to look at Jadwiga and Rumpf with new eyes. They were Chosen Keepers? Descendants of the Alexandrian librarians?

"What . . . how . . . do you mean—"

"I should clarify that," the major said. "They are members of the *International* Brotherhood of the Chosen Keepers, rather than the British branch. Does that help clear things up?"

"Best go explain it to them," I said, pointing at the

wedjadeen who had collected around the men's horses, swords drawn.

Major Grindle hurried forward. "No, no! They're with us."

Khalfani joined him, explaining to the wedjadeen that the Brotherhood was indeed an ally, if not an actual part, of the wedjadeen organization. His poor men looked as confused as I felt.

When I finally reached the small group gathered around the newcomers, I was struck by shyness and hung back a bit.

"How did you find us?" the major asked the two archaeologists.

Rumpf threw a quick glance at me, and then I had my sixth or seventh shock of the day. "We followed the girl's cat."

"Her cat?"

"Isis?" All my fear and longing and utter homesickness crowded in my throat so that I ended up squealing her name.

"*Ja,* your little black cat." Jadwiga reached into his coat and the wedjadeen scout closest to him raised his spear.

"Lower your weapon," Khalfani bellowed at the scout.

"But, sir!"

"Lower it. These men are now our allies."

The scout scowled but retracted his spear so that Jadwiga could reach into his coat and pull Isis from the depths of his jacket. "She got tired of walking. It is a long way for such little paws."

Dear Jadwiga! His voice sounded as if every one of those steps had bruised his heart.

As I reached for her, she twisted gracefully and launched herself from Jadwiga's lap into my arms. I caught her and hugged her close, reveling in the soft silkiness of her fur, the fierce rumble of her purr. She was as happy to see me as I was to see her.

"Is that true, sir?" Rumpf glanced sideways at the scouts. "Are we working with these men now?"

"Yes, it's all true, and have I got a whopper of a story to tell you." Major Grindle rubbed his hands together in anticipation.

"Yes, well, before you do, I need to let you know that we've found where the Serpents of Chaos are hiding."

A slow smile spread across Major Grindle's face, and he turned to Khalfani. "Which means they have also found the boy."

The men dismounted and Jadwiga clucked and removed his coat, placing it around my shoulders. "Why do they have you running around in your petticoat?"

If I hadn't had my arms full of purring cat, I would have hugged him. "It's not a petticoat—it's a ceremonial shift. I'll explain later. How is Mother?" I was worried for her and how she was taking my disappearance.

He tried to protect me from her misery, but it simply

wasn't in his nature to be cheerful. "She is doing all right. She visits the police station and the consulate offices twice a day, haranguing that they should do more to find you."

"She notified your father right away," Rumpf said. "I believe he left the next morning. He should arrive in Luxor soon."

Before I could ask for more details, we were all pulled into the great swirling commotion that surrounded the newcomers' arrival and the announcement of the wedjadeen's newfound alliance with the Brotherhood.

Jadwiga looked down at me. "Are you ever going to let go of your cat?" he asked. I couldn't be certain, but I think his mouth held the faintest hint of a smile.

"No," I said, looking down to where Isis was purring contentedly and kneading in my lap. Her tiny claws pricked at my stomach through the thin material of my dress, but I didn't mind—I was too happy just to have her back. The truth was, I refused to let go of Isis the entire time, even when Sefu came to see what was going on. I decided that if the wedjadeen and the Chosen Keepers could learn to get along, so could the monkey and my cat.

Once all the wedjadeen had been told of the new developments, they were dismissed and Major Grindle, Jadwiga,

Rumpf, and I were summoned to the *mudir*'s tent with the soldiers and Weret Hekau. Khalfani and the *mudir* were already poring over a map. Khalfani looked up as we entered the tent. "Can you show us on this map where the followers of Set are?"

"Ja," Jadwiga said, stepping around me and going to the table. The rest of us followed, eager to see the exact location. Jadwiga peered at the map a moment, then plunked a thick finger down on an intersection of streets in Luxor. "Right here."

Major Grindle looked at him. "Right in the middle of the black market. It makes sense, as most of those men either have worked for Chaos in the past or benefit greatly from their traffic in stolen antiquities."

"How do you know this?" Khalfani asked.

"That is part of our work in the Brotherhood, keeping an eye on cursed artifacts and preventing the dangerous ones from falling into the hands of Chaos," Major Grindle explained. "Many of the black-market men are your people. Do you have any idea how many are sympathetic to Chaos?"

"Most likely all of them," Khalfani said. "There are not many occupations here that pay what selling *antikahs* to tourists pays. You cannot blame them. They have families to feed. It makes no difference to them who takes the treasure from their land."

Major Grindle met Khalfani's accusing gaze steadily. "No, I do not blame them."

"But don't they fear the Eyes of Horus?" I asked. "Aren't they afraid of what you'll do to them for siding with others?"

"Not if they think the others will win," the *mudir* said.

Honestly, you'd think the leader of an organization would show a little more confidence than that!

"So how many are there?" Major Grindle asked.

Rumpf shrugged. "It was hard to get an exact count because there was so much coming and going," he explained to the others.

"And the boy? Did you see a young boy?" Khalfani asked.

Rumpf shook his head. "There is something else you should know. The British officials are blaming the locals for the girl's disappearance. They are rounding up your people and questioning them, rather roughly. This has stirred up quite a bit of resentment."

Fenuku slammed his hand down on the table. "I say we storm the area," he said. "Bring destruction down on their heads." I wasn't sure if he meant the heads of the Serpents of Chaos or the British officials.

Khalfani threw him a wry glance. "I fear they will slit the boy's throat at the first signs of attack. Even if they do not, there is too great a chance he could be harmed in the fighting."

Major Grindle studied the map. "We need to be more subtle than that."

Khalfani looked up. "What are you thinking?"

"We need to eliminate their home-field advantage."

"And how do you suggest we do that?" Fenuku challenged.

The major looked up and met his gaze. "By luring them out." He turned to the *mudir*. "They have no doubt learned that the tablet we gave them was a fake. Its magic only lasted until the moon set that night. Send them a message saying that the girl and I were not the ones they needed to deal with in order to retrieve the tablet. That you are the ones who hold it in your possession and that they must deal with you. You offer them a second chance at the tablet, in exchange for the boy."

Khalfani nodded slowly as the plan took shape in his mind. "Yes, that would draw them out. And the best time to strike would be when they are transporting the hostage to the exchange point. That is when we will strike."

"Exactly," Major Grindle said.

"Very well. We move out tonight, under cover of darkness. We will take ourselves to the stronghold at Karnak and plan the rest of the operation there, where we will have greater access to their comings and goings."

CHAPTER THIRTY-TWO
ON THE MARCH

WE LEFT QERERT IHY as the moon reached its zenith, its silvery glow spilling across the landscape and giving us some light to travel by. I tried to coax Isis up into my lap to ride on my horse with me, but she was having none of it. She insisted on traveling behind us on her own four paws. The wedjadeen's blood was running high and they were filled with rising hopes that they could retrieve their pharaoh. And if hope failed them, they had plenty of grim determination to see them through.

We had timed it so we would arrive in Luxor under the cover of nightfall. Our horses slowed as the city drew near, and Khalfani had us detour around the city proper and any possible scouts Chaos might have posted. We came in through the East Gate of the Karnak Temple and silently filed past the sacred lake to the small Temple of Osiris that abutted the south girdle wall.

Hashim dismounted, then came over to speak to me. "We leave our horses here," he explained, helping me dismount. "A handful of servants shall lead them just out of sight. They will set up a Bedouin camp, which will explain our presence should anyone notice."

"Are we going to camp here in the temple grounds?" I asked, looking around for signs of habitable space.

He flashed me a quick grin. "Not exactly."

The wedjadeen unloaded their horses and gave last-minute instructions to those charged with setting up the decoy camp. As that group disappeared out the East Gate, the rest of the wedjadeen drew apart to let Khalfani and Baruti come forward. They entered the small Osiris temple, and the rest of the men followed them. As they disappeared inside, I turned to Hashim in surprise. "We're going to sleep *inside* the temple?" I asked, faintly shocked at the idea.

"Not exactly," he said again, then motioned for me to precede him.

After checking to be certain Isis was still behind me, I followed the others to a hatch of some sort near the back of the temple. Khalfani and Major Grindle pried it open to reveal a sunken staircase. I glanced at Hashim, who only smiled and took a lit torch from the fellow handing them out.

Ever curious, Isis slipped in front of me to sniff at the passageway. After a slight pause, she disappeared down the hatch. Comforted by this, I followed the others down the deep, narrow stairs and tried to ignore the light flickering eerily on the walls. As I stepped into the small antechamber at the foot of the steps, the men used their torches to light the oil lamps positioned around the room.

We were in a vast underground chamber that stretched out as far as my eye could see. Dark, shadowy shapes danced along the walls, and I shuddered. Those were not mere shadows, but whether they were *mut* or *akhu* or simply remnants of the gods or earlier wedjadeen who had passed this way, I could not tell.

Major Grindle nearly broke his neck trying to see everything at once. His face was alight with wonder. Rumpf's face shone, too. Jadwiga merely looked as if he expected the entire thing to come down on our heads any moment.

"Does this run the entire length of the Great Temple?" I asked Hashim.

"Nearly."

Small rooms opened up off the larger chamber. Some of them held supplies, such as jars of oil, honey, and grain. Others contained a jumble of artifacts and furniture, while

still others held roll after roll of scrolls and papyruses.

"Is this where you plan to hide the Emerald Tablet?" I asked Khalfani.

"No." He laughed. "This is much too close to others and much too easy to find. There is a mountain, hidden deep in the desert, that contains many artifacts of the gods."

"It wouldn't do much good to hide a map *with* the treasure it leads to, would it?" I asked, puzzled by this strategy.

Khalfani gave me a sly glance. "Did I say we would hide the tablet there?"

Come to think of it, he hadn't.

"This place that you see is one of our sanctuaries," Khalfani explained. "A place for us to gather away from prying eyes or to wait out unpleasantness."

"Marvelous," Major Grindle breathed. "You can go to ground here until trouble blows over or pursuers give up the chase."

"It is also an excellent place from which to launch an attack. Come." Khalfani led us to a large table in the back. He retrieved a map from his saddle pouch and unrolled it on the table, anchoring it in place with small stones on each corner.

"Gamal, Rashid, I want you to scout out the black-market area. See if you can find any signs of where they might hide a valuable prisoner. Also try to determine how many men are loyal to the followers of Set." They bowed, then left the room.

Khalfani turned back to the map. "The question is, how do we let them know we have an exchange we'd like to offer? Even if I were to march down their street myself, they would not know me or my face and I would most likely not gain an audience with the man in charge. At least, not alive," he amended. "Do they know your men by sight?" he asked Major Grindle.

The major glanced at Jadwiga and Rumpf. "They do not, and I am loath to have them break their cover. Years have gone into building these identities for them."

"They'd talk to me, wouldn't they?" I asked, my voice sounding very high and thin in the cavernous room.

"I'll go," Major Grindle said, as if he hadn't heard me.

"You?" Fenuku asked, clearly suspicious.

"Me. I'm the only one they've seen, other than Miss Throckmorton, and I'm sure we're all in agreement that she is not marching into their midst."

"Agreed," Khalfani, Jadwiga, and Rumpf all said at the same time. Fenuku was the only one who kept silent.

"But sir," I said. "You've already thwarted them once. Won't they kill you on sight?"

Khalfani studied Major Grindle a long moment. "Not if he carries the Orb of Ra with him."

Major Grindle's face lit up like my brother Henry's on Christmas morning. Honestly, if I didn't know better, I'd think he was just here for the toys.

"You cannot be serious!" Fenuku sputtered. "Hand over one of our most precious artifacts to the *Inglaize?*"

Baruti laid a hand on Fenuku's arm to calm him. "He must have some means of ensuring their cooperation. Besides, we are brothers now, remember?"

But it was clear from the look on Fenuku's face that he would never call the *Inglaize* "brother."

"When could you be ready to deliver the message?" Khalfani asked.

"Immediately, of course," Major Grindle said.

CHAPTER THIRTY-THREE
A NEW WRINKLE

THERE WAS A FAIR AMOUNT OF DISCUSSION as to what Major Grindle should carry with him into the heart of the enemy. "The Orb of Ra, most definitely," he and Khalfani agreed. It was pistols and knives they were in disagreement over.

"They are not going to let me waltz in there carrying a pistol," the major pointed out.

"We do not know this. It is worth trying to slip one in," Khalfani said.

"Then we risk losing what little trust our white-flag venture might gain us."

Khalfani sighed and I almost stepped in to tell him it was hopeless. I was sure that Major Grindle's skewed sense of sportsmanship had much to do with his decision, and how could one argue with something as odd as that?

In the end, it was decided that he would walk in carrying the orb so they knew he meant business. Of course, this necessitated a whole new debate: carry it concealed or out in plain sight?

Khalfani argued for plain sight. That way, everyone who saw the artifact, even if he didn't understand its power, would know that it was very valuable. It would ensure the major got to the top levels of the organization quickly. Second, Grindle could access it more easily should he need to use it.

"Do you know the proper sequence to tap in order to activate it?" I asked.

Khalfani shot me a glance. "Our Rekhet never ceases to surprise with the vast scope of her knowledge."

"Tell me about it," the major muttered.

"There are many sequences that can be used, but the one to emit a controlled burst is this." Khalfani's fingers twitched out a sequence over the orb's surface, careful never to actually touch the orb itself.

I leaned as far forward as I could without tipping over and watched as he went through the sequence a second time.

Major Grindle nodded. "Got it." He repeated the maneuver three more times (also careful not to let his fingers touch the orb) while Khalfani watched. Then it was time to go.

"Will they bring a horse around for me?" the major asked.

"No," Khalfani said, eyes sparkling. "We have a better way to travel unobserved." He led Major Grindle to one of the far doorways on the south side of the chamber. No one told me not to follow, so I did.

Khalfani stopped in front of the doorway. "This is an underground path that leads directly to the Luxor Temple. It mirrors the Avenue of the Sphinxes."

"By Jove!" Major Grindle was agog at this marvel. "You can come and go between the two temples with no one the wiser."

"Exactly so. It will bring you up just outside the Luxor Temple, and then it is but a short distance to the market area."

I meant to wait up for Major Grindle's return, because honestly, who could sleep at a time like this?

Apparently, I could. I was absolutely knackered after the long march through the desert. The minute I collapsed onto a bedroll, Isis hurried to my side, as if she, too, was wanting a bit of a nap. With her warm presence cuddled next to me, I closed my eyes and slept like the dead.

I was awakened by a flurry of excited voices. Someone called out, "He's coming!" I sat up and pushed my hair out of my eyes, disoriented for a moment by the dark chamber and the flickering torches. It took me half a minute to realize I wasn't stuck in a nightmare involving the Arcane Order of the Black Sun and was, instead, stuck in a rather shocking bit of reality.

Wondering where my cat had gotten to, I pushed to my feet and straightened my frock just as Major Grindle strode into the chamber. Jadwiga, Rumpf, Khalfani, and the others pressed around him, hungry for news of what had happened.

I hurried over so as not to miss out.

"It is exactly as Jadwiga and Rumpf reported. The market area runs the entire length of the street and spreads out to include the streets on either side. It is a veritable rabbit warren of crumbling buildings, dilapidated shop fronts, and men with hardened eyes and no smiles. It's hard to say how many live there. It could be one hundred; it could be three hundred. There's no telling."

Khalfani swore in Arabic. At least, I think he was swearing. He sounded an awful lot like Father when he is swearing. "Then we cannot risk slipping in and rescuing him by stealth?"

The major shook his head. "I don't think so. Not without risking many of the women and children who also live in that area." Major Grindle's face looked drawn and grim. I could not help but feel that a second shoe was about to drop.

"Did they agree to the exchange? Did they let you see the boy?"

Slowly, Major Grindle raised his eyes and looked straight at me. My stomach dropped all the way down to my toes as I prepared myself for his next words.

"They would not allow me to see the two prisoners."

"Two prisoners?" Khalfani asked.

The major's sorrowful gaze never left my face. "I'm afraid they have taken a second prisoner. Your mother," he said gently.

My mother. His words reverberated in my mind, so horrible that I could hardly absorb them.

"When they could find no sign of you or me, and none of the locals they questioned would give them any information, they decided to up the ante in an effort to lure us out of hiding."

I think I actually swayed on my feet, and then Jadwiga was there, his big solid presence at my back like a fortress. I let myself lean back against him, just the teeniest bit. Von Braggenschnott was sweet on Mother, I reminded myself. Surely he wouldn't hurt her.

Khalfani's face was full of sympathy. "Were you able to verify this with your own eyes?"

The major gave a brief shake of his head. "I was, however, able to hear them speak, and I recognized both their voices."

"What about the exchange?" Khalfani repeated. "Did they agree to that?"

"In a manner of speaking, yes." Major Grindle slowly pulled his eyes from mine and turned to Khalfani. "They agreed to the exchange. However, because of the first botched attempt, von Braggenschnott said that the price had gone up. The new price for releasing Gadji and Mrs. Throckmorton is the Emerald Tablet and the girl. He wants Miss Throckmorton as part of the deal."

There was a moment of dead silence that was filled by the thundering of my heart. Me?

"That is impossible," Khalfani said, and I began to breathe again. I hadn't realized I'd been holding my breath, but the truth was, I had no idea what my actual standing was with the wedjadeen. I'd been half afraid they would have said, *Certainly. Here she is, and thank you.*

"I'm glad we agree," Major Grindle said.

Fenuku threw me a look that said he did not agree. "Then what do you propose we do to get the Son of Re back?"

"We will alter our plans, that is all. We never intended to let them get as far as the exchange point anyway. We will continue with our plan to intercept them on the way to the exchange and they will never even have to see our Rekhet," explained Khalfani.

Major Grindle cleared his throat, and Khalfani scowled. "What?"

"They have a few more conditions. They will need proof that this tablet is not a fake." His old cheeks pinkened slightly with embarrassment at this reminder of his earlier trick.

A brief smile flickered across Khalfani's face. "Do not worry on that score. Our magic will hold better than yours."

"And they will have scouts in place to ensure Miss Throckmorton is indeed part of the exchange before they will step foot outside their compound."

Jadwiga shouted out, "Impossible!" with such force that it made his mustache quiver.

Khalfani swore again and Fenuku looked almost pleased. "They are not fools," he pointed out.

"No." Major Grindle fixed him with a hard stare. "But they are evil."

Fenuku had the grace to look away.

"We will have to risk storming the market after all."

"But we still have no idea where they are keeping the prisoners," Major Grindle reminded him. "You can be certain they were moved immediately after my departure."

"Not to mention untold innocents may be harmed," Khalfani murmured.

"I am not so certain anyone there can truly be called an innocent," the major said.

"True. But not all are followers of these men of Set."

"We can't risk it." My high voice cut through all their deeper ones. "We were going to trick them anyway; now we'll just add one more element to the trick—I'll be in place long enough for their scout to observe me."

Major Grindle and Jadwiga started to argue, but I held up my hand. "It's *my* mother they're holding. And I feel partially responsible for Gadji's capture, although it was not all my fault." I cast a sideways look at Fenuku to be sure he heard that part. "All I have to do is be in position long enough for their advance scout to spot me, then give the signal to the rest of the Serpents of Chaos that everything is in order, correct?"

Major Grindle nodded slowly. "Correct."

"Or," I said, a new thought occurring to me, "we could do what they did when you asked to see Mother and Gadji. Just let them hear my voice."

Khalfani and the major exchanged a look.

"There's got to be tons of places where I can hide in that big temple. Then, when they show up, I'll just shout out a hello, and they'll know I'm there."

Major Grindle stared at the map and stroked his chin. "That could work, I suppose."

"Of course it could. And with so many wedjadeen for reinforcement, what could go wrong?" I asked brightly.

"Everything" was Jadwiga's morose reply.

CHAPTER THIRTY-FOUR
BAU BAU,
BLACK CAT

THE NEXT FEW HOURS WERE SPENT in a frenzy of men poring over maps and plotting out every possible route from the black market to the Luxor Temple. They wanted to allow for all possibilities, and who could blame them?

A second group of men were busy in one of the smaller chambers, fashioning a new faux tablet. Major Grindle was hanging over their shoulders, drinking in every word. Normally, that's where I would have been, too, but for some reason, the magic wasn't holding my interest. I was too filled with a gnawing restlessness that had me pacing the long length of the chamber and practically clawing the walls.

That's where Baruti found me. "Peace, Rekhet," he said.

"I am at peace," I told him as I turned and began my umpteenth lap of the chamber.

Baruti fell into step beside me. "You are making the others on edge, child. They do not like to see the Rekhet so nervous. Even your cat has given up on you."

I looked behind me to see that Isis was no longer following. Indeed, she was no longer in sight, apparently having decided to go off and explore one of the many chambers and underground passages.

"Well, the Rekhet's mother is one of the hostages, so forgive me if I'm not a cool, calm warrior like the others are."

Baruti raised his eyebrows. "Come, let us sit down over here. Perhaps it would help if you talked. And talking would certainly make me feel less dizzy."

Perhaps he was right. Perhaps if I were to sit calmly, my pulse would stop racing.

He led me to a far corner of the chamber where thick pillows and a pile of blankets had been shoved against the wall. He creaked down onto the floor, and I joined him. The thick, cool stone of the wall felt comforting at my back. Surely many such battles and skirmishes had been planned here—and won, since the wedjadeen were still around.

"What troubles you, child?" Baruti's face was kind and concerned and I was suddenly violently homesick for Awi Bubu and Lord Wigmere.

"It's the Serpents of Chaos, sir," I whispered. "They always seem to get the upper hand."

"Ah. Chaos," Baruti repeated, leaning back against the wall. There was a long moment of silence, and then he spoke again. "Chaos is not always evil, child. Sometimes it is simply chaos. And remember, chaos has many sides. Much good has come from chaos. The world itself, the gods—both were formed from chaos. It is only when men turn it to their own ends, or create it on purpose, that chaos flirts with being evil. But even then, it can be turned to good, for that is the very nature of chaos. Neither good nor bad in and of itself, merely . . . chaotic."

Isis came wandering back from her explorations and crawled into my lap.

Baruti reached out to pet her, and she let him. "Even your cat has many sides. To you she is a beloved pet; to those she hunts, a terrifying predator. To the gods she is a vessel into which they can pour their will to have influence over the physical world."

"She's what?" I asked.

Baruti looked surprised. "You did not know she was a *bau*?"

I stared at Isis, purring contentedly under the old priest's gnarled hand. "I guess not, since I don't even know what a *bau* is."

"It is a divine messenger sent by the gods to lend aid. Or, very occasionally, harm."

"You mean my cat has been sent by the gods?"

"I believe so, yes. She is no ordinary cat."

I thought back to when Isis had first walked into my life. For that's exactly what had happened. One day, she was just . . . there. I'd been only seven years old and had just begun visiting the museum with my parents and experiencing the shivers and chills that I could not yet explain. We had thought one of the workmen had left a door or window open, and she wandered in out of the cold. Instead, she'd been sent by the gods. I could hardly wrap my mind around it. If I hadn't spent the past week witnessing all manner of mystical and inexplicable events, I might never have believed it.

Major Grindle and four Weret Hekau came out of the smaller chamber. "The tablet is ready," they announced.

"Very well." Khalfani rolled up his map and shoved it somewhere inside his robe. "It is time, then."

"It is time," the men repeated.

"My presence is required for this, I'm afraid," Baruti said.

"It is?"

"You did not think I came along merely to comfort you? I have duties I must perform. To help these men prepare for battle and pray to the gods." He patted my arm, then hoisted

359

himself to his feet. As he crossed the long room, he seemed to grow taller, stronger, less frail. I rubbed my eyes, wondering if it was a trick of the light or some architectural illusion.

Isis leaped off my lap and followed the men as they all filed into a separate chamber. Having nothing else to do, and not wanting to be alone in the cavernous, shadowed room, I went, too. (Oh, all right. I was abuzz with curiosity. I admit it.)

The chamber turned out to be a chapel of sorts. A tingle of alarm went down my spine as I recognized the three statues seated at the front of the room: Sekhmet, Mantu, and Seth himself. Surely three of the most aggressive and violent Egyptian gods.

Major Grindle, Jadwiga, and Rumpf joined me against the back wall. "This should be most enlightening," the major said quietly, taking up position beside me.

"*Ja,*" Jadwiga said. "If the gods don't smite us for witnessing something that is no business of ours."

"You can always wait outside," Major Grindle pointed out.

Jadwiga merely turned his melancholy gaze upon the major, as if disappointed in him for having pointed out the obvious.

At a word from Baruti, the wedjadeen (about thirty of them, all told) slipped off their thick black outer robes, exposing the less voluminous tunics they wore beneath. They pulled their arms out of their sleeves and uncovered their torsos, letting the top half of their clothing hang from where it was cinched to their waists with their belts.

"I'm not sure you should be here for this," Major Grindle murmured.

I gave him a look, one that essentially said, *Just try to make me leave.* He harrumphed and turned his attention back to the wedjadeen.

All of them bore the distinctive Weret Hekau serpent tattoo running up the inside of their wrists. All of them were extremely powerful magicians, then. The Serpents of Chaos shouldn't stand a chance.

Fenuku and four other priests joined Baruti up front. Fenuku lit a small pile of incense in a bronze chafing dish and a thick, sweet, spicy smell filled the room. Next the four priests went to a small shrine and collected four palettes and sistrums, which they placed on top of the shrine. They each took a palette and began moving among the wedjadeen, stopping in front of each warrior of Horus. It took me a moment to realize that they were painting symbols on the warriors' bodies. Symbols of power and strength, it looked like.

They painted the vulture, Nekhbet, protectoress of Upper Egypt, across the warriors' backs. A feather of Maat went up their necks, indicating that their fight was to restore justice and balance in the world.

On their left arms went a flail and crook, to grant them majesty and dominion over their enemies. Over their hearts, a fiery Eye of Ra, encircled by a loop of rope with no beginning and no end.

"Isn't that dangerous?" I whispered to Major Grindle. "Invoking Sekhmet like that?"

The major shook his head. "That's why the eye is encased by the *shen* symbol—to contain her power. They want the fierceness of Sekhmet but contained, so that she does not harm the innocent," he whispered back.

Lastly, a winged solar disk was painted on each of the warriors' foreheads, the exact form and shape that Horus took in his battles against Seth.

No one would mistake them for Bedouin now.

When each of the men had been covered in tattoos, the four lector priests set down their palettes, took up the sistrums, and began rattling them. The sound of the ancient rattles had been designed to call the attention of the gods. It worked.

The atmosphere in the room grew heavy. The air was so full of *heka* that every hair on Isis's body stood on end. She looked far bigger and more ferocious than I had ever seen her. Shimmering forms filled the room, insubstantial ephemeral visions that I wondered if anyone else could see. The pressure of the *heka* built and built, pressing down on us, and I had to struggle to breathe, as if something huge were sitting on my chest. Baruti chanted some words in ancient Egyptian. The wedjadeen repeated them, and the pressure grew so heavy that it felt as though my body would implode.

Never taking his eyes from the men, Major Grindle leaned over and whispered in my ear, "They are inviting the gods into their bodies, asking them to lend their wisdom and strength so that they may overthrow Chaos."

"Can you feel that?" I whispered back. "All that pressure building?"

Major Grindle pulled his eyes from the wedjadeen and looked at me. "No, can you?"

"Yes. It's very nearly unbearable."

Major Grindle looked distinctly jealous.

The priests shook the sistrums once, twice, a third time, then set them down. They clapped once, and the shimmering air popped, all the pressure releasing. I looked around the room. Where had it gone?

Baruti said another prayer, then dismissed the wedjadeen. They quickly pulled their clothes together and donned their robes. As they filed past me out of the chapel, every one of their eyes seemed to shine with a fierce light.

Suddenly, I knew exactly where all that *heka* had gone.

CHAPTER THIRTY-FIVE
THE EXCHANGE

W E SILENTLY MADE OUR WAY DOWN the underground shaft that mirrored the Avenue of the Sphinxes above. Isis let me carry her exactly halfway before becoming restless and wanting down so she could explore on her own. I knew she would be safe enough, what with her being a *bau* and all, but I could have used the extra dose of reassurance that holding her always provides.

When we emerged near the Temple of Luxor, all but five of the wedjadeen proceeded to the black market to arrange their ambush. Major Grindle and the other Chosen Keepers were in that group due to their knowledge of the streets of Luxor. Also, they had no shadowy hiding skills like the wedjadeen did and would have stuck out like a handful of sore thumbs at the Luxor Temple.

Major Grindle was not happy about this; he didn't like leaving me. But he also recognized that he might be more of a hindrance than a help. When it was time to part ways, I felt as if we should have a solemn goodbye, just in case something went dreadfully wrong and we never saw each other again. But he was having none of that. "See you on the other side, Miss Throckmorton." He gave me a solid pat on the shoulder, then strode away.

Jadwiga and Rumpf were more circumspect. They shook my hand solemnly, and Jadwiga patted me on the head with his big paw of a hand. I'm sure he meant it as a gesture of affection, but he nearly gave me a concussion.

The underground passageway brought us up to the surface on the west side of the temple, just outside the outer wall near Hypostyle Hall, where the old chapel of Khons used to be. It was nothing but ruins now.

The bulk of the party peeled off and dispersed into all directions, making their way to the streets and alleys surrounding the black market. My five wedjadeen escorts and I stepped over the rubble and entered the temple. "Where will the men hide?" I asked Fenuku. I was still not happy that he was the one in charge of our part of the mission. However, he was the second-most powerful Weret Hekau, next to

Khalfani, and Khalfani was the leader of the men, so I got stuck with Fenuku. My only consolation was that he was just as unhappy about it as I was. That and he now had the Orb of Ra. Surely that would give us the upper hand with Chaos, no matter what.

"In here," he said shortly, then led me through the ruined chapel and portico into the second antechamber. A tiny annex opened off the west wall. Fenuku poked his head in to examine it. "Here is where you and the tablet will wait.

"The others," he said, indicating the four trailing wedjadeen, "will hide over here." He led us into the next antechamber, which had once been the sanctuary of the barque but had been plastered over and remade into a shrine of Alexander the Great. Pictures of him dressed as pharaoh decorated the walls. Fenuku stopped and pointed to the lintel over the doorway. I looked at him, a faint flutter of panic stirring in my breast. There was no hiding place here! He was trying to sabotage this, wasn't he? "They'll be spotted, sir."

He gave me a disgusted look, then waved at the men. They leaped forward and removed a series of stone panels from the wall, revealing a rather large hidey-hole. "It was built to hold two men, but four can fit in a pinch, if they won't be there too long."

Without a word of complaint, the men found footholds in

the wall and shimmied up to the hiding place. "What is the compartment for?" I asked. Did they really have that many occasions to hide hostages or extra soldiers in the ruins?

Fenuku gave a wry grimace. "It was used for our oracles, once upon a time," he confessed. I wondered if they'd had one of these in the Temple of Horus at Qerert Ihy, where we'd just come from. Was that how the Seer of Maat had spoken to all of us?

"Once the followers of Set have confirmed you and the tablet are here, they will send off a messenger to tell the others to proceed. I will move with the remaining follower of Set to wait out in the vestibule. You will then slip out of the annex and take your place up there in the hidden chamber. The men will come down and wait in the annex with the tablet. The followers of Set will have an unpleasant surprise waiting for them, I think. You"—he speared me with a look—"shall remain hidden until you are told to come out. We do not need you making things more complicated."

I wanted to protest that I never made things more complicated, but I was learning that that wasn't as true as I'd once hoped. "How long do we have until the scheduled rendezvous?"

"Their first scouts should be here shortly. It would be wise to get you and the tablet in position, in case they are early."

I tried not to feel claustrophobic in the small room, but it was hard. The walls were thick, crumbling stone and there were no windows. The only light came from the narrow doorway. I felt like a sitting duck with no avenue of escape should things go wrong.

Sensing my distress, Isis returned from exploring parts unknown and came to sit in my lap. Her warm presence calmed me somewhat. As I petted her soft black fur, I told myself that it wasn't that I didn't trust the wedjadeen. It's just that in my experience, things invariably go wrong.

I pushed that thought from my mind and concentrated on petting my cat and praying it would all be over soon.

The verification scouts were indeed early and arrived not ten minutes after we'd all taken our positions. I heard their voices out in the vestibule. "Where is the tablet? And the girl?"

"Right this way," Fenuku said politely.

A moment later, Fenuku ushered two men into the annex. One of them was Carruthers, from the museum. "Hello," I said, trying to look scared and defeated. It wasn't difficult, to be honest.

Carruthers sneered. "You are not so very precious, then, are you?"

"No, sir," I said in a meek voice, wishing I could slap that smile off his face.

He glanced at Isis, curled up on my lap. "Your cat will not be coming with us. Best say your goodbyes while you can." He jerked his head and the second man came forward and knelt by the tablet. He took a small knife from his pocket and scraped the surface of the Emerald Tablet. I winced, both worried that the magic would give way and insulted that he would risk defacing such a priceless artifact.

Apparently satisfied, Carruthers sent the other man back to von Braggenschnott with a message that all was as agreed upon. The idea of coming face-to-face with von Braggen-schnott again made me feel ill. I had to remind myself that it was all a ruse. He wouldn't even make it to the temple, not with scores of wedjadeen waiting to ambush him in the streets of Luxor.

Fenuku was able to convince Carruthers to wait out in the vestibule so they could watch for the rest of his men. Carruthers seemed perfectly content with this as he knew as well as we did that there was no way out of the temple except through the vestibule where he'd be waiting.

As soon as their voices receded, I set Isis on the ground, jumped to my feet, and hurried to the doorway.

Silent as shadows, the wedjadeen slipped out of their hidden chamber. Three of them moved noiselessly toward me. One hung back, waiting to assist me into my hiding place.

I hurried over to the wall, and the fourth remaining wedjadeen gave me a boost up. Using the subtle hand- and footholds that had been carved into the wall, I worked my way up to the space over the lintel. I nodded at the man to let him know I was ready, and he quietly replaced the slabs of stone. I was completely hidden from view.

I was heartily glad to see there was a peephole; I wouldn't be completely in the dark up here. I peered around until I found Isis, sitting so still and silently against the far wall that she looked like little more than a shadow herself.

Have I mentioned that I think waiting is the hardest part? It seems we are forever rushing, then waiting. Rushing, then waiting. I tried to entertain myself with imagining the look of surprise on von Braggenschnott's face when he found four wedjadeen instead of me, but the vision kept being interrupted by worries for Mother and Gadji. What would he do to them when he saw I wasn't there?

Calm down, I told myself. Surely there was nothing I could do that four wedjadeen couldn't? Not to mention that things shouldn't even get that far.

Just when I had finally managed to convince myself of that, I heard Fenuku's voice speaking loudly from the vestibule. "Here come your followers of Set," he said.

"I can see that," Carruthers replied, somewhat nastily. But of course, Fenuku hadn't said it for Carruthers's benefit. He'd said it to warn me and the four hidden wedjadeen. If Chaos was coming, it meant the ambush had failed.

"Who are all those people with them?" Fenuku asked.

"Did you not hear?" Carruthers answered. "There was another nationalist demonstration this morning. We thought it best to keep the streets crowded today, in case you planned any surprises for us. We find it pays to stay involved in politics."

My heart sank like a stone. The wedjadeen had not been able to pull off the ambush. Now what? How was von Braggenschnott going to react when he didn't find what he wanted?

Minutes later, I heard the sound of dozens of footsteps outside in the vestibule. Von Braggenschnott's voice rang out. "Where are they?"

"First I must see the woman and the boy," Fenuku reminded him.

"Bring them," von Braggenschnott called out.

There was a pause, and then Fenuku spoke again. "I see that they are unharmed. Good. Let us make the exchange in here where the girl and the tablet are waiting."

"You saw them yourself, Carruthers?" von Braggenschnott asked.

"Yes, sir. I did."

"Very well. Bring the woman and the boy."

"They can't all come with us," Fenuku protested. "For one, the room is too small. And as you requested, there is only one of me here in the temple."

There was a pause as von Braggenschnott considered whether to honor his original agreement or not. "You six, come with Carruthers and me. The rest of you wait here."

"But that was not the agreement," Fenuku protested.

There was another pause. When von Braggenschnott spoke again, his voice had taken on a reasonable tone. "This is not your argument. Give me the tablet, take the boy, and be gone. The rest does not concern you."

There was a surprised silence—at least, I was surprised—before Fenuku spoke. "You are right, follower of Set. This is not our fight to win or lose. Come, let me show you the tablet and I will take the boy and leave. You may do what you want with the woman and the girl."

I nearly gasped in outrage at his treachery. Had he tricked the other wedjadeen into believing he would go along with this plan, when all along he had intended to hand me over to Chaos? What betrayal did he have planned to get rid of Major Grindle, I wondered? And would the other wedjadeen go along with his decision?

Seething, I shoved my eye into the peephole, desperate to

catch a glimpse of Gadji and Mother, to see with my own eyes that they were safe and unharmed. And there they were. Bedraggled, but alive and safe. Joy at the sight of them surged through me and it was all I could do to bite back a shout of happiness.

Carruthers held Gadji, and von Braggenschnott had a tight grip on Mother. Fenuku stepped aside. "Your tablet, gentlemen. And the girl," he lied.

Still holding on to Mother, von Braggenschnott disappeared into the annex, while Carruthers crowded at the doorway. "Where is sh—"

A shout went up as Fenuku pulled out a club hidden in his sleeve and cracked Carruthers on the skull. He yanked Gadji well away from the crumpling Serpent of Chaos and shoved him toward the door. At the same time, muffled shouting came from the annex as the hidden wedjadeen tried to subdue von Braggenschnott without hurting Mother. Fenuku reached in, grabbed Mother's arm, and pulled her out of the fray. "Run!" he told Mother and Gadji.

Confused, they took three faltering steps toward the vestibule, stopping as more Serpents of Chaos began pouring through the door.

"The other way!" Fenuku called out. "Rekhet! Come get them to safety! If our gods were foolish enough to bestow you with gifts, show they weren't wasted and *use them!*"

Still stunned that he hadn't betrayed us, I kicked the slabs from my hiding place and dropped to the ground. The shock of the impact jolted through my legs, but I bit back the pain.

"Theodosia?" Mother blinked, her mouth dropping open. "Wh-what are you doing here?"

"Rescuing you two. Come on." As I reached out for Mother and Gadji, I looked up to see von Braggenschnott straining to get past the wedjadeen, trying to get to me. Our gazes met, and unspeakable threats shone in his eyes.

Isis darted from her corner and disappeared through the small door immediately to our right. I didn't know where she was taking us, but it was away from Chaos and that was enough for me. "Come on." I tugged at Mother and Gadji.

"Where are we going?"

"We need to get away. Fenuku is buying us some time and we need to use it. We might not get another chance." I grabbed her arm, confident that Gadji knew enough to follow along without being pulled. Isis was just disappearing through a second doorway that led deeper into the temple. Without thinking about it, I followed.

It was a birthing room, I realized, and I immediately began searching for another doorway. There! Isis had found one. Just as I took a step to follow her, an explosion rocked the temple and knocked us to our feet.

CHAPTER THIRTY-SIX
THE MIGHTY ISIS

"WHAT IS THAT?" Gadji cried out, throwing his arms over his head to protect it from a chunk of rubble.

"The Orb of Ra," I told him.

"The orb of what?" Mother asked. "Theodosia, I demand you tell me what is going on, right this minute."

"Mother, I'm just trying to find a place where we can hide until help arrives." My mind worked furiously. I paused, listening. Had that blast killed every living thing in the vicinity?

From far away, I heard a groan, then a rumbling and scraping noise as if someone was pulling himself out of the rubble and dragging himself across the floor. A muffled German curse rang out.

Oh dear heavens, no. Don't let *him* have survived!

I took Mother's arm again (she seemed to be a bit stunned) and pulled her along. Isis waited for us in the next room, a small chamber lined with four alcoves. When she saw that we had followed, she took an immediate right into the next vestibule, the Hall of Hours.

I peered through the twelve columns in the room. "Where'd she go?"

"Through there!" Gadji pointed to yet another doorway. Honestly, this was as bad as a labyrinth!

"Go!" I said, and Gadji disappeared into the heart of the temple, with me and my mother right on his heels. Once inside, we stumbled to a stop. The room was small and dark, and there were only narrow slits up high to let the faintest bit of light in.

"The Holy of Holies," Mother whispered. She glanced fearfully over her shoulder. "A dead end."

"There is no way out, Mother. Not on this side of the temple. Chaos—Borscht's men—are blocking our only exit." But if Isis brought us here, there must be a reason.

"But we'll be trapped like—"

"Shh!" I poked my ear outside the door, trying to hear if von Braggenschnott was following us. And if so, how close behind he was. I heard nothing, which was good. Just how far away were the wedjadeen, anyway? "Gadji, you take the door. Tell me if you hear anyone coming."

"Yes, effendi miss."

Fenuku had told me to make use of being a Rekhet, but I had no practice being one. I'd really only removed curses and nursed Sefu back to health. But as we'd run through the temple, a plan had formed in my mind. It was a long shot, but it was all I could come up with. I glanced down. "I'll need you," I told Isis.

She meowed and flicked her tail, as if that announcement was not news to her. And if she was truly a *bau*, like Baruti had claimed, then it probably wasn't.

"Mother, do you have a pencil or a pen nib? Even a hairpin will do." I reached into my pocket for the compact of sandstone from the inside of a pharaoh's tomb. "Isis, up here." I patted the plinth where the statues of the gods once sat. The power was greatest there, and if I was going to call on them for help, I needed to get as close as I could.

"Here." Mother handed me a hairpin. When I took it from her, our eyes met. Her gaze held fear and confusion. I could only hope the fear wasn't directed at me. Best not to think about that now. "Thank you, Mother. Now please go stand on the other side of Gadji, away from the door."

"Theo . . ." Her eyes pleaded with me, and I couldn't tell

if they were pleading for me to make this all go away or to go back to being only slightly peculiar rather than downright scary.

"We don't have time, Mother. Please trust me on this." Our gazes held and I tried to open my soul to her, to let her see that while I was about to do some very strange things, I was still her (hopefully beloved!) daughter. She nodded, and I let out my breath and turned to my cat.

"Are you up for this?" I asked Isis as I set the silver compact on the stone plinth next to her. She purred, which I took as a very good sign.

Rituals and rubrics, spells and mysteries, swirled in my head—all the wonders I had seen and experienced for the past five days. I closed my eyes and breathed deeply. I could do this. I could. I opened my eyes again and faltered.

But maybe not with Mother watching. "Mother, would you mind facing the wall?"

With an impatient sigh, she did as I asked and I turned back to Isis.

"I hears footsteps, miss!"

My heart stuttered. "One set or many?"

He listened more closely. "Only one set, miss."

Bother. It most likely wasn't the cavalry, then. We were being pursued.

Shutting all visions of von Braggenschnott out of my mind, I did my best to focus.

I licked the hairpin to wet it, then dipped it into the tomb dust. As quickly as I could, I began to sketch a figure along Isis's back. It was difficult, because fur is a tricky writing surface at best, but I kept dipping and drawing, dipping and drawing, replenishing the pin with dust so that a faint, shadowy outline of the great goddess Sekhmet began to take shape on Isis's back.

It was the only thing I could think of, trying to tap into the gods' *heka,* just like Baruti had done when he'd prepared the wedjadeen for battle.

"Footsteps is being closer, miss!"

"Almost done, Gadji. And when I say so, throw yourself back against the wall with Mother."

I dipped the pin one last time into the dust and traced an Eye of Ra over Isis's heart, then enclosed it with a *shen* symbol, the rope with no beginning and no end that would contain Sekhmet's fierceness. There. That was all I could do.

I had no sistrum, no drum, no incense. Only my hands and fervent pleas. I clapped three times very loudly, the small chamber causing the noise to amplify.

"Theo," Mother hissed. "You'll give away our hiding place."

I should have reassured her, but I was too enthralled with

what was happening on the plinth before me. Isis was writhing and hissing, her body pulsating, growing larger.

"Uh-ohs," Gadji said.

Unable to stand not knowing what was happening, Mother turned away from the wall and bit back a scream.

Isis spilled onto the floor, power running along her fur in ripples. She was now the size of a small dog. "H-has she gone rabid?" Mother asked, plastering herself against the wall in an effort to avoid touching my cat.

"No, she's just protecting us." My voice was a little high and breathless, either from all the magic in the air or because I was just the teensiest bit worried.

"Footsteps is being in the next chamber, miss!" Gadji shouted, then darted onto the other side of Mother.

"*Fräulein?*" The ragged whisper was more chilling than any shout. "Fräulein, there is no way out. You cannot escape me this time."

Just then, a lion-size Isis gave a snarling scream that had the others cowering against the wall. I looked at her, her eyes no longer familiar or recognizable. They were filled with destruction. "Go," I whispered. "Keep us safe."

With a throaty roar, the giant Isis bounded out of the chamber.

Von Braggenschnott's shout of surprise was cut off with a snarl and a gurgle. Low growls were followed by a loud thud as something connected with one of the columns. Von Braggenschnott, perhaps? Isis let loose with a roar that shook the roof, and then we heard the soft pad of her paws as she bounded away. I closed my eyes and said a silent thank-you.

After a few seconds, more roars and screams erupted from somewhere near the front of the temple. I poked my head out. "It looks clear," I told the others. "Let's get out of here before we're trapped again." I grabbed Gadji's hand, then held my other out to Mother. She stared at it, and for one horrid moment, I was afraid she wasn't going to take it. Just when I started to wilt inside, she grabbed it, and I savored the feel of her hand in mine. We ran.

We tore out of the small room into the Hall of Hours and raced back the way we'd come. I could hear the sound of fighting far off—in the main courtyard, perhaps—but steered well clear of that. We finally made it to yet another wretched vestibule, then out into the open air. I paused for a moment, trying to catch my breath.

Another loud roar came from deep inside the temple, followed by shouts and yelling. I was relatively certain that Isis wouldn't hurt *me*, not even in her Sekhmet incarnation, but I wasn't sure about Mother and Gadji. "Come on," I said.

"Where are we going?" Mother asked.

"There." I pointed with my elbow.

"Where?" Her voice wobbled a bit.

"There, Mother, into the crowd."

"Theo, I really don't think—"

"Mother. Trust me. We are far safer with those angry demonstrating Egyptians than we are with the men back in the temple."

"Right." She nodded once, then began hurrying alongside me.

"And you," I said to Gadji, "should be right at home!"

He gave me one of those cocky grins I'd missed so much. "Just like old times, eh, miss?"

And then we reached the fringes of the crowd. I plunged into the masses, bumping into one body, then another, murmuring, "Excuse me," every ten seconds as I wormed my way farther and farther into the crowd. No one seemed to pay us any mind at first, and then slowly, space began opening up between us and the other demonstrators as they realized there were two English women in their midst.

I stared at the puzzled, angry faces, and I could not fault them a bit. Not only had we come into their country and plundered their treasure for our own museums, they were the first we blamed when one of our own went missing. We had done them a great disservice. I could only hope that by restoring Gadji to the wedjadeen, they would be able to put him on Egypt's throne one day and give their country its own ruler, one they deserved.

As the voices around us died down, however, I began to feel extremely uncomfortable. In the sea of white and black robes, there was an occasional black veil. And then I had a great big wonderful idea. Surely our housekeeper would not miss a demonstration such as this.

"Habiba!" I called out. "Habiba?" I turned around, searching the other side of the crowd. "Habiba, are you out there?"

There was stunned silence, and people began to look at one another, shaking their heads. "Habiba!" I tried one more time, dead tired and wanting nothing more than for all of this to be over and for me to be back in our little bungalow. "Habiba!"

Slowly the crowd parted and a hesitant black-swathed figure crept forward, glancing at those beside her and shrugging her shoulders, as if she could not account for the craziness of the *Inglaize*. As she drew closer, her hand flew to her mouth. "Young miss? Madams?"

"Oh, Habiba!" I pulled my elbow from Mother's grip, hurried over to the stunned Egyptian woman, and threw my arms around her neck. "Thank you for finding us!"

CHAPTER THIRTY-SEVEN

EXPLANATIONS AND GOODBYES

THE DEMONSTRATION QUICKLY DIED DOWN as word spread that one of their own had found the English ladies. The sea of people parted as Habiba led us to the nearby police station, where we could explain what had happened. Or parts of it, anyway.

They were rather overwhelmed by our somewhat hysterical tale of a German national who'd been impersonating a member of the Antiquities Service by the name of Borscht. It wasn't until Major Grindle's name was mentioned that they began taking us seriously.

Word was sent round to Father at his hotel, but Major

Grindle arrived before he did, with a rather battered-looking Jadwiga and Rumpf. When Jadwiga spied me, a slow grin spread over his face, the first I had ever seen.

Before we could greet each other properly, we were distracted by the police's seizing of Rumpf, thinking he was the German national who'd kidnapped us. Honestly, did they really think he'd just waltz right into the police station and make their life that easy? Chaos didn't work that way.

The only good thing about their harassing poor Rumpf was that it created an opportunity for me to speak with Gadji. As I settled onto the bench next to him, I asked, "So now do you believe you are the last pharaoh?"

"Oh, I always believing it, miss." He shrugged. "Just didn't care so very much."

"I have some good news for you." His little face brightened. "Sefu and your sister are both safe and waiting for you."

His jaw dropped open as he gaped at me. "How you be knowing this?" he demanded.

This is what would make him a good ruler, I thought. It was people he cared about, not the trappings of power. "I saw her with my own eyes. She's very nice, and she's keeping Sefu for you until you return."

He digested this news quietly for a moment. Unable to

contain his joy, his legs swung back and forth vigorously. "Effendi miss is not needing me now that the bad mens is gone?"

"No. And even if I did, there are others to help me." I glanced over at Major Grindle, who was arguing fiercely in defense of Rumpf. I had no doubt he'd win, eventually.

There was a whisper of movement in the hallway next to us as a familiar black cloak swished in the shadows. I glanced up, relieved to see Khalfani. "You made it," I said quietly.

He nodded. "And you." Then he turned his gaze to Gadji, the wedjadeen's relief palpable. "We owe you much, Rekhet." He glanced over at the arguing officials. "Even so, I think the boy and I should be gone quickly."

"I agree." Before Gadji could squirm away, I gave him a quick hug. "Be safe."

"I will, effendi miss. You too!"

As I blinked back tears, Khalfani bowed. "Do not worry, Rekhet. You will see him again—when he leads his country to independence!" He flashed a rare grin, and then, with a swish of black cloak, he and Gadji slipped out the back door just as Father arrived at the front.

There was a lot of shouting and hugging and kissing. Father insisted on giving Habiba the reward he had posted for information leading to our rescue. However, one of the police tried to suggest she had had us kidnapped in order to collect the reward. Honestly, was he related to Mr. Bing? Father set him right double-quick, and that was that.

But not quite.

I was still desperate for a chance to speak with Major Grindle and find out what, exactly, had happened that had made everything go so terribly wrong. And if the looks he kept throwing me were any indication, he had questions for me as well.

We finally had our chance when the police decided they wanted to take Mother's and my statements separately, to be sure they matched. Mother was still just this side of hysterical, so Father went in to accompany her. At the door, he hesitated, and I was somewhat relieved to see that he was thinking twice about leaving me alone.

"I'll just sit here with Major Grindle," I assured him. "I'll be fine." I gave him a bright smile. Then he did the strangest thing.

He left the doorway and came over and planted a kiss on the top of my head. "I know you will, Theo. You are made of remarkably strong stuff." Then he returned to Mother's side and shut the door.

Major Grindle and I were alone at last. Well, relatively alone, if you didn't count Jadwiga and Rumpf sitting on the bench across the hall or the various harried-looking police officials racing back and forth, carrying reports of violence done during the demonstration. There were also reports of a small earthquake centered at the Luxor Temple, so they dispatched some of their men to see. There was even one crazed report of a lion being spotted in the desert, just on the outskirts of town. That one they ignored.

When I was certain that everyone was too wrapped up in his own business to pay any attention to us, I turned to the major. "What went wrong? How did Chaos get past all of you?"

"We hadn't counted on the nationalist demonstration," Major Grindle said, his voice laced with bitterness.

"They arranged that, you know."

"I'm not surprised to hear it. The streets were clogged with people—innocent people—and we couldn't even get close to our arranged ambush points. We had to stand helplessly by while Chaos let the crowd carry them to where they wanted to go, safely surrounded by a shield of innocents.

"Once we realized all the ambush points had been neutralized, we rushed to the Luxor Temple with all due haste." He gave me a glance both curious and shrewd. "Imagine our surprise to find a bloody panther on the loose, tearing through Chaos agents as if they were nothing but a field of mice. It seemed to avoid the wedjadeen, for some reason."

"Did you find von Braggenschnott, sir? Was he"—I swallowed hard—"dead?"

Major Grindle sat up straight, his nose quivering in indignation. "Von Braggenschnott! No—where was he?"

My heart sank as I explained how he'd followed us to the temple's inner sanctum. "Isis—the panther—attacked him first, but we were in such a rush to escape, I didn't check to see if he survived the attack."

"I will send someone round at once."

"It was the only way I could think of for us to get away."

"It was downright brilliant, is what it was, and if we had the time, I'd insist you teach me how you did it."

I glanced nervously at the door. "But Mother saw . . . so much. How do I explain it to her?"

Major Grindle's bright blue eyes studied me intently. "Your heart will know, Miss Throckmorton."

"Yes, but will it know *soon?*" I asked. "Because they will want a full explanation sooner rather than later." It was too much to hope that Mother would forget what had happened or that she would refrain from telling Father. "Do you have a family?" I asked.

He gave a brisk shake of his head, and it suddenly became crystal clear to me why he didn't. He knew the true costs of the life he lived. The family he'd never have, the friends he'd always have to keep at a distance, the secrets he could never share. Impulsively, I turned and threw my arms around him, giving him an enormous hug. "Thank you, Major Grindle.

For everything. But especially for my grandfather," I whispered.

He hugged me awkwardly, as if he hadn't done much hugging in his time. Then he pulled back and chucked me under
the chin. "So much like your grandfather, and yet so very
different. Any man should be proud to call you his daughter." He glanced at the closed office door. "Remember that."

"What will you do now? Has your cover been blown? Will
they reassign you?"

"Ah, I think not." He glanced toward the window.

I followed his gaze and saw one of the wedjadeen waiting
outside, looking like a loitering Bedouin. "You're going with
them, aren't you? You're going back into the desert to study
what they know?"

He smiled. "I've always said nothing much gets by you,
Miss Throckmorton. Yes, I believe I shall. It is the opportu-
nity of a lifetime! To learn all the arcane magic and ancient
ritual! My whole life has been working toward this point.
Who knows, I might even see if I can become the first
British Weret Hekau. Wouldn't that be an accomplishment."

I had no doubt he'd succeed.

"But I'll never see you again," I said around a lump in my
throat.

"Ah, now, don't say that, Miss Throckmorton. Who's to
say your involvement with the Eyes of Horus has come to

an end? Or perhaps one day you'll choose to come find us in the desert and continue your education."

I blinked at him. Now, there was a thought. "When will you leave?"

"As soon as we get this mess all sorted out, I'll be on my way. Mr. Jadwiga and Mr. Rumpf will remain behind to clear up any loose ends and keep an eye out for any lingering bits of chaos we might have missed."

The office door opened and Father stood there. "Theodosia? They'd like to speak with you now."

"Go on." Major Grindle gave me a gentle nudge. "Your family needs you."

I stood up, then threw my arms around him for one last hug and tried not to let my tears get his uniform wet. "Goodbye, my dear," he whispered in my ear.

I let go and he stood up straight, then saluted me. Ignoring my father's curious gaze, I saluted back, then turned and made my way into the office that held both my parents and my future.

At least for now.

Mother and I spent the next two days sleeping while Father clucked over us like a mother hen—which would have been amusing if it hadn't been so necessary.

I kept waiting for Mother to say something, to call me into her room and ask for an explanation of what had occurred. When we met in the hall or at the dinner table, her eyes would glance over me without truly looking at me, as if she was afraid. Or disgusted.

To make matters worse, Isis still hadn't returned. I had never imagined when I had put that spell on her that I would be seeing the last of my cat. I'm not sure if I could have done it, knowing that. Honestly, you'd think after pulling off a ransom exchange that involved the last pharaoh and my own mother, I would have been riding high. Instead, I was down in the doldrums, afraid I would never come out.

On the third day, Father decided we'd "recovered" long enough and that a nice outing was what we needed. He was dying to see what we'd found at Deir el-Bahri and talked Mother and me into getting dressed and leaving the house.

I was struck by how peaceful the city seemed, as if that big catastrophe had released some horrid pressure that had been building and building. Had it been because of Chaos's presence here? Or was it just a cycle that we humans went through? And would I never know the answer to that?

When we reached Deir el-Bahri, Mother was dismayed to see that the small earthquake had sent an entirely new load of rubble down over the temple we'd discovered, completely

side, I

been,

ound.

n this

been

more

ther,

some

nged

avior

oses.

oth

la

ew. We couldn't even see any sign of a sin-

1 queer look, as if she thought I was some-

for this, or perhaps she merely wondered if

t that my newest discovery had just up and

Whatever the case, I suddenly realized she

ok at me the same way again, and our future

before me, impossibly long and forever sepa-

orrid chasm.

1 faint rumble as a small section of rubble on

gave way, tumbling down the mountainside.

a small squeak and backed up, and I wondered

would ever recover. Then I heard another sound,

wonderful sound. I turned around and saw my

cat creeping out of the rubble. "Isis!" I said.

Mother repeated, then took another step back-

nored her and ran forward. My cat was covered in dust

looked a little bedraggled, but she was perfectly tame

an allowed me to pick her up. She began to purr.

Had she been hiding? I had thought the reported earthquake had been from the explosion of the orb, but perhaps
Isis had brought down the hillside in her carnation as Sekhmet. I buried my face in her dusty fur. I would probably

never know. As I rested my cheek on her silky black
stared back at where the temple of Thutmose III had
remembering that magical, hidden sanctuary I had
Just one of many pieces of living magic I'd discovered
trip to Egypt.

I'd come here hoping to visit the temple where I'd
born. Instead, I'd found a heritage and a destiny, and
answers than I had ever dreamed of. I glanced up at M
at her lovely, worried eyes. Perhaps I should provide
answers of my own.

There had been so many times in the past when I'd lo
to confide in my parents, to explain my peculiar beh
and tell them what was going on right beneath their n
But the hugeness of explaining it all when they knew
ing about it had been overwhelming. How does one exp
being able to see magic and curses or being chased by
cret societies and Egyptian magicians?

But it turned out they had known some of it all along.

Now that I knew, really truly *knew*, that there was a
son for my abilities, that I wasn't in danger of going rou
the bend, it would be easier to explain. Reality was, after all,
on my side.

Holding Isis close for strength, I squared my shoulders
and took a step toward my parents. "Mother? Father? I have
something I need to tell you . . ."